Because he married young, Sam Groves never got to play the field. But seventeen years later something happens to make him feel he's missed out. It isn't too late, though, and he's always believed you should go for what you want. After all, what's wrong with that, provided nobody gets hurt? Now Sam Groves feels he's found a foolproof way to happiness – and maybe in the end he has. Just not the one he'd been expecting.

The Golden Voyage of Samson Groves is Stephen Benatar's seventh book. His last novel *Recovery* has now been optioned for the cinema.

Reviews of Stephen Benatar's
Previous Novels

RECOVERY

... Stephen Benatar's haunting new book. Clever as he is in constructing this fantasy, Benatar is less interested in the technicalities of time travel than in the evocation and exploration of regret... which, here as in earlier novels, he records with such grim immediacy yet transcends with such grace.

Michael Kerrigan, Scotsman

A mammoth talent... He is a writer who can thread reincarnation and a time-travelling Lucifer through a fantastical 90s morality tale without once stretching the bounds of credulity... Benatar manages to observe the mind-numbing minutiae of end-of-millennium life and paint our tiny triumphs and failures onto the canvas of two thousand years of flawed humanity... Book of the month... discovery of the year.

James O'Brien, G-Spot

FATHER OF THE MAN

Benatar's writing captures the absolute dailiness of real life without being in the least mundane itself, and he is particularly good at capturing life's small lifts and cringing embarrassments. This oddly distinctive and affecting novel... intertwines the farcical and tragic.

Sunday Times

SUCH MEN ARE DANGEROUS

Extraordinarily powerful. An absorbing read; a novel to make you think.

Times Literary Supplement

Beautifully written... a delight... a joy to read.

Tribune

WHEN I WAS OTHERWISE

The book is remarkably convincing... One's first reaction on finishing the novel is "Goodness, how sad!" One's second is "Goodness, how funny!"

Francis King, Spectator

An intriguing, funny, sometimes exciting and, finally, sad story; the elegant idiosyncrasy of the author's viewpoint, which made *Wish Her Safe At Home* so enjoyably inventive without discarding a carefully controlled narrative, here creates a moving story from what might at first appear to be the elements of a black farce.

Christopher Hawtree, Literary Review

WISH HER SAFE AT HOME

With this marvellous book, character and poetry return to the English novel... Rachel is one of the great English female characters, like the Wife of Bath or Flora Finching: both an individual and a species.

Times Literary Supplement

A remarkably odd and chilling story, the effect of which I found difficult to shake off.

Anthony Thwaite, Observer

THE MAN ON THE BRIDGE

Handles tricky material with conviction and assurance.

Robert Nye, Guardian

Absorbing throughout... a haunting book. The subject is treated in depth and is finely characterised.

Pamela Hansford Johnson

Great understanding and depth of feeling.

New Statesman

9.9.98

For Kafarzyna
Happy birthday!

The Golden Voyage
of Samson Groves

Stephen Benatar

Stephen Benatar

Dear Pappy
I hope it's not tosh
Your Pyppy

Welbeck Press

For John and Pauline Lucas

First Published in Great Britain, July 1998.

Welbeck Press
19 Devonshire Avenue, Beeston, Nottingham NG9 1BS.
Telephone: (0115) 925 1827

Design, typesetting and print by Goaters, Nottingham.
Cover photo: © Piers Benatar
Author photo: © Andrew Palmer

ISBN 0 9528976 1 X

1

My assistant had gone to lunch so I myself was serving. There was only one customer. She had been browsing for maybe twenty minutes and I had been watching her for maybe nineteen. At last she brought a fruit bowl to the counter.

"Nine pounds fifty," I said, smiling, peeling off the sticker. She looked as good close up as from a distance.

"This place is rightly named," she said.

"Thank you. To be honest I wasn't quite sure. I sometimes thought it might be twee." *Treasure Island.* Winning out by a whisker: over *Fantasy Island.*

"Then you're its proprietor?"

"You look surprised."

She hesitated. "I somehow expect the owners of shops like this to be dusty old gentlemen."

"Why?"

"Because as a child I was always enchanted by junk shops and it seemed that the men who owned them..." She broke off. "But perhaps that wasn't tactful?"

"What?"

"Junk shops."

"Why not? What else could you call it?"

"Oh. Many things. A cornucopia. An Aladdin's cave." She spread her hands. "A treasure island."

"A junk shop."

"Right."

We laughed.

"And of course," she said, "one man's junk is another man's joy."

"Unquestionably."

"Astonishing I didn't go in for it myself — this line of work. As I say, I spent so much time... and so much pocket money... We lived in Camden Town. It was a good area for junk shops."

"And dusty old gentlemen."

"Precisely."

"Plus an interesting place to grow up generally? Regent's Park and the Zoo. Theatres, cinemas. Museums." I added museums mainly to impress her.

She nodded. "How long have you lived here?"

"My whole life."

"This must've been a good place, too, in which to grow up. Country and sea. Enviable to grow up by the sea."

"The grass being always greener?"

"Well, perhaps. But for instance... are you a swimmer? I mean, a proper swimmer?"

"Yes."

"I thought you might be." She sounded wistful.

"Are you a dancer?"

That was a crazy thing to say but she seemed to release me from my inhibitions.

"A dancer? Why?"

"I don't know exactly. Something to do with the way you move. The kind of aura you give out. The clothes you're wearing."

"Are these the clothes that dancers nowadays wear in Deal?" In fact it was merely a cream silk blouse and a black skirt, very simple and well cut, undoubtedly expensive. Her beads, her low-heeled shoes, her shoulder bag; they too were black. The effect of colour came almost entirely from her hair, lustrous and shoulder-length and tawny, and from her eyes, which were a striking beautiful green.

"That isn't fair," I said. "Sometimes it's very difficult to pin down an impression. Was I nowhere near?"

"You were exceedingly close."

"Really?"

"I'm an interior decorator."

"Ah, yes. Of course. I can see how exceedingly close."

She smiled. "My mother saw *The Red Shoes* shortly before I was born and because she enjoyed it so much named me after Moira Shearer. Also, perhaps, because my colouring

8

was similar."

I gravely nodded my approval. I said: "I always wanted life to imitate the movies. Are you successful?"

"I do the work I like, at any rate. The same as you. And yes. Without false modesty I think I am." She handed me a ten-pound note. By now I'd wrapped the bowl in tissue paper.

"Aren't you going to haggle? People often do."

"Not on this occasion," she said. "The first time I go anywhere I always behave *beautifully*."

I experienced an absurdly quixotic impulse to return the ten pounds and make her a present of the thing. I really did feel tempted; and afterwards wished I'd done it. But anyhow I knocked off one pound fifty.

"That's very kind," she said. "It's a gift for the friend I'm staying with. She's going to be delighted."

"Then you're only on a visit?"

"Yes; but haven't I picked the right weekend?" She glanced behind her through the window.

I agreed she had.

"Especially as I hope it's going to be the first of many. I've been seriously thinking of taking one of those small houses in Silver Street."

"Oh, excellent."

"Thank you. I find it a fascinating quarter, down there by the front. Easy to believe it was a thriving haunt for smugglers!"

"'Brandy for the Parson, 'Baccy for the Clerk... Them that asks no questions isn't told a lie. Watch the wall, my darling, while the Gentlemen go by!'" I laughed. "Never anyone like Kipling."

"No," she said. It was friendly rather than committed.

"He also wrote my all-time favourite piece of poetry."

"Did he? I remember how the camel got his hump and how — "

"*If,*" I said.

"Your all-time favourite? We did that at school. But shamefully little has stuck. Oh, yes. 'You'll be a man, my son.'"

9

Again, I didn't mind the hint of mockery. "If pressed I reckon I could still recite the bulk of it."

"Perhaps next time you can give me a performance?"

"I'll start rehearsing."

"Well, it's been nice to meet you, Mr...?"

"Groves. Sam Groves."

"I'm Moira Sheffield." If the bowl hadn't been cradled in her right arm I felt we might have shaken hands. "I think I must've rediscovered my natural habitat. I told Liz I'd be away ten minutes!"

When she'd gone I likened her departure to the flight of some rare bird whose sleek, exotic plumage had momentarily lit up the shop. But if this were indeed her natural habitat and she proposed to buy a house wasn't it on the cards that someday she'd fly back? *Next time*, she had said. I was always chatting to my customers — one of the perks for secondhand dealers — but I couldn't recall a single encounter which had given me more pleasure.

2

After a slack lunchtime we grew busy again. Spring had come. None too soon...April nearly over. People seemed readier to spend. But several times I stood in our doorway and was mesmerised by that glinting expanse at the end of the road. I smelt the tang of seaweed. Gulls were lifting and the houses above the beach would all be looking white and clean as if anticipating the time when towels and swimwear would hang again from balconies. A woman went by in a summer dress. This seemed premature but I enjoyed looking at her and could readily sympathise with the urge to cast off heavy clothing. A lot of passers-by smiled at me, although I thought there wasn't one of them I knew. I wondered if you ever got this reaction in places where the weather was more settled. California, say. I had frequent pipe dreams of escape to California. California dreaming.

I myself felt happy. Still did so when I got home that evening. As usual on hearing the gate Susie ran round from the back; panted and jumped up and wagged her mongrel tail; rolled over and waited to be tickled. Often my response to all this was perfunctory but tonight I squatted down and really fussed her. Asked about her day; told her a bit about my own. And as sometimes happened at such moments her lips parted and she appeared truly to be smiling. We stayed like this for several minutes and I enjoyed the sensation of being close to the moist earth and of smelling its freshness, of being able to squat for so long without strain, of seeing the clean strong line my thighs presented in their newly laundered jeans, of noting too the way my hands and fingernails looked good against the dog's white fur and how the brown leather of my righthand loafer, despite a long day's wear and tear, still had a satisfying gloss. I enjoyed also my awareness of the bottle of Burgundy and the bunch of yellow roses I'd set beside me on the path.

The front door opened. It was Junie. "I was beginning to think I must've been mistaken."

"Hello, my love. No. Just a spot of heavy petting."

"I can see. D'you want me to go away?"

"What do you say, Susie?"

Susie merely went on grinning, after a moment of distraction. My wife said absent-mindedly: "Who loves her master then? I know it isn't ladylike to inquire but are those roses meant for me?"

"Yes. So long as you come to have your tummy tickled."

She exclaimed both over flowers and wine. I rose to my full height, then bent again and kissed her.

"I love you, Junie Moon."

Briefly she rested her head against my chest. I couldn't remember now if those five words, for twenty years my catchphrase, were taken from the title of a movie or some stage production. Whichever, we hadn't seen it. But even at sixteen she'd been softly rounded and moon-faced and if she wasn't any longer quite so dewy-eyed and misty, having herself these days two children of practically that same age, she was still plump and pearly-skinned; with hair which, by turning prematurely grey, enhanced that opalescent look.

"I love you, Samuel Groves."

The one endearment triggered off the other. Unfailingly.

After a minute we went inside the house — the three of us — into the living room; I settled in my usual chair and Junie poured us both a drink. This was also a part of the ritual. "How's it been today?" she asked.

"It's been good. The sun made such a difference. This morning I finished turning out that house I told you about."

"Any exciting finds?"

"Yes quite. One or two nice dresses dating back to the twenties. But they'd fall apart if you tried cleaning them. Some fairly good china. A first edition of *The Cruel Sea*."

"What's that?"

"A novel. Well-known novel. Oh, and a pleasant woman

came into the shop at lunchtime. Interior decorator. From London. Intends to take a place here for the weekends."

"In what way pleasant?"

"Easy to talk to, I suppose."

"Attractive?"

"Very."

"Married?"

When I shook my head she asked how I knew.

"No wedding ring."

"My! You are getting observant in your old age."

"*She* thought I looked young."

"What made her say that?"

"Oh. She'd expected the owner to be venerable and dusty."

"Well, the main thing is: was she a good customer?"

Was that the main thing? In my case, not certain why, I upped the profit on her patronage.

"Thirty pounds?" exclaimed Junie. "Not bad. What did she buy?"

"A lot of bits and pieces. But principally a bowl. Present for the friend she was staying with."

"Boy friend?"

"No. Some woman."

"Perhaps she doesn't like men."

I stared at her. This seemed so wholly out of character. And was distinctly irritating. "Why the hell should you think that?"

"I honestly don't know." She, too, seemed disconcerted.

"Just because she may be in her mid-thirties and unmarried and happening to spend a few days with a woman mate of hers…"

"I agree. I wish I hadn't said it." She stood up. "I must go and look at supper."

And the ironic thing was: it was far more my own kind of remark. I remembered how Junie had recently surprised me by saying in the company of friends, "Oh, these men! They think if a woman isn't married by forty she's got to be either hideous or gay! They simply won't believe she might prefer

13

to lead her own life and not be weighed down by commitments and demands!"

Till then I hadn't realised Women's Lib had so much as trickled underneath our door. Also it was the first occasion I'd heard Junie attach its modern connotation to the word 'gay'. Mike and Sandra too had looked surprised. But times were changing and it was inconceivable even Junie or Sandra should remain untouched. Yet it hadn't become a problem. Thank God. When we'd got back from the restaurant I'd asked Junie if *she* ever felt weighed down.There had been only the slightest hesitation. "Oh, don't be silly. I was talking in the abstract. It was simply that Mike sounded so very smug and I just had to let go." I hadn't much enjoyed the evening and was teetering on the abyss of a mood but unexpectedly, in the end, it had proved to be all right.

And anyhow I knew well enough Miss Sheffield wasn't gay: I could visualise the way she'd looked at me.

Instinctively my head turned towards a set of shelves. This was mostly taken up by books and a CD player but I stretched across and pulled out our earliest photograph album and opened it three pages in. I found a double spread commemorating my sporting achievements when I'd been eighteen: the same year I'd left school: the year before I'd married Junie. There were pictures of Sam Groves, bowler, batsman and wicket-keeper; Sam Groves, centre-forward; Sam Groves on the diving board; Sam Groves in the boxing ring (arm upraised to show he was a champ). In each of them you saw either a grinning or else a grimly determined fair-haired giant: healthy, handsome, unstoppable. Poised to win cups, set records, beat the world.

It all seemed a long time back. Another life. Yet tormentingly close, too: practically within feel, within smell, within earshot. In and out of present-tense immediacy. Eighteen years ago. Midpoint exactly.

But really I hadn't changed that much. My hair was only a little thinner, my stomach remained hard. A few laughter lines; light creases on the brow; no apparent middle-age spread. I was a man now, of course, not a stripling. But essentially I hadn't changed.

I wasn't aware of June's presence until I realised she was at my elbow. I closed the album with a snap.

She smiled. "You look as if I'd somehow caught you out!"

"Moonshine!"

"Would you like another drink? Supper ready very soon."

She replenished my glass. "But you haven't told me yet about *your* day," I said. "And where've the children got to? This house seems suspiciously quiet."

"Ah. Matt's still sitting in the garden working on his project. Panic stations: it has to be handed in on Monday: somebody telephoned to remind him! And Ella decided to spend the night at Jalna. She went off after lunch."

"And what about their mum?"

"Well, as for me..." Did I imagine it or was she sounding nervous?

"Yes?"

"Well, as for me, I began on the big spare bedroom!"

"What!"

She nodded. "I got all the wallpaper stripped off and sanded down the woodwork. Also I put undercoat on the door and skirting boards. I didn't get as far as the window because it was growing late and I had to start the meal."

"But...?"

"It must've been the sunshine or something. I felt like it. You don't mind, do you? I was hoping you'd be pleased."

Pleased? I was certainly amazed. The decorating had always been my province; not the choosing but the actual work. I'd been planning to embark on that particular bedroom the following Tuesday evening.

But on the other hand.

It wasn't that I lived for colour schemes and renovation.

"Yes. Of course I'm pleased." Perhaps there wasn't much conviction in my tone; and yet it could have been the truth. "Very pleased." I grinned. "Tell me, though. Whatever

15

happened to Baby June?"

There was a ritualistic answer to that one, too. "Oh, something rather horrible," she said. She laughed. "You know, I really quite enjoyed myself. Sang lots of songs, thought lots of thoughts, listened to the radio a bit. Was almost sorry when it was time for the potatoes and a lightning-quick bath and making myself all fresh and gorgeous for you."

"Unutterably gorgeous."

"You know I never contradict!"

"I love you, Junie Moon."

"I love you, Samson Groves."

That was a frequent minor variation. Samuel and Samson were fairly interchangeable.

3

Ella not being at supper Matt got her share of the wine; which even when added to his own still wasn't much; so naturally he complained if only as a question of form.

Matt was our twelve-year-old, large-boned and darkly blond, favouring me, whereas Ella, at fifteen, took after Junie.

He was so like my youthful self the resemblance could make me wince. And at such moments I often experienced a sharp longing for my mother — adored, adoring mother — who'd died of cancer a few days before my thirteenth birthday. He had my mother's blue eyes (my own, like Junie's, being brown) along with the freckles which I hadn't inherited either.

Now at table he turned on me those trustful peepers and I knew at once there was something he wanted.

"Dad?"

"No. Whatever it is — the answer's no."

He grinned. "After supper *will* you help me with my project?" I had forgotten. Before we'd sat down he had been told: We'll see.

"I … suppose so."

"Oh, thanks, Pop. You're a good bloke."

"For the moment."

"Oh, no, for always."

It gave me a warm feeling, being a good bloke for always, even if he did inspect his fingers to let us see they were crossed.

While his mother and I were having coffee I told him to run to a nearby shop to buy a couple of Aeros and a couple of bags of crisps — for Junie shook her head with regard to herself — so that we'd both have something to nibble as we laboured in his bedroom.

"Can I get a coke as well?"

"*May* I?" I spun one of the coins I'd been about to hand him. "If it's tails — yes."

It landed on the carpet with the Queen uppermost.

Blithely disregarded.

"Great!" He gave my cheek a fervent kiss. "We'll have a sort of midnight feast."

"Just so long as it finishes some three hours early."

His bedroom was as untidy as ever but oddly appealing, his divan placed beneath the window with brightly coloured cushions thrown along the length of it — two propped against the corner where his head would rest. The walls were covered with travel posters and postcards, with magazine cutouts of mainly sports stars, and pictures of animals he'd drawn himself. Books and records filled not only his shelves but overflowed onto his desk; also onto the carpet where they mingled, much at risk, with cars and tennis balls and a seaplane in the process of construction. It was a junior, domesticated version of a treasure island, eminently father-friendly. I sat on the floor, my feet tucked underneath me, and Matt drew up his comfortable but battered armchair. In his lap some loose-leaf paper rested on a boys' adventure annual — circa 1950.

"Now then," I said. "The six people whom you'd most like to change places with... Six seems rather a lot, doesn't it?"

"Well, I suppose we've had a month to do it. Too long really. If it were just a week I wouldn't have forgotten."

"Mmm," I said. "In any case. Who are the five you've got?"

"Greg Rusedski, Alan Shearer, Darren Gough... David Duchovny and Noel Gallagher. But I couldn't think of much to write about Noel Gallagher."

Alan Shearer reminded me of Moira Shearer. We'd hang onto Alan Shearer, even if we dispensed with all the rest of them.

"It doesn't seem an awfully varied list. Three sportsmen. Two bods out of show business."

"Yes, but different branches of sport and different

branches of show business. And nobody said it needed to be varied."

"But no politicians... doctors... women..."

"What do I know about politicians or doctors? Miss Martin said she wanted it to come from the heart. And the girls will probably write about the women: odds-on it's Mariah Carey, Demi Moore and the Spice Girls." He gave a heartfelt "Yuk!"

"If all of you are writing on the same people it's going to be a bit boring for Miss Martin."

"That's her problem."

"Yours too — if you're aiming to rise at all above the common herd."

"Listen, Dad. I've done those five. I don't have time to change them."

I looked at his face and saw how obdurate he was and decided not to push it. His top-grade mark could still perhaps be saved.

"Okay, then. So the sixth has to be a snorter. A real humdinger."

"Gosh! How you do keep up with all the modern phraseology!"

"Quiet, you." While we searched for candidates we opened our bags of crisps; munched them companionably. He offered me his can of coke but I shook my head abstractedly. "Do these people have to be alive?"

"Oh, Dad, I'm not going to write about Julius Caesar or Napoleon. Or William Shakespeare either. Or Robert Louis Stevenson. Forget it."

"How about Ghandi?"

"No thanks."

"But with all of history to choose from can't you see your list seems very... unimaginative."

"She said from the heart."

I had a burst of inspiration.

"Hey! Superman!" I exclaimed.

"What? Oh, for Pete's sake, Dad! Get real."

"Well, wouldn't you change places with Superman?

19

I would. And I bet she didn't exclude people out of fiction."

He looked at me pityingly. "I wouldn't change places with Superman. Superman is creepy. He's a pain."

"Christ! You're difficult to please."

"Watch it," he said, more happily. "I'll tell Mum."

We settled back into ruminative munching. "I hate to feel restricted, though."

"Then don't."

"Got to find the real McCoy."

He seemed gratified by the degree of importance I was attaching to it. Held out the coke again. I accepted. I think we both felt very close.

"Hey, Matt! I've got it! A fellow no one else will think of. Do him justice and you're guaranteed to shine."

"Who is it? You?"

"Well, that hadn't actually occurred to me. No. Theseus."

This time Matt was puzzled rather than outright dismissive. "Theseus? You mean, the Minotaur Theseus? Why d'you think I should want to be like him?"

"Dozens of reasons."

My son looked sceptical.

"Firstly, young Matthias, he rid the world of the greatest evil hanging over it. Saved hundreds of lives. Thousands. Maybe millions if you bring it up to date: the cumulative effect of unborn children…"

"Dad, it's a myth! But you certainly do believe in things, don't you? Once you get going?"

He sounded half admiring, half uneasy. I ignored it. I gave him a moment to relate all this to modern times: to think in terms of nuclear warheads and the like; of tyrants such as Pol Pot and Saddam Hussein; I hoped he'd make his own connections.

"Secondly, he delivered people from other kinds of oppression."

I thought Nelson Mandela might come into his mind. Or Martin Luther King; Mother Theresa; Albert Schweitzer. He probably hadn't heard of Dag Hammarskjold or Pope

John XXIII.

"Sounds a bit like Jesus Christ."

I decided to ignore this, too. It was no part of my aim to encourage irony on such a subject.

"Thirdly, he had a marvellously romantic love affair. When he set off to kill the Minotaur, Ariadne held the thread which would later guide him out of the labyrinth even though she was betraying her family by doing so."

I paused again, endeavouring to remember all the great twentieth-century love stories in which a woman provided similarly heroic assistance. Beyond doubt a plethora. I could only come up with *Spellbound. Pandora and the Flying Dutchman.* And Jean Kent throwing herself in the path of a bullet intended for Stewart Granger.

"Fourthly, it seems to me he led a golden existence; full of adventure and achievement and a steady sense of purpose; right from the moment he started preparing to go off in search of his father."

"Imagine actually going off in search of your father!" declared Matt.

"Ha ha! Very funny."

I waited.

"But tell me, what do you think of it?"

"Well, I don't know. Just Superman in shorts and sandals...tunic and sandals."

I began to feel seriously impatient. "But I don't believe you wouldn't want to be like him. And why the heck should he be creepy? Oh, forget the movies, can't you?"

He remained indecisive.

"Here. Pass me the paper and your Biro."

That made up his mind for him. He surrendered them immediately. Gave me the annual, too. Thoughtfully unwrapped his Aero and then began to cut out the shot-putter from an empty packet of Scott's Porage Oats; at much risk to his mum's sharpest pair of scissors.

It was a time for wandering in the garden; Junie and I strolled hand in hand across the grass. The air felt gentle and a blackbird, singing in the branches of one of our apple trees, was answered, counterpointed, by a thrush. We made a tour of the estate: admired the goldfish in the fishpond and the splendour of a clump of daffodils upon a bank; the tiny buds of blossom that were now appearing overhead: we had pear and cherry trees as well as apple. It was a beautiful half-acre, bounded by a high wall of weathered brick. We sat on a wooden bench in a small natural arbour, stretched out our legs, looked back in the declining light at the soft red brick of the house itself.

"You know, I never take this place for granted," said Junie. "Do you? That's one of the things I was thinking about today. How fortunate we are."

"Especially if you consider what's going on in other parts of the world."

I should have been a moralist.

"Yes, but I wasn't meaning that. I meant — without comparison."

She gave my hand a squeeze.

"Remember how we so much liked this house," she said, "we used to make detours on our way from school, simply to look at it? It wasn't grand or anything but I just knew any family must be happy here. At peace with themselves. I imagined flagstones on the kitchen floor, rows of jams and pickles in the larder, breakfast in the garden, flowers on a polished table in the hall, sunlight filling every room." She laughed. "And in some ways it's been even better than that. For instance I hadn't reckoned on that bright red Aga: practically the hub of the whole house…"

"You hadn't reckoned on the house at all. Whoever would

have thought we'd end up in a rectory?" I smiled, wryly. "Without my taking holy orders?"

But it certainly been extraordinary. (Miraculous, said Junie.) Suddenly we'd heard a new rectory was being built, actually in the church grounds, half a mile away; this present one would soon be up for sale. We'd known instantly that it was meant for us. Yet our utter conviction hadn't saved us from anxiety; nor obsession. We'd likened it to being in love. It was in fact far worse. I'd never experienced such fear of ultimate frustration: there could exist no other house so wholly right for us. It was ridiculous how childish we had been. Well, no — not me. Junie. *Now* she had grown placid but that was only because of years of trust in my protection. *Then* she had seemed as mercurial as I myself had been stoical and strong.

And resourceful. We went to Junie's parents; asked for help. I was in the mood to barter: an unacknowledged pact. They'd known me for five years, had all but adopted me. Groomed me, tagged me. They themselves had married young and been as happy as lovebirds. Likewise they'd always claimed I had no need of university. 'Gilding the golden boy,' was what they called it. (Golden Boy: my epithet at school.) More honestly they could have called it: giving me the chance to fall in love with other girls. No, they said. Better to settle down in a good job, get married, start a family, stay in Deal. The Fletcher clan was nothing if not patriarchal.

Sorry, Freudian slip.

Matriarchal.

The house belonged to the Church Commissioners, who knew there were other parties interested; and decided, finally, upon a sealed bid auction.

We had no idea, of course, what our competitors were offering. We became reckless. Didn't care if we went too high. Didn't care how long it was going to take to pay back Junie's parents.

Pay them back, that is, the difference between the sum

we'd offered and the far smaller sum a building society had offered *us*; in order to be eligible I had hurriedly applied for a position at Lloyds Bank in the town.

The day we learnt we'd got the house should have been, as Junie said, one of the most exciting of our lives. It was only a pity I suffered from toothache during most of it — and perhaps, too, a small bit, from reaction.

"Yes, we've been lucky," I agreed. I prodded thoughtfully at the lawn with the tip of one shoe. "This grass will soon need mowing." I hadn't cut it yet this year.

Then I yawned and withdrew my hand from hers and stretched my arms out sensuously. It was an evening that induced contentment and gave a pleasant preview of approaching summer.

"You wouldn't feel like walking Susie with me?"

"Oh, that would be nice, darling, but I can't. For one thing I've got some pies in the oven: pies to take tomorrow. And for another it would mean leaving Matt on his own. I know he's quite a big boy now and we wouldn't be away for long but all the same..."

"He is quite a big boy now. Do you realise it's his birthday in under a fortnight?"

"How can I forget? He gives us plenty of reminders."

"If we were Jewish he would then be fully adult." I was aware my feelings were confused.

"It's *my* birthday in just over a month. I think I'll be fully adult, too. Oh, I'm not sure. Maybe."

"As you know, he wants some dumbbells. If you like I'll order you the same."

"Why not take him on your walk?"

"He's just got in a bath. To celebrate completion of his project. He's been lent a Stephen King and means to have a wallow."

I called the dog and went out on my own.

We walked down to the sea. I found a stick for Susie to chase along the shingle and during intervals of hurling it tried to skim flat stones across the waves. Moonlight set a path upon the water and the sky was packed with stars. For a full minute I stood there with my head thrown back. I imagined I was Captain Kirk, commander of the starship Enterprise, now speeding boldly through the galaxies. It was nice to think of him up there, busily protecting us.

"Good evening, Mr Groves."

It was Moira Sheffield and another woman. I'd been so caught up in space I gave a start.

"I'm sorry. I feel we interrupted some important metaphysical reverie."

"Yes. I was whizzing through the stars along with Captain Kirk."

"Oh, in that case it was important. It's just that seeing you I didn't stop to think. Small world," she added. "Isn't it?"

"Not when you're looking up at the stars," smiled her companion. "Good evening," she said to me.

"Mr Groves; Mrs Dawlish. But I believe you two already know each other."

"No, no," said Mrs Dawlish, who was fortyish and pleasant-looking but — in this half-light at any rate — totally unfamiliar. "I've been into the shop on several occasions, that's all; no reason why you should remember me. It's by far the most enthralling shop in town."

"Thank you. Yes, of course I remember you." We shook hands. It occurred to me as strange I should be shaking hands with *her* when I had never done so with Miss Sheffield.

"And by the way," she said, "I love the fruit bowl."

Then Susie came bounding back from wherever she'd been

and jumped up at all three of us. I called her off sharply; and to my pleasure she obeyed.

"Oh, that's all right," said Miss Sheffield, bending to stroke the chastened animal. "But why Susie? I'd have thought you'd call her Patch."

"Susie's short for Black-Eyed Susan."

"Ah."

I was pleased to be discovered not totally predictable.

"Isn't it a heavenly evening!" said Mrs Dawlish. "I feel we scarcely had need of our coats."

"Mr Groves is evidently a hardier type."

"Or more improvident," I said.

"Doesn't your wife," asked Miss Sheffield, "tell you you ought to wear your coat?"

"How do you know I've got one? A wife, that is. Or come to that — a coat?"

She laughed. "Oh, don't be so difficult. I may as well tell you: you were the subject of a spot of speculation. I said you didn't look as if you could be married. Liz said she was sure you were."

I'd wondered whether they'd have spoken of me. And clearly Miss Sheffield's impression had been favourable: *D'you suppose he's married?* I felt so gratified that — ludicrously — I began to get an erection.

"First...why did you think I couldn't be? Did I come across as queer?"

"Good heavens, no," she smiled. "Not at all. You looked too..."

"Young?" I said, hopefully.

"Let's just say, too unbowed by care and the responsibilities of family life. Too boyish — no, that isn't right. Too happy, maybe? I don't know what it was, really; merely a feeling."

"And you, Mrs Dawlish? Did I always impress you, then, as appearing to carry the world on my shoulders?"

"He's playing with us," said Miss Sheffield. "Now that isn't very nice. It's not the hallmark of a gentleman. We made ourselves vulnerable and he betrayed our trust."

"Perhaps I'm simply not as cynical as Moira is," said Mrs Dawlish.

"Yes, she is cynical," I said. "Isn't she?" I was aware that I was flirting — almost as blatantly as her friend was.

"Also I think to myself," went on Mrs Dawlish, "that if a man is in his thirties and interested in women and (well, I may as well say it) as attractive as you are...then certainly he's married. There rests my case."

"And I suppose," said Miss Sheffield, "that if into the bargain he has a dog... None of it conclusive but, yes, I admit I'm gradually coming around to your way of thinking. I'm going to lose my 20p."

"You had 20p riding upon this?"

"Finally — most damning bit of all, the bit that really clinches it — he won't tell us. Now why should he be cagey?"

"Okay, I'll come clean, then."

"Well?"

"No, I'm not married."

"*Not?*" exclaimed Miss Sheffield.

"No. You win your 20p."

"Living with somebody?"

"No."

"Not even that?"

"Not even that."

"Which just shows, doesn't it, about the truthfulness of first impressions? One shouldn't lose one's confidence."

"Well, what about *my* first impressions?" asked Mrs Dawlish, reasonably.

She didn't get an answer, though. "But Mr Groves. How in heaven's name have you escaped so long?"

"*More* cynicism, Miss Sheffield?"

"Oh, possibly I'm justified. I mean — having been married myself at one time."

"Really?" I added slowly: "Well, waddayaknow?"

"So where does that leave me?" asked Mrs Dawlish. "I still am. Married."

"Plainly it was Mrs Sheffield," I answered, "who was handing out those burdens which make a person bowed. Plainly it's Mrs Sheffield who represents the kind of woman a husband must escape from; a potential husband, that is." Then I recognised how tactless I was being: an actual husband had already done so. I almost apologised but was frightened to compound my gaffe.

"Wrong," said the butt of all that mild disappointment. (Yet why should I feel disappointment?)

"Wrong?"

"Yes. You had it right the first time. *Miss* Sheffield. I went back to my maiden name. But as a way of breaking free from all such confusion — how about Moira?"

"Sam," I said, automatically.

"I know."

"And Liz," said Mrs Dawlish, "if the fact of my not merely being married but even fairly contentedly so doesn't altogether rule me out. At the moment I *am* a grass widow, which ought to count a little in my favour."

"Actually, I — "

"We were just filling our lungs with sea air," said Moira, "before tripping along to *The Lord Nelson* for a quick one before closing. You wouldn't care to join us?" Even in only the moonlight — especially, perhaps, in only the moonlight — her smile was surely as entrancing as any smile of Lady Hamilton's. Her skin looked velvety and flawless. I felt a longing just to touch it; to brush my knuckles slowly down her cheek.

"Well, thank you; yes, I'd enjoy that," I answered; pensively. "I — oh, hell. I've got no money on me." I'd given the last of my small change to Matt; had left my wallet in my jacket pocket.

"I shall treat you," she said. "Out of my winnings."

"And if we have time for any second round," said Liz Dawlish, "I shall treat you, too. But I shall have to do it, unhappily, simply out of the goodness of my heart."

"And how about you, Susie? What's yours going to be?

A refreshing pint of five-star water?" Susie had been patiently sitting on the pebbles throughout all this. Now, as Moira spoke to her, she cocked her head inquiringly, as if desperately anxious to understand, and her long white tail swept rhythmically across the stones. Moira bent a second time to stoke her.

"Good dog," she said, as she straightened up. "I expected you to testify for Liz!" We began to mount towards the promenade, the shingle slipping noisily away beneath our shoes with every hard-won step.

Here was my opportunity. For the retraction of a lighthearted act of derring-do — because I'd wanted to see if I could get away with it and how it would have felt. My opportunity, after that fortuitous entry into a forbidden world (O brave new world: already having drinks bought for me, unilaterally, by women in a pub!) and into that heady kingdom of what might have been. A brief, ten-minute trespass.

But far *too* brief. Impossible to leave so soon.

So why not make it an hour? Playful rascal back to solid citizen by midnight. Contrite but forgiven. And understood. Reassured he hasn't lost his finery.

"What's this?" I said. "Susie, star witness for the Dawlish camp! Then can't a single man who's lonely be permitted to possess a dog?"

"It truly didn't occur to me he couldn't — not at first. But subconsciously, perhaps, I still think of dogs as belonging to families. Stupid of me. I'm sorry."

"Actually she belongs to our neighbours," I told her. "They're fairly elderly and sometimes I walk her for them." Gilding the lily and the golden boy as well. It all came to me so easily. No trace of guilt. Before it had been fun. Now it was exhilarating.

"Our?" she repeated. "*Our* neighbours?"

That gave me pause. But she misread my hesitation: thought I hadn't understood the question.

"Do you still live at home, then? With your parents?"

"Oh, no. My parents are both dead." Gilding be blowed; when hoping to deceive you must stick as closely as you can to the truth. "My mother died when I was a boy, and my father..." I hadn't realised I would mention this but I found it wasn't difficult. "Well, my father died just two days afterwards. From then on I was brought up by my grandmother."

But now I was faced with a choice: should I resurrect Gran and give my life a flavour of nobility and sacrifice — the grateful grandson paying back his debt — or should I tear away completely from the thought of apronstrings (implicit however uncritically in the surprised tone of the question) and perhaps invent a commune: a way of living which, ideally, had always quite appealed to me — especially if located on some sun-drenched far-off island? And of course lodgers were another possibility; slightly more mundane.

"Your father died just two days afterwards?" The cynical Miss Sheffield was very clearly shaken.

I still kept my tone casual. "Well, they talk about people dying of a broken heart. And you never saw a husband who..." But I found I couldn't keep it all that casual.

"And people really do die, then, of broken hearts?" she asked after a moment, quietly.

I nodded. "Especially when assisted by the right number of aspirin."

"Oh —dear God!"

Mrs Dawlish also drew in breath.

But in the space of scarcely a minute this had all got too heavy. "Maybe it wasn't quite as bad as it sounds." Which was unquestionably the biggest lie I'd told them yet. "I managed to cope with it. At school. Threw myself into my studies. Into sport, as well. Became a bit of an all-rounder." Well, that was certainly true; though I made it sound almost as if I had *benefitted* from being an orphan.

"And then it was your grandmother who looked after you?"

"And now I look after my grandmother." There was a pause. Possibly liars, too, abhor a vacuum. "She's eighty-six years old."

She would have been, anyway. And if this were so I'd still have been looking after her. Naturally. As I'd been doing — as Junie and I had been doing, that is — until about seven years earlier.

"But now I vote we change the subject," I said.

"Of course. Forgive me. I didn't mean to stir up painful memories."

For a minute in fact there wasn't much conversation at all — merely the clatter of cascading stones. But we were almost on the front. I re-attached Susie's lead. We were opposite an ice-cream parlour; apparently business was brisk. Liz spoke of the holiday atmosphere. At first all our comments sounded forced but soon the easiness returned. Moira was looking out to sea. "Have we been pardoned yet for dragging you down from the stars? I still feel it was mean."

"Nonsense. The stars will be there anytime. But you madam, go back to town tomorrow night."

"That was extremely gallant."

"A bit creepy, actually." I nearly said — so very nearly said— As my son would undoubtedly be the first to point out. "But sincere," I added, with a flush.

She smiled. "Oh, by the way, I've definitely decided to go ahead with that cottage in Silver Street."

"I thought it was decided already."

"No. I was dithering. Finally made up my mind over coffee after lunch."

In the lamplight the red hair with the green scarf that matched her eyes was one of the loveliest things I'd seen.

"So when do you move in?"

"It could be soon, the house being empty." But then it appeared she'd thought of something. "Perhaps, Sam, you'd like to take a look at it? I could do with your advice."

"I'd be pleased to."

"Do you mean that? In which case... well, how about next Sunday?"

I had to think quickly; but though, often, my brain seemed

only to function in slow motion, tonight it slid smoothly on castors. "Sunday would be great."

"Or on second thoughts — how about tomorrow?"

I'd have given almost anything to be able to say yes.

"No, I'm sorry. That I can't manage."

"Next Sunday then."

"Right." I forced myself to play it fairly cool but I suppose I was in the grip of a kind of fever. Practically a madness.

This wasn't the time for a reversion to solid citizenship.

This was my time for living dangerously.

6

When I got home Junie was in bed. "You must've gone on a long walk!" she said. "Did you both enjoy it?"

"Mmm." I was careful to keep my distance in case she smelt the beer. (Though it wouldn't have mattered: she would only have laughed at my feeling too ashamed to tell her.) "When we set out I hadn't the least idea I'd ever go so far."

I went and made our bedtime cup of tea and sang while I waited for the kettle.

"You sound very pleased with yourself. I could hear you all the way from here. I thought at first it was the radio."

"I'm sorry."

"What for? It's good to hear you sing. You couldn't fancy a biscuit, by any chance?"

"I'll get the tin." But while I was downstairs it occurred to me she might prefer a sandwich. I made us both a cheese-and-cucumber.

"Oh, what treats!" she said. "How wicked!"

This was the kind of midnight feast Matt would approve. We sat up in bed eating our sandwich and slice of chocolate cake (I had decided to go the whole hog), sipping our tea and reading our library books. In my case it was *The Shape Of Things To Come* but I should think I read barely a dozen lines and took in the meaning of barely a dozen words. I wasn't even aware Junie had looked up from her own book and was studying me.

"Penny for them," she said.

"What?"

"You were miles away. I'd love to know what you were thinking."

"How insulting! Only valued at a penny?" I held up my novel. "Just doing a spot of time travelling." From now on

I should have to be more careful.

"And obviously having fun. It was mean of me to pull you back."

That was ironic, I thought. I always prided myself on being alive to irony.

"Poor darling," she said. "So pathetic."

"What is?"

"You wandering off into your own little dream world and me trying to pull you back — no, not trying — but at any rate bringing you down with a bump."

"Yes, is there no privacy anywhere? May a man never hope to escape? I shall go to clean my teeth!" If I'd had a cloak I would have swirled it; any self-respecting audience would have hissed.

Cleaning my teeth I gazed critically at my reflection. I should never have eaten that sandwich, nor that piece of cake; not to mention the Aero bar and bag of crisps. (The pints of beer had been permissible.) Starting tomorrow I must cut down both on sugar and fat. I could probably lose several pounds in a week and several pounds would be sufficient.

But then I squared my shoulders and held myself erect. Oh, what the hell. Eating was one of the pleasures of life (except at those periods when I grew compulsive) and anyway I looked all right. To become obsessive over a few odd pounds — and I swiftly grew obsessive over anything I went in for, health regimes, language-learning, economy drives — struck me as being life-denying, negative. Entirely out of tune with the way I felt at present and from now on (meaning to savour every moment, open my arms to all the munificence every day would have on offer) intended to feel for ever. Yes! *Yes*! *YES*!!!

Why, even cleaning one's teeth could be an enriching experience! I thought about toothpaste. I'd never given much thought to toothpaste. What was it made of; how long had they had it; how was it coaxed inside the tube? I thought about the rest of mankind cleaning its teeth, in times of peace and in times of war, sharing with me this unhymned facet of being a member of the human race. I felt warm towards the human race. How many thousands, I wondered, were spitting out into the basin at this precise moment, declaring themselves my brothers, uniting in the great adventure. I felt I might have garnered some rare new insight; however difficult it might have been to put a name to it.

I felt warm towards the human race; warm towards my wife. When she too had been to the bathroom and switched off her lamp and murmured a drowsy "Good night, sleep tight," turning her back towards me, I slid across and put my arm about her and nestled up close. Compliant as ever — although she herself, sadly, seldom initiated anything — she turned again and I levered my other arm beneath her. I pulled up her nightdress.

"I wish you'd take this thing right off." I myself hadn't worn anything in bed since I was seventeen; much to my grandmother's disapproval.

"Aren't you feeling sleepy?" she asked.

"No, not a bit."

"Me, I'm feeling sleepy."

"You won't do in a moment, love. My erection pledge. I'm going to make you *sing*! Every inch of you."

"That's good," she said. "Furthermore... I know just what I'll sing. Every inch of me."

"What?" But I wasn't quite sure if I'd heard correctly; owing to her yawn.

"Let's Put Out The Light And Go To Sleep."

Junie had a sense of humour but she wasn't generally witty. Her sally was so spontaneous and surprising — surprising to herself just as much as me — that we got the giggles. We rolled about in utter helplessness until it really did begin to hurt; and even after that the laughter kept resurfacing. I was reminded of the lyric from another song: 'You've got a sense of humour... and humour is death to romance!' But Mr Irving Berlin had got that wrong; or at least in this case. Junie was so aroused by our merriment and by the pleasure of her own success — aroused in both its senses — that she sat up and threw off her nightgown while I was still wiping away my tears. She slipped down again and I felt her radiant warmth and swinging breasts — especially glorious on first contact, both the warmth and what contained it — move in and settle against my chest; settle luxuriatingly. I let out a long and well-contented sigh.

"I wish you'd learn to sleep nude."

"It's too cold."

"Not tonight. I think summer's on the way."

"Besides. You know I don't like to be looked at."

"But that's silly. You've got a nice body."

"Podgy."

"No. It feels wonderful."

"I'm glad you think so. You're very sweet. You feel good, too."

In essence, we had had this conversation often.

"Why do I feel good?" I asked. "Explain why I feel good."

"You just do."

"But why? I know why you feel good. You're all powdery and soft and comfortable."

"Comfortable!"

"Like a peach with a warm and fragrant bloom to it. Ripe deliciousness; juicy perfection. I wanna be a wasp!"

But the buzz I made was more like that of a bee; and the lip-smacking little nips probably like those of no insect or animal on earth.

Junie giggled again and feigned alarm at falling prey to so resolute a sucker. Feigned anxiety, too. "But won't fruit that's ripe and juicy soon be past its use-by date?"

"What a pessimist!"

"Realist?"

"And not just *any* fruit! Weren't you paying attention? I was being specific."

"Yes. I was a lovely, dusted, hothouse peach! I don't mind you being specific."

"Well, then. *Specifically.* I really like your tits: they're full and heavy and mature. Specifically, I like your bum. I like your cunt. I honestly can't say which bit I love the best." The lyric poet might here have slipped away but every part I itemised received a fondle and a kiss. "I think my cock would probably pick your cunt." Junie murmured happily with each fresh pause in the progression. "So tell me now which bit of me you like the best! Tell me now why *I* feel good."

"Oh... because you're all hard and lean and *strong,*" she said. "You've got such a nice chest and arms and legs. All muscled and gorgeous. And my cunt likes your cock, too — you know that. Yummy." She yawned again. "I am sorry."

This dialogue, as well, wasn't completely new.

But her yawn had warned me I ought to cut back on the talk and proceed with the action. I carried on kissing and caressing every part of her. She stroked whatever bit of me her hands came into contact with.

"Is this pleasant? I asked. "Are you enjoying it?"

"Mmm. Nice. Sorry if I don't seem terribly responsive."

"Any particular requests?"

"No. You choose. Anything."

"Like your back massaged?"

"Lovely. But you're doing all the work."

As usual! The thought was involuntary.

"I don't mind that. Your turn next. Roll over."

"I don't know where you get your energy."

She'd always said I had a talent for massage and as I worked she stretched beneath the arch formed by my thighs and burrowed down voluptuously into the mattress, sighing deeply. I kneaded and pummelled and felt my sweat breaking out. During a moment's respite I turned the lamp on and she protested only feebly. As I moved slowly down her back I glanced from time to time into the mirror on her dressing table. I got as much excitement from the sheen of my own body and the taut look of its muscles as I did from the increasing responsiveness of hers. When I reached the base of her spine I gave her bottom a couple of tentative smacks and finding she squirmed pleasurably beneath them gradually stepped up their power. Eventually I pushed her legs apart and introduced two fingers. She was moist by now and soon she raised herself, drew up her knees, for better penetration. Our movements grew more frenetic, until at last she was whispering, "Harder, harder!", and I was pumping my two fingers just as fast and far as they would go, feeling the tension in my bicep.

When finally she came we both flopped down exhausted. I felt smug, triumphant. She turned over after a while and I put my hand back on her crotch.

But this time she didn't want my hand. She wanted my penis.

I wondered how many millions of my brothers might be keeping me company. I rejoiced in it. Male solidarity. All those bums going up and down in unison with mine.

However, I'd been inside her scarcely half a minute — to a count of merely sixty-nine — when I found it impossible to hold back.

Which was immensely disappointing.

"I'm out of practice," I said. It must have been well over a month since we had last made love.

"Never mind; so long as you enjoyed it. I did."

"But listen," I said. I raised myself upon my arms so as not to weigh down too heavily. "We mustn't alow ourselves to get out of practice any more. Mustn't. Understood?"

"Understood." She smiled at me, relaxed and satisfied and pink and creamy in the lamplight. "So what are you going to do about it?"

"You'll see!"

"Good. Do you know, with your back arched like that, you look all glistening and golden and masterful up there?" She ran her hands across my chest, innocently tweaking dampish curls, then stroked my shoulders and my arms. I felt myself begin to stir in her again.

"And don't I always?"

"Always," she agreed.

"Shall I tell you what I am going to do? Henceforward? Gonna fuck you in the morning — fuck you in the evening — fuck you at suppertime... Yes, ma'am, kindly take note, ma'am. I hereby file intention of turning into the world's greatest lover. Bar none."

If she had replied, "But you already are," or, "I think you're practically there," then the stirring might have strengthened into hardness. "Well, sounds all right to me," she murmured.

I sighed. "I love you, Junie Moon."

"I love you, Samson Groves."

Then I gave her a parting kiss on the cheek and leant over and pulled out a wad of tissues. After we'd mopped up and she'd reached for her nightdress and struggled into it she switched out the lamp. I turned on my side, away from her, and she snuggled up against my back.

"Thank you for that, my darling," she said.

"Thank you, my love."

"You know what the trouble is, Sam? Most days I get so tired. By bedtime all I can do is lie here like a sack of flour."

"Moonshine. You're a marvellous lay."

"That's very dear of you but even so... Well, just wait until the children have grown up and left home and then you'll see how much more energy I'll have and what I'll do with it. Not that I'm wanting to wish any of our lives away, obviously; or to get rid of the children either." She sighed and I felt her long release of breath, cool, fanning my shoulder blades.

"You shouldn't have taken on that extra job today. The decorating," I mumbled. "You'd better let me finish it."

"Oh, but I told you. I find that creative. Oddly fulfilling."

"Matt won't be leaving home for six years. Six years at the earliest. I'll be forty-two by then."

"What's so wrong with that?" She laughed. "And besides. It'll give me plenty of time to lose weight."

"I warn you: I'm not waiting six years until our next fuck. I might just get — with a lot of self-restraint — until the morning."

39

"No, you silly, I didn't mean that, of course. I meant, until you chase me naked through the house again…"

"Ah. Good night, Junie."

"Sleep well, darling."

She turned again, and, retreating to her own side of the bed, soon settled into easy slumber.

7

But I didn't sleep — not for a long while. I lay on my back, hands beneath head, and stared into my crystal ball, bright with warm enchantment. Was she awake too, sparkling-eyed, there at the Dawlishes', a strong man's stone's throw away: a judge of Israel's? I pictured her red hair tumbling on the pillow; her slim dancer's body sprawled langorously, and bare; arms stretching in sudden exuberant abandon, as she, like myself, contemplated the future and felt an irresistible urge to express something wonderful. I was confident that if she *were* awake she'd be thinking of me; nearly as confident that if she were asleep my shadow would be pressing on her dreams. And her dreams would be in Technicolor.

I was going to be so *good*, so worthy of those dreams. A new man. Dynamic, cheerful, kind. Patient; under-standing. Aware. Truly the Rock of Gibraltar Junie sometimes called me.

Away with gluttony. Meanness. Lack of charity. Away with jealousy and fear; small-mindedness. From now on I'd be living entirely for others. The doorway to life was so blazingly obvious once you'd discovered the key; I could only feel amazed and regretful I hadn't done so sooner. But at least, thank God, it had happened while I was young. With perhaps a second allocation of thirty-six years still to look forward to.

Yet even if there wasn't and there was merely one of ten years, or five, or two... even this would be enough. The short happy life of Samson Groves. Even one year — broken into sufficiently small segments — could seem illimitable.

Of course there'd have to be deception. But purely for the common good. It was through Moira I was going to grow and blossom and bear golden fruit; through me she'd meet with love and passion and fulfilment — very much the same thing. Junie would wake to find an incomparably more thoughtful husband. Ella and Matt would wake to find the best damned father on record. It was as simple as that. I aimed to become the kind of dad I myself had used to dream about.

I remembered not so long after the death of my parents watching a film on television: *Down To The Sea In Ships*. The story concerned a boy of about my own age — an orphan, like me. With a grandfather who died. But by the end he'd discovered not simply a friend but a father-substitute in the young Richard Widmark, whom he (and I) had slowly come to idealise. And, oh, the envy I had felt! An unremitting ache which for days — weeks — had left me with a sense of deprivation not exactly more real but somehow more insistent, less susceptible to the healing properties of the schoolroom, than the one I'd experienced a month or two earlier... and of course still was experiencing. I don't know quite how serious I had been but I'd climbed out of my bedroom window overlooking the back garden of my grandmother's house and stood there on the sill — in February, in my pyjamas and for fully twenty minutes — trying to find the courage to hurl myself off.

Even for some time afterwards it had remained: that hollow feeling in the pit of my stomach. Totally unreachable. Seemingly permanent.

I suppose that for a boy of thirteen I was being remarkably immature. I could hardly imagine Matt, who sometimes gave the impression of being practically a man and who, I had noticed only that evening, was already — and disconcertingly — filling out his jeans; I could hardly imagine Matt ever fantasising he was the son of Alan Shearer or David Duchovny or — who were those others he had chosen? Well, if he did, all that was going to be different from now on, anyway. Move over, David Duchovny. Here comes Samson Groves.

I brought up my wrist and looked at my watch with its illuminated dial.

It was getting on for three.

Very carefully I got up — went downstairs to the sitting room — did half an hour of vigorous exercising; then I ran myself a bath. Several times I started to sing in the bath; had to check my song abruptly. Washed my hair. In fact I'd washed it less than nineteen hours previously but I felt like total immersion. Total cleanliness, so far as that was possible. Baptism.

Mens sana in corpore sano.

Likewise, although again they hardly needed it, I trimmed my toenails; looked for a cuticle I should remove. Looked for any visible hair inside my nostrils. Rebrushed my teeth. Was almost going to shave but decided this was maybe overdoing it. Anointed myself in Cool Water.

It was ten-past-four when I went back to bed. This time I knew I'd sleep. Still marvellously happy, of course, but physically and mentally relaxed. Not that I worried about sleeping or not sleeping. Sleep didn't seem important. Tiredness was nothing but a state of mind.

And as if in confirmation I was awake again by half-past-eight and feeling great. Sunlight buttered the edges of the curtains and I stretched and lay in blissful comfort, thoroughly conscious of my state of well-being, drinking it in along with a dozen more tangible things: usually unnoticed details of the flowered wallpaper; the reproduction Pissarro above our mantelpiece, the faience candlesticks, the gilded and becherubbed mirror which I'd also brought home from the shop; my own bunched biceps as I stretched again, the well-shaped contour of my arms when I straightened them once more, the light gold sheen from wrist to elbow. I turned my head and let my right hand fall across the pillow above Junie's hair. She stirred and my fingers gently intruded into the short, thick, silvery mass. It was time for her to wake.

"I love you Junie Moon..." I put my arms about her and she burrowed into me, all warm and sleepy. I kissed her eyelids and her nose and mouth and cheeks and she made

43

small noises of contentment. When I entered her she still wasn't properly awake but made the same agreeable squeaks, wore the same soft beatific smile. This time I counted up to three hundred and twenty-eight. By the following Sunday — I had precisely a whole week — I would have increased the score to at least a couple of thousand. I felt utterly confident. It had happened before but now the difference was it would be permanent. And now I wasn't doing it simply for myself; though I don't suppose I ever had been — not exactly. But maybe a little unfairly I had the feeling Moira would appreciate it more than Junie; I mean, appreciate it more consistently and more wholeheartedly. Yet in any case... one thing was sure... they would both benefit. I'd be doing it for the three of us.

I went and washed, then came back for my bathrobe. "Darling, stay there," I said. "I'll bring you up your breakfast."

"Really?"

"Got it all planned. One of a thousand small decisions I made during the night. From now on I'm going to pamper you."

"But you already do."

"You're very precious to me, Junie."

"You, too."

It was a good, it was the right, beginning to the day.

"What were the other nine hundred and ninety-nine small decisions?"

"Mainly to do with loving you more and taking better care of you."

"All right then. I approve. But I'm sorry if it means you had a sleepless night."

"Don't be. I'm not."

I fetched *The Observer* from the mat.

"Better watch it," she said. "You'll make me even more dependent than I am already."

"That's a curious remark."

"I only meant... you mustn't spoil me too much, must you?

44

What would become of me if you ever dropped dead or something?"

I laughed, and went down to the kitchen. Susie uncurled herself from her basket and stretched and came forward to greet me. I fell to my knees and put my arms around her neck; gave her the sort of fussing she'd received on my return from work. "Did you sleep well, Susie? Did you dream of chasing bunny rabbits? Or of lapping up beer and wolfing down crisps? Tell me all about it." She loved being spoken to in this way; in my mind I slightly adapted that couplet by John Masefield: "He who gives a dog a treat, hears joy bells ring in heaven's street." I wished that Moira could have seen us. (Almost pretended that she could.) The quarry tiles were cold and hard against my shins but such minor discomfort was well worth it for the sake of seeing Susie's expression: somehow different, yet not quite definably so, to her look of the previous evening. It was a pity, I felt, dogs couldn't purr.

Moira was still strongly with me as I washed my hands and started to collect things from the larder. I began to sing. Although over the years, obviously, I had given Junie breakfast in bed on many occasions, it had never before been a *cooked* breakfast — and I was glad of that: the chance to be doing something for her this morning for the first time. It would be good, in fact, if every day could hold some new experience. That or a new thought, new insight, new item of knowledge. This was a further resolution to be added to my list.

Perhaps that list ought to be committed to paper before long, expanded on, made concrete. To paper? Why not a journal? Lists were dry but a diary could comprise a swallow dive — functional *and* aesthetic — into a whole fresh concept of behaviour. (Fresh to me, that is.) God! It was amazing how once you'd decided to enter the water headfirst the right ideas came bubbling up at you. It made you feel there was a charge in the air, you were a lightning rod, a channel for something dynamic. Made me feel I should never have laughed at that man who claimed he had been used to score a melody for Mozart; nor at the woman who said she'd many times met Freddie Mercury — but only since his death. There were melodies by Mozart lining up for me. Meetings with Freddie Mercury. With Audrey Hepburn. William Holden. Princess Di. Princess Grace. President Kennedy...

But first I had to concentrate on breakfast.

I prepared two trays, one for Matt as well as Junie, and I went out in the garden, barefoot, for a daffodil to lay on each. Then I cooked four eggs, sunnyside up, after I'd done some mushrooms and tomatoes and — since there were no sausages, nor bacon, in the house — fried bread and baked beans. Luckily there was some fruit juice. I decided to take this main part upstairs and then return to do the toast and coffee.

It suddenly occurred to me what tune I was humming: an old one from *Annie Get Your Gun* with which I had used to serenade Junie when we were in our teens.

> "The girl that I marry
> Will have to be
> As soft and as pink as a nurseree
> 'Stead of flittin'
> She'll be sittin'
> Next to me
> And she'll purr like a kittin..."

I smiled. I remembered her saying, "Yes, I like the idea of being a doll you can carry!" And I *had* carried her — all round the house, all round the garden, all round her parents' house as well! (Even, once, out in the town. In retrospect people had seemed surprisingly indulgent. All the world loves a lover.) "I'm so glad I've got someone I shall always be able to lean on. Lots of girls haven't, you know. You can't think how pleased it makes me."

I delivered Junie's tray first. The intake of her breath, the soaring of her hands, was genuine. "But what *are* you trying to do?" she cried. "Fatten me up for Christmas?"

"Why not? Every ounce of meat upon those bones, ma'am, is so quintessentially choice."

"You're sweet. You're a liar but you're sweet."

46

"Do you love me?"

"Ever so. Millions and millions."

Matt, too, was happily surprised. He struggled to sit up in bed and did so with the air of still being in the midst of dreams.

Like me he didn't wear pyjamas. In the light of what I'd noticed yesterday I thought his shoulders were also looking broader. A shadow lightly spilled across his chest: the possible forerunner to a quantity of fuzz. One thing was certain. If he meant to throw himself into his training with the dumbbells I should clearly have to intensify my own programme of exercises.

Soon, of course, he'd start to take more interest in the girls. And vice versa — obviously. Already I could see he was becoming quite a hunk.

"Young Matthias," I said. "I reckon you need building up." I handed him his tray and briefly ruffled his blond hair.

He, as well, had occasionally had breakfast brought up to him by me but even so… "Gosh! Eggs? Fried bread? Did *you* cook them?"

"Who else?"

"Not bad. Not bad at all. Where's the bacon?"

"Sorry; I must've forgotten it."

"And the sausage?"

"Sorry."

"But thanks, Pop, this is cool. You're a good bloke. Ta."

"No crossed fingers?"

"No crossed fingers. But next time…"

"What?"

"Don't forget the bacon."

Standing in the doorway I lifted two fingers at him; and they weren't crossed, either. He giggled. "I'll tell Mum…"

I made the toast and coffee — real coffee. I found some honey in the larder, which I knew to be Matt's favourite. Honey on butter! (*Anything* on butter was the kind of extravagance I normally frowned upon; but not this morning. Nor, indeed, ever again.) I even prepared Susie a

47

piece of buttered toast with honey, which I put outside the back door, on the path. She guarded it between her front paws and looked askance at me, as though I might be passing through some kind of crisis.

"Have *you* eaten anything yet?" asked Junie.

"No; it's ready and waiting."

"Well, go and have it, please. Your eggs'll be hard. Mine were delicious. It was all delicious — every mouthful."

I didn't mention I wouldn't be eating eggs. Despite my decision of the previous night I'd now resolved to shed those extra pounds. Not wholly for the sake of appearance; asceticism got catered for, as well. Less self-indulgence in the future... *comprenez?* Bit more discipline. A feeling of being in control: of your own appetites; digestive juices; destiny. No polished apples rotten at the core *here.*

Therefore I drank some orange juice and coffee but ate only two slices of toast. No butter. Hardly any honey. Felt satisfied by my meal; and more especially — by my moderation.

Then I went and collected the trays, with offers of more toast and coffee. But not even Matt took me up on the toast. Junie had another cup of coffee.

"You'll wear your legs out running up and down those stairs. You can't guess how very grateful I am. But your own breakfast wasn't spoilt, was it?"

"Not one iota."

"And did you enjoy it as much as me?"

"No. I enjoyed you more."

"Did you get as much enjoyment out of your breakfast as I did?"

"Yes, thank you. I got at least as much enjoyment out of my breakfast as you did."

"No, I'm sorry. I simply don't believe you." She took my hand. "It's sad. You've stopped being trustworthy. As well as being a complete idiot."

"I'm glad. It's sharp of you to notice. Yes, I have stopped being a complete idiot. Haven't I?"

I did the washing up and looked out at the garden as I did so. All that blossom. It was perfect. For a minute I propped myself there, my hands resting on the edge of the deep stone sink, and gazed out longingly, trying to take in every detail, imprint it clearly for all time, down to the robin on the branch of one of the cherry trees, the celandines and daisies underneath it, the Solomon's seal with its clusters of white flowers, the neighbours' black cat already basking on our brick wall. If you saw it on a postcard or the lid of a chocolate box you might wonder if it hadn't been retouched.

I wiped the window with the back of one hand — which dispelled a certain gauziness of effect. It could scarcely dispel a modicum of my appreciation but I felt mildly sorry I had done it.

Even apart from the view, I enjoyed the washing up, the sensual warmth of the sudsy water, the recollection, which I often had at such times, of sailing my yacht across a park pond, on holiday with my parents in Torquay. Sometimes as I grew older I seemed to miss them more — I mean, more at thirty-six than at thirty. But it didn't seriously cause melancholy; I simply wished I had more photographs — and still possessed that little yacht, which, oddly, I could never remember sailing on any pond in Deal.

My eyes misted... so contrarily. Now why on earth? But in fact it made me smile. Sorry, Dad. I haven't forgotten. Big boys don't cry.

When I'd cleared up I shaved and dressed: a short-sleeved shirt today: first of the year. I recalled how yesterday, seeing that woman in her summer frock, I'd considered short sleeves premature. Now I apologised to that woman in her summer frock. Caution was for the timid, the untrusting. Caution was not – no, certainly – not for the treasure seekers.

Then I performed my regular Sunday chore: took a shovel round the garden, a shovel and a stick, collected Susie's turds. Normally during these five or ten minutes my expression must have been one of distaste — particularly if the poor thing had suffered from diarrhoea — though distaste not unmixed perhaps with self-protective humour. This morning I actually sang. Actually executed several lively dancesteps — though not, I hasten to add, after the shovel had become well-filled. Matt was in the garden, feeding the fish, putting out more nuts for the squirrels, replenishing the bird food; fortunately the neighbours' cat was elderly and somnolent. Matt looked at me in some wonder, shook his head and tapped his temple. I would have sung whether he'd been there or not; have gone in for all those silly clownish antics. But it was good to have an audience.

8

We left the house at half-past-eleven; for some reason later than usual; on Sundays we customarily went to Jalna. (Jalna was the only place I knew which had a double-barrelled name: Jalna — The Dovecote: always scrupulously observed on envelopes by close friends and members of the family. Most members of the family.) Sometimes I would moan like hell about having to go. Sunday is my one day off, I'd say — or, rather, shout — to Junie and the children; why can't I have the freedom to enjoy it? This is worse than going to church, I'd shout. This is worse than going to prison! (It's the same as going to prison!) I'll join a potholers' association! Ramblers' club! Witches' coven! Anything... so long as its meetings invariably fall on a Sunday! Exclamation marks appeared to fly thicker than arrows over Agincourt; or over one of Junie's uncorrected letters.

The kids would mostly giggle; or do their best to suppress the urge to giggle; depending less on me than on their mother. Junie could be bent to my will in nearly anything that hadn't to do with her family but now she'd assume an indulgent smile which was infuriating (relegated me to third child, whom she must patiently seek to propitiate!) but which could generally coax me back towards a sheepishly grinning — if residually grumbling — form of acceptance. Until the next time.

Yet occasionally I'd take a real stand: sweep the children off to ride on a steam railway or see some distant castle or visit the Tower of London. To a degree, Junie could sympathise, but would usually decline to accompany us; and her sympathy was intellectual — not of the heart. Occasionally too (for this, please bear in mind, was happening over many many years) I'd insist I needed to get on with the decorating; or needed to go to clear the contents of some house. Once when I was feeling outstandingly bolshie I'd declared I should like simply to spend the day in bed and take a little holiday, inaugurate a Samuel Groves Day, to be celebrated at least biannually, with fireworks and bacchanalia and a service of thanksgiving. I don't know — being much too grand even to inquire — in what form the message finally got through. (But I remember they sent me back a cakebox filled with iced fancies and cheese straws and sausage rolls. However, I refused to be touched — let alone humbled. I gave them to the children.) I thought how marvellous it would be just to pass the day like any normal family, reading the paper, popping to the pub, despatching the children to Crusaders, spending the afternoon in bed.

Not that you couldn't do all those things at Jalna (The Dovecote) save perhaps the last. And not that when I was there I didn't generally have a good time — a better one than I might well have had at home. It was just its inexorability I complained of. Its claustrophobia.

Its in-breeding.

And yet before Junie and I had got engaged it was precisely this closeknit quality which had most appealed to me; one of the factors, even, which may have influenced my hesitant proposal. I'd had no family of my own except for my grandmother and had always longed for a sibling — ideally, for several. Junie was the youngest of five sisters; and the others, though all married, still lived in the locality. I suddenly found myself drawn into a young, charming and good-looking group whose members were full of fun, mutually devoted, and around whom existed an aura of almost storybook enchantment. Drawn in, I mean, on equal terms. I'd of course met Junie's parents countless times before — and most of their daughters and their daughters' husbands at least once — but though they were ostensibly the most hospitable couple I had ever known, and were obviously fond of me, even hopeful of me, their hospitality didn't truly extend beyond their own children and their own children's families; for whom Sundays were kept sacrosanct

52

and unadulterated. Only following our engagement did the sabbath walls of Jalna finally fall before me. The outsider put away his trumpet and belonged.

But after a few years, when most of the initial glamour had worn off, though not without leaving a pool of variable affection, I'd once asked Junie if there weren't some unpublished list (or maybe even published; why not?) outlining the requisites for the perfect Fletcher son-in-law: a willingness, say, to remain for all time within easy reach of Deal; to subscribe ninety percent of his Sundays, seventy-five percent of his Christmases, and a goodly portion of his annual vacations? (These last to be subsumed into the family's summer reservation on the Continent.) I'd ventured that at present most bank holidays were optional, as were — again, for the moment — the majority of Saturdays; but that all birthdays and wedding anniversaries were inalienably the property of Jalna. Junie had laughed and admitted in a tone of faintly clannish pride I maybe hadn't got it all that wrong. I'd suggested with a degree of self-congratulation and mordantly black humour that the son-in-law who really wished to make it big should somewhere along the line have managed to cast off both his parents.

But today I neither moaned nor meant to wax satirical. Instead — as we drove towards Jalna — I thought about the diary I was going to keep. I must have been to Junie's childhood home roughly a thousand times but I decided I would try to look upon this as my very first visit — or else, perhaps, my last (on the theory that you should live each day as though you would be dead tomorrow) — and attempt to catch it through the viewfinder of my opening entry. "What's the date?" I asked.

"I think it's the twenty-seventh," answered Junie, after a pause. "Or possibly the twenty-eighth."

"April the twenty-seventh...or possibly the twenty-eighth," I repeated slowly, taking my hand off the steering wheel and laying it briefly upon hers, which was resting in her lap. "Nineteen hundred and ninety-seven or ninety-eight

53

or thereabouts?" ("It truly isn't kind to mock," my wife suggested, primly.) "In any case, a day to conjure with. Momentous. Uniquely historic."

"Why?"

"Simply because it is."

"Oh, Mum," cautioned Matt, wearily, from the back seat. "He's going to say that this particular day will never come again — ever — ever. That's why we've got to savour it. He's going to tell us that history is being made today, just like any other day which we may read about with bated breath. Dad's in one of his *improving* moods. Can't you tell? Don't you know your husband yet?"

"Ah... Does anyone ever know anyone?" I enquired — improvingly.

(But that was purely to point up a general truth. I certainly knew his mother. I knew his mother almost like I knew myself.)

"He'll probably go on and mention that today marks the very beginning of the rest of our lives," said Matt, in the same tone of quietly tolerant resignation.

"Newborn like the spring!" I added.

"Newborn like the spring," he explained.

"Well, I can't help it. You blasé wretch. I *feel* newborn."

"Yeah. May you have a long and happy life."

"Thank you, Matthias — my precious sweet love. I really do intend to."

"I give you till about lunchtime."

"As long as that?"

"Going on past experience."

"Ah, but today's different," I assured him. "Today is different; *I* am different."

"How different?"

"As different as possibly can be. You'll find out."

"All right, then. Let's put it to the test. Make me a present of five pounds."

I smiled — and pulled the car over. "What are you doing?" asked Junie.

54

"Looking to see how much money I've brought." In fact I knew perfectly well. I'd again left my wallet in the bedroom but had neatly folded a couple of notes and transferred them to a pocket of my jeans. Now I fished one out. "Yes, you're in luck," I said. "Except we'll have to make it ten."

"Darling, you're crazy," said my wife. And although she was smiling she honestly did sound a bit appalled. "I think you may've gone out of your little mind."

"Well, *I* think I may've just come into it." I started up the car.

"Come on, Dad. You'd better take it back." Matt prodded me on the shoulder. The folded note was in his hand.

"No, Mattie, it's yours."

"D'you mean that?"

"Yes. For being so intuitive and clever and mature. For expressing yourself so well. For remembering all my tiny pearls of wisdom."

"If it goes on like this," he said, "I may start writing them down and memorising them for homework."

"Wise fellow. Just tell me, though, who's the spiffiest father in all the world? Or do I mean spiffingest?"

Matt had pocketed his ten pounds.

"Ask me again in another week."

I laughed. So did Junie.

"But I've got to admit it, Pop. Since last night you do appear different. Somehow." (I didn't say so but I found this tribute more gratifying than he could ever have imagined.) "Is it going to be okay, Mum, d'you think… for me to keep this loot?"

"Well, why ask me? It's your father's money. I've got nothing to do with it."

Yet Matt still seemed unbelieving. "Dad, I'll get it changed at some point and give you back your five. That'd be fair, wouldn't it? After all, I only asked for five."

"Then perhaps it will have taught you not to set your sights too low? Not to ask too little out of life? In any case, my darling, I want you to hold onto it."

I added: "And let me say that I admire you for your integrity... for your reluctance to exploit a situation."

He leant forward and kissed the back of my neck.

Already, I thought. Already three small items for the diary. *Cooked breakfasts. Ten-pound note. Demonstrative affection.* I smiled at him in the mirror.

Acknowlegement of difference.

Unsolicited to boot.

We drew up outside the house. There were two other cars parked along the verge and a further two standing in the driveway. Jalna was in a quiet and tree-lined cul-de-sac; ten-minute drive from home. A quite attractive house, built during the thirties, mock-Tudor, moderately imposing — but in no way as beautiful as ours. I'd never have considered swapping.

Ella came to meet us. She'd been sitting on the swing in the front garden awaiting our arrival. "You're late!" she announced, moodily.

"Hello, darling," cried Junie, through her open window. "Have you been having a good time?"

"Hello, Mum. Oh, not bad. I suppose. Hello, Dad. Hello, Susie."

"Hello, Matt," said Matt.

I went round the car (which, as always, I had parked for an easy getaway), lifted my daughter and gave her a big hug. She seemed to have grown heavier since the last time I'd done this. Nothing daunted — indeed, responding to the challenge — I then hoist her well above my head and swung myself round a couple of times, laughing up at her. "Hey, why so physical?" she asked, when I had set her down.

"You're my little girl, aren't you?"

Matt, beside her at the front gate, said, "He's acting pretty weird today. If only I cared for you a bit more I'd tell you something to your advantage."

"Like what?" She was now busy stroking Susie, who was jumping up at her as though they'd been apart for weeks.

"Like, for instance, see what happens if you ask him for a

piggyback or something."

"You must be nuts. Why should I want a piggyback?"

"Or *something*," he repeated, almost hissing out the words. "Anything."

"I don't get you," she said.

"You're so thick," Matt told her, dispassionately.

Though neither of my own children wanted a piggyback, or to ride upon my shoulders, or to be whirled around like aeroplanes, there were plenty of other children that day who did — and some of them not a whole lot younger. "Oh, *poor* Uncle Sam!" was a cry heard many times during the course of the afternoon. "Won't you please have mercy on him... monsters?" But this wasn't just because of piggybacks. Whilst all the other fathers dozed in their deckchairs, who was it who organised a crude treasure hunt round the garden and after that a game of hide-and-seek in some nearby woods (with Susie proving something of a liability to those in hiding) and after *that* played several bouts of tag — even having to throw off his shirt and wipe himself down with it, he was perspiring so heavily? "Now doesn't that put the rest of you to shame?" asked Jeanette, whose husband was pasty-faced and stolid and looked forty-five although he wasn't yet forty.

"Oh, he's only making up for lost time," he answered good-humouredly; Raymond's glamour might have gone but not his geniality. "He's feeling bad he didn't get here soon enough to help mark out the tennis court. We've got to be kind to him."

(And here I'm going to edit a little: shall make these characters pipe up in turn.)

"Yes, indeed; the least we can do is give him this chance to salve his conscience," agreed Ted, who also wouldn't have looked any great shakes these days without his shirt on. "Life doesn't always provide us with a second chance. We urge you to go for it, Sam. Just go for it!"

Unlike these other two, who were businessmen, Robert was a librarian. The poor chap suffered from anaemia and ought by rights to have found each Sunday's get-together more wearing than I ever had; but either he drew strength from togetherness or else was seriously well trained.

"Sammy, I get scared," he said; "so painfully worried you might burn yourself out. Too much, too fast, too soon! *Then* who's going to creosote the fence and paint the greenhouse and build the rockery and attend to all the other little things that doubtless Mimsy and Pim will organise to keep us entertained throughout the summer?" He shook his head — sadly.

"Listen," said Jake, who was the most intellectual of my brothers-in-law and actually had a thick book of poetry open on his lap. "Why are you standing there as though you had nothing better to do — just blocking out the sun? Take the children on a long hike." He added graciously, "That way you can atone for the disturbance you created a short time ago with all that running about and screaming."

I said: "You're like a bloody barbershop quartet. You're like a troupe of performing seals. Hasn't anybody ever told you?"

"Yes, they're a thoroughly smirky lot," Yvonne confirmed, with grudging laugh. She was next up in line from Junie and like all the Fletcher girls was short and bouncy and big-chested. "Well, I wouldn't take it. You're larger than they are, Sam. For my part I give you full leave to grab Ted and teach him a good lesson."

Sonia and Debbie also granted me permission to educate — respectively — Jake and Robert. Jeanette chipped in, as well.

"But I thought they were my friends," I opined; piteously hanging my head.

"Well of course we are," crooned Raymond. "Now if we weren't we'd hardly be putting you forward for Uncle of the Year? Would we, guys?"

"Uncle of the Year? Would you *really* do that for me?"

"You have our word on it."

"Oh… shucks! I don't know what to say."

"You don't have to say anything, Samuel. Just run along now. Perhaps to Sandwich. Jake will get the kids lined up in pairs."

"Oh, yes? Let him but try." Sonia, who'd objected to my using my shirt as towel, was now shaking it out forgivingly, about to bear it off to a clotheshorse or ironing board, despite Junie's half-hearted remonstrances that I shouldn't be so pandered to. Or mothered. But Sonia had become my champion; roused, she twirled my shirt about her husband's head as a baton of subdual. She was like the Devil Girl from Mars; Drum Majorette from Hell. I timidly expressed the hope this mightn't be allowed to interfere with the placing of those nominations.

Soon, though, it was teatime. My dieting plans had gone awry: I needed to maintain my energy. "Today I want the biggest piece of everything to go to Samuel," proclaimed Myrtle Fletcher, raising plump and dimpled forearms. "And the smallest piece of everything to go to Robert. I heard what he said about creosoting fences, et cetera. So did Pim. He won't get much of a glass of sherry, either."

"You on the other hand, Sam," said my father-in-law, "can have a tumbler if you'd like it." He was a small man, rosy-cheeked, bald-pated, amiable. Always synchronised his viewpoint with his wife's; at any rate in public. "The old girl's got a longer reach than I have!" He'd been kind to me and I was fond of him; wasn't proud of the fact I'd come increasingly to feel contempt. Subservience in a husband troubled me. Even adoration. I can't have realised it when first I knew him. Maybe hadn't done so for a full decade.

"Oh, Lordy, Lordy," said Robert. "Even the walls have ears."

"And the kitchen has open windows, too, where Pim and I were preparing tea...for ingrates. I'm sorry to have to inform you that your own two daughters were amongst those of us who heard."

We stayed in the garden. The children, whose ages ranged from seven to sixteen, either sat on the grass, on rugs or cushions, or roamed at will eating their sandwich; or their scone, or their tartlet, or their toasted teacake. I sat next to Jake. "The Brain and the Brawn," he said. I slightly resented this — well, as much as I could've resented anything on such a sunny afternoon. As much as I could've resented anything that part of me found flattering.

He was certainly the scrawniest of the sons-in-law; sharp-nosed, long-chinned; rope-veined. But he always seemed straightforward. Open-minded. Was probably popular with pupils.

He'd been preparing one of his lessons.

I protested.

"Just because you have the Oxford Book of Something-or-Other to use as a tea tray! That doesn't mean you're the only one round here with an appreciation of poetry!"

"Oh, sure," he said. "'If you can keep your head when all about you Are losing theirs and blaming it on you, If you can trust yourself when all men doubt you, But make allowance for their doubting too...'"

"Here!" I said. "You mustn't knock Kipling."

"I don't. But I bet you couldn't recite me four lines of anything more weighty. Excluding Shakespeare."

"Is that so? Then what about Dryden?"

"Could you recite four lines from Dryden?"

"Would that impress you?"

"Enormously."

"Okay. Listen to this...

> 'I strongly wish for what I faintly hope:
> Like the daydreams of melancholy men,
> I think and think on things impossible,
> Yet love to wander in that golden maze...'

Word perfect, I assure you."

"Yes," he said, slowly. "I can believe it. I'm not actually familiar with that passage — "

"*Rival Ladies*," I said. "But my point is: not all of us are total dunderheads."

"After nearly twenty years do you imagine I don't know that? And after nearly twenty years don't *you* know yet when I just might be — ever so slightly — pulling your leg?"

I smiled. "Yes, of course I do."

But my education had always been a touchy subject.

Perhaps because I'd never gone to university. One of these days I hoped to set that right.

Go to university and get to be a rowing blue.

Well, anyway. No harm in hoping. You gotta have a dream.

"How much more of it can you recite? Old memorybags!"

"Of *Rival Ladies*? None. But you only asked for four lines. What about two from Alexander Pope? Also impressive? 'Know then thyself, presume not God to scan; the proper study of mankind is man.' Lastly I can offer the whole of *The Whiffenpoof Song*. But sadly not its etymology." I sighed and went round with the macaroons and flapjacks.

As it happened, a few hours later I did in fact give voice to those little black sheep who had lost their way — baa, baa, baa! (And wouldn't get home till the Judgement Day... baa, baa, baa!) But not as a solo. We'd built a fire in the garden and after a light supper we ate buns and drank cocoa round it; some of the children would later place foil-wrapped potatoes in the embers. Ted told a not-very-scary ghost story; though most of the adults pretended to be terrified. Then we had a spelling bee and played 'I Spy'. Everyone seemed smiley and relaxed; especially as the night grew darker. Cosy, too — we all had woollen jumpers. Beside me lay Susie, well-fed and content and interested: eyes constantly on the move, snout resting on her paws. (How could all those other households honestly prefer cats?) Young Gary sat with thumb in mouth and head against his mother's breast and Sonia absently stroked the hair back from his brow. I wondered if Jake ever suffered from claustrophobia. He or any of the others. Impossible to tell. I never did while I was there; or only very seldom. I smiled at Junie and my daughter, both sitting straight across from me. People said there was no such thing as a perfect day — and of course they were right — I suppose — yet I really didn't see how this one could've been improved upon. Our initially lusty singsong was now petering out but as I looked at all those friendly faces in the firelight, faces so familiar I usually took them more or less for granted, I suddenly felt regretful that next Sunday I shouldn't be amongst them. Although I knew this was merely sentimental and would no doubt be fleeting, nonetheless I couldn't shake it off. What's more, it happened even before somebody, I think it was Mimsy, led the rest into something I hadn't heard for ages. "Here's a happy tune, you'll love to croon, they call it ... Sam's song." What *was* ironic was that it was followed, immediately, by *Don't Fence Me In*.

No; no day is ever quite perfect. At about eleven, when this one had barely an hour remaining, I took Susie on her evening walk. "Is it necessary?" asked Junie. "She's been charging around all day. I would have thought she was exhausted."

"Just look at her," I said. She had gone to the front door and was gazing back with soulful trustingness in the integrity of man and a tail that wagged in tentative anticipation. Anyway, I myself fancied a stroll: a short time in which to ponder without interruption, plan, dream, take stock... or simply be. I often meant to do all this in bed but either fell asleep or was distracted by Junie's frequent resettlings or — sometimes — gentle snoring.

"Poor little thing," I went on. But now I was condoling with the animal; not reasoning with her mistress. "How could she ever be so cruel as to mean to take away one of your few simple pleasures?"

"Oh, Susie. Is that what I was meaning to do? Take away one of your few simple pleasures? Then it's a good thing somebody around here has a bit of heart. Isn't it?" To me she said: "But you won't be going far?"

"No. Only round the block. Won't even take the lead."

In fact I'd been considering returning to the beach; to sanctify my day with a tranquil half-hour listening to the ebb and flow of the ocean running over shingle. But it was too far; so now I chose to wander in the back streets. They were deserted at this time on a Sunday: houses all in darkness. Tonight, I could again smell the sea. I loved the smell of it; the feel of it; everything about it. The sea probably represented my biggest single reason for staying on in Deal. I'd always been a son of Neptune — years before becoming a son of Richard Widmark: the sea was the setting for some of my greatest exploits, both actual and imaginary. Sometimes I felt — and by no means only when wretched or despairing — I should like to wade out and simply swim and swim, until either I became entirely one with it, turned in my dreams into a kind of water sprite or merman, or else finally walked ashore, all glorious and shining (though pleasantly exhausted), onto some lush tropical island with silvery sands, exotic fruits and Gauguin's available maidens. The sea was purifying. The sea was a transmuter of base metals. It was eminently right that by the sea, and underneath the stars, I should've been brought, fabulously, face-to-face again with love.

The car came quickly and it didn't stop.

I could hardly believe it had happened. One moment I was attending some glamorous cocktail function with Moira: being introduced to many of her smart friends: arousing wonderment and envy. The next I was staring down at Susie's blood-mangled body. Separating the two had been the heartstopping and animation-suspending thud of impact, and then the bastard's tail lights were already burning into the distance on that long and empty stretch of road. So not only knocked down but run over. Or possibly sent flying.

Yet she was still alive. The whimpering and the slavering and the frenzied breathing, the bared teeth and the smell of panic, all testified to that. I squatted beside her and stroked her head and spoke her name, spoke it softly and repeatedly, while trying to think what I should do; and she gradually gave over snarling, and feebly attempting to struggle up.

I knew that the vet lived on the seafront, in a flat above his surgery; indeed we were halfway there and it might be better to carry Susie straight to Mr Dodd rather than back to the house — also quicker and less frustrating than trying to get a lift. No lights had been switched on. No windows had been opened. Everything remained as quiet. Almost. The only difference being a crying baby and a whimpering dog. Nobody had come to his front door.

I would have come to my front door.

I felt an urge to stand there and throw back my head and howl. Howl until the incident was marked. Its inhumanity acknowledged. In some way shared in.

So would Junie and Ella and Matt and nearly everyone I knew: have come to their front door.

So, without question, would Moira.

Moira.

The very thought could give me strength.

"Here we go, Susie; here we go, old girl. Easy does it. Don't be afraid. You're going to be all right."

All right, Susie — you're going to be all right. This was the refrain that ran through the whole of my half-whispered monologue during the next ten minutes; I felt it was essential she should hear my voice. "You're going to be all right, Susie. Mr Dodd will take away the pain. You're going to be as good as new. As right as sixpence. Dear God." But that was dishonest. I had nothing but scorn for anyone who only at moments of stress turned to a god he didn't normally believe in. God played no part whatever in my own world. I didn't need him. I was not the type to lean. (I was the type whom others leant upon.) "You — are — going — to — be — all — right — Susie. Do you hear?" Moira kept pace with me along the pavement, bearing us supportive company. She had kept pace with me throughout the day.

Susie was still conscious but a dead weight and my arms were aching long before we reached the vet's. She smelled dreadful. She was dribbling copiously onto one of my cable-stitch sleeves and there was blood and heaven knew what else across my chest and stomach. I saw scarcely anyone. I passed the ice-cream parlour we had passed the night before but now it gave the impression of still being shut for winter. It was odd to think that only a little over twenty-four hours ago we'd been there in *The Lord Nelson:* Susie making up to Moira rather than bothering with me. Even if you tacked on roughly a further ten hours for the period since Moira had come into the shop mere human ideas of time could convey hardly anything of how long I felt I'd known her.

To my relief there was a light in one of the windows over the surgery; it showed pinkly through thin curtains. Not that it would have made any difference if there hadn't been.

Mr Dodd looked like a young man out of an American soap. He had striking — if somewhat vacuous — good looks and thick blond hair combed back into a peak. But then you noticed the skin at his throat: not baggy so much as crumpled and crisscrossed and crêpey: and later on you learned he was a grandfather and you set him down as one of the creepiest people you had ever met.

(Superman, I can assure you, Matt, could never hold a candle to Mr Dodd!)

Tonight, as on every other occasion I had seen him, winter or summer, he was wearing a shirt not merely open at the neck but generously open at the neck. And that was the second thing I found utterly amazing about him: with an artfully arranged scarf or some high rolled-over collar he could perhaps have gone on looking thirty-five for ever. So did he suffer from some inexplicable blind spot? Or purely from that self-destructive urge we're all supposed to have but which — speaking for myself — I could never really recognise? 'O wad some Pow'r the giftie gie us To see oursels as others see us! It wad frae mony a blunder free us, And foolish notion.' (Another four lines I could have quoted happily to Jake; and would have done, had Mr Dodd been present.) Yet the poor man was always thoroughly agreeable; besides being a first-class vet. And right now, of course, my mind was not on quirks of personality or appearance, nor on poetry or philosophy, nor on anything at all other than the fate of my gravely injured animal.

And when he came to the door he instantly took in the situation; opened up without the least show of reluctance; and while I held Susie down and averted my eyes as far as possible from everything the harsh surgery light was cruelly exposing conducted a painstaking examination.

"I'm afraid she's badly hurt."

"Well, I can see that! But she's going to be all right, isn't she? She is going to pull through?"

"It's not these gashes on the body we need worry about. It's the damage to the head."

"Concussion," I said. "Concussion heals with time."

"Unfortunately, it's more than that, Mr Groves. I'm sad to have to say it — "

"No!" I shouted.

"But I truly feel — "

"I am not going to have my dog put down!"

"But I don't believe that she can make a full recovery. I am sorry. I appreciate what you're going through — "

"No!"

The sound of my tone. The set of my features. Obdurate like Matt.

"Very well, then." Without a shrug he still conveyed the feeling of a shrug. "In that case, I'll give her something to help her sleep till morning."

"Don't you see? We love her. My wife —my children... It wouldn't be like home without her. It wouldn't be right."

"Of course. I understand that. Yet I still think when you've had a chance to reconsider... I know none of you would wish to condemn her to a life of — a life of — "

"But how can you be sure? *Can* you be sure...?"

"Short of a miracle," he answered. "Yes."

I paused.

"All right, if that's the way it is," I said, heavily, "then there's nothing else for it. Is there? I shall have to pin my hopes on miracles."

He drove us home; assured me with an air of concern he would come to look at Susie in the morning. Burrowed in the pocket of my jeans, opened the front door for me and then departed.

"Samuel — is that you? Do you realise you've been gone an hour? I've been getting so worried; and so cross. I'm livid. You said ten minutes, damn you! I'm almost coming to think I can't trust you any more."

I called back up the stairs. In other circumstances I'd have got secret satisfaction out of being able to vindicate myself so fully; even now there was a sneaking sense of righteous indignation. Junie was still pulling on her dressing gown as she came running after me into the kitchen. Her hand was on my shoulder, squeezing in mute apology, while I settled Susie in her basket. At the same time I added all the salient details. "I think I may sit up with her," I said.

"But, darling, there isn't any point. Not if Mr Dodd's sedated her and told you it'll last all night."

I allowed her finally to lead me up to bed.

"We mustn't let her die," I exclaimed. "It wouldn't be right. She's had barely half her life... " I was aware how inadequate this sounded.

"I promise you, we'll do our very best to save her. But try to keep your voice down, love. It's far better the children shouldn't hear. A minor miracle I didn't wake them earlier," she smiled, ruefully.

There! That word again! It struck me as auspicious. And at the top of the stairs there was a horseshoe hanging on the wall. I brushed my hand against it as we passed. Then suddenly I turned and gave her a ferocious hug.

"Darling, it's going to be all right; don't worry," I said. "Keep faith with me. I love you, Junie Moon."

10

And I slept well; even extremely well. I woke at half-past-six feeling refreshed and practically as optimistic as I'd felt yesterday. Drew back the curtains to discover another bright sky; then ran downstairs to take a look at Suze. She appeared inert but her breathing was less stertorious. She was really going to recover — just as I'd predicted she would. I squatted and stroked and spoke to her as normal, because, although I naturally expected no reaction, it would have seemed like betraying a trust if I hadn't done so. I carried on our conversation as I filled the kettle. I doused my face in cold water. Then, cheerfully impulsive, I went out in the garden and had a long pee on the grass. It was the first time I'd ever done this and it made me feel romantically close to nature, standing there erect and naked in the early morning sun and watching my urine arch like a fountain from a piece of statuary, shoot up prismatically before it frothed amongst the daisies; and if anyone in either of the neighbouring houses had happened to be glancing from an upper window at that hour... well, just too bad. Waiting for the kettle to whistle I meandered round the garden savouring the earth beneath my feet and the air between my loins. I did a few physical jerks: toe-touching, running on the spot, swivelling at the waist with legs apart and arms in line with shoulders. I'd have done more but the water boiled. I made the tea, put a couple of Petit Beurre on both our saucers, was careful not to slop as I returned upstairs, and, having wiped my soles on the carpet, got exuberantly back into bed. I hadn't bothered to take anything to the children; it wasn't yet seven. As usual Junie only came to properly whilst drinking her tea but all the same she'd instantly asked about Susie and been relieved by what I'd told her. I fetched us both refills — though I didn't really want mine and didn't finish it; then made love to her (count of six hundred and seventeen) and went to shave and have my bath. A perfect start to a second — potentially — perfect day; not taking into account, of course, that bloody motorist and the effects of his swift uncaring passage through our lives. I wondered if he were feeling in the slightest bit remorseful. Yes, 'he'. Impossible to imagine — ever — that it could have been a woman.

Reclining in the bath I thought about possible openings for my diary. 'Today I peed naked in the back garden and frightened the horseflies.'? No, perhaps not.

I got to the shop at a minute to nine. Mavis didn't work on Mondays. Until high season she came in only on Thursdays and Fridays and Saturdays. But at five-past-nine I rang her. Knowing she'd be up. Knowing she was strapped for cash.

"You're saying," she repeated, "the whole week? Five days? *Already*?" She had a breathy voice. Her emissions fairly rustled down the line.

"Six, if you like."

"But, Mr G, you can't afford to take me on full-time. You know you can't. Not as early as this."

"Here! You let me worry over *my* finances and I'll let you go bananas over yours! Wouldn't it be useful?"

"Breathlessly." This didn't seem totally the right word but I was pleased to hear her say it. "And apart from the money you know how much I enjoy just being around."

"Great. Then when'll you start? This morning?"

"D'you really mean it?"

"Of course."

"I can be with you in thirty minutes! Or in twenty if you're wanting to go anywhere...?"

"No, no, take your time. Why not come in after lunch and we'll count it as a full day?"

It occurred to me afterwards I could simply have doubled her wages. But supposing she'd viewed this as blatant charity? Besides, it gave her pleasure to be here; didn't she say so? Got her out of the house. Provided an escape from

70

her demanding mum.

And in a month or two — when she'd have been coming in full-time anyway — it might have turned into a problem: the business of her wages. I wasn't sure it hadn't done so now.

But it had seemed the proper thing; and no doubt we should survive. Live every day as though your last. (Maybe *this* was the true opening to a journal!) Really commit yourself to whoever depended on you. Like when you'd been the captain of a team and your eleven or fifteen players had all relied upon your guidance. Now I had a crew of only four. A tiny ship but for all hands, hopefully, a good one and a safe one; caringly — protectively — responsibly navigated.

Partly thinking this, I walked slowly up and down our two broad aisles, renewing my acquaintance with the stock, picking up several objects at random, speculating on their history; studying a daguerreotype taken at the Great Exhibition; experiencing, as usual, pleasurably mixed feelings, an awareness of the transience of things and of my own mortality, but also of my own unutterable good fortune. This morning, for the second time, a boy's catapult suddenly bore me back to childhood — to the remembered sunlight and long country days, to the adventurousness and unappreciated safety; to a stream where I went fishing and to the warm smell of a local bakery, gone now for quarter of a century.

This morning, too, I saw the shop through someone else's eyes. Moira had been here. Her feet had trodden this blue carpet. Her eyes had seen these pictures stacked against and hanging on the walls, the books, the clothes, the records, furniture; the glass-topped cases displaying jewellery, medals and old coins; the various tables strewn with all the clutter of forgotten lives. Between the tables ran a network of passageways. Moira had traversed them all. Now I slowly threaded them myself, imagining that by so doing I was drawing closer to her. Shared experience. I was definitely drawing closer in another sense. In only five days' time she would be coming back to Deal!

Only?

At half-past-twelve I rang home. Wanting to know if Mr Dodd had been.

"Yes; and he sounds more hopeful than he must've done last night. She's drunk a little milk, and eaten a few scraps of meat, and she knew the garden was the right place to go and do her business. And she remembers where it is — I mean, on the other side of the back door. Also it's obvious she can recognise her name. Mr Dodd seems fairly pleased with her."

Oh, hadn't I said! Hadn't I said! I swivelled on my office chair and — free of the table on which the phone rested — held my legs out straight and clicked my heels in joy. "Where is she now?"

"Back in her basket. She's still a bit whiffly, though. Will you be able to bath her this evening?"

"You bet. There's a meeting of the Players but I can easily bath her before supper."

"Were your sandwiches all right?"

"Haven't eaten them yet. Sure they'll be wonderful." I'd always said Junie's sandwiches were as varied, inventive and chock-a-block as the finest New York deli's... although I often wished I'd been in a position actually to check. "Ambrosia in wholemeal," I added now; conservatively.

"I've made a start on the wallpapering."

I still found that incredible — both oddly discomfiting and oddly reassuring. "Great! I'll be looking forward to seeing it," I said.

"Just don't expect too much, though. I'm only a beginner."

"I'm only a little lamb, sir." *Tales of Toytown,* handed down to us by both my parents and hers.

"Well, I suppose I'd better let you go now. I think I'll stop and have some lunch myself. And don't worry about Susie. Try to have a decent afternoon."

"And you." Her voice had suddenly sounded a little flat.

Mavis came in soon after one. She was a large unwieldy

type of woman who affected a girlish manner but had a genuinely sweet expression which declared her both easy and eager to please. Yet she had absolutely no dress sense and more than a smattering of facial hair. She was only in her forties; I didn't understand how anyone could be so careless. I suspected she was lesbian. I had taken her over with the shop twelve years ago, when, with the aid of a loan from the bank (now mercifully discharged), I had managed to buy the business.

"Mr G," she said, "you are the best boss ever. Did you know that? I shall write to the papers to suggest a nationwide survey: Boss of the Year Award. Presentation dinner at the Dorchester."

Well! Yesterday, Uncle of the Year; today, Boss. Tomorrow? Husband or Father or — wey hey! — how about trying this one on for size? *Lover*.

Or should I settle comprehensively? Simply go for Man?

Anyhow, as a foretaste of this greater glory Mavis had brought me a rum baba to eat with my sandwiches. She was ebullient and this fact alone even more than the baba or the Dorchester award — no, actually we had decided on the Ritz — provided ample justification for what had been a mildly impetuous gesture. But I had learned by now the danger of not acting when the spirit moved. The road from Deal is paved with good intentions!

With this in mind, during the afternoon I wrote two cheques for charity. When, later on, I popped out to post them I left the shop hard on the heels of three old ladies who had stopped outside to rearrange their headgear and didn't realise I was just behind. "What a delightful young man! So charming and so handsome! I only wish you met a few more like him in the world these days, don't you, my dears?" I ducked back through the door, and felt sure they hadn't noticed, but I think I must have blushed.

Returning from the letter box, driven by a whim, I made a detour into the small old-fashioned stationer's around the corner. That journal. At home I'd found a book which may have dated back to school. Unused but scruffy; with its cover deeply creased. But it appeared to me now that perhaps this brand-new project deserved as much respect as this brand-new fellow who aimed to make it so reflectingly his own.

And almost at once I saw something in Ramsey & Whittaker's that my heart could joyously respond to.

It was a tooled leather volume in green, thick but pocket-sized, the tops of its pages gilt-edged. And shockingly expensive. But an *objet d'art*, I told myself, which would maybe end up as an heirloom or else communicating truths to strangers; in either case ensuring that the best of me, the zest of me, was given its due chance for survival. Besides. Whereas on the one hand I should be able always to have it near me, even on my deathbed, this precious distillation, bright gilt-edged memorial — on the other, if I suppressed my current instinct, I should soon lose track altogether of the money I had saved. And I'd regret it. With us ordinary individuals it was the things we *didn't* do which had the greater power to nag. So I took a breath and clutched the book and bore it to the counter.

When I got home that evening (with an attractively chunky bracelet for Ella, since one had to try to even things up a little, whether Matt spoke of his ten pounds or not) I was fervently hoping Susie would rush round to greet me. But, no, as I walked into the kitchen she remained leaden in her basket, awake but not even raising her head. She had eaten her supper, however, and had apparently spent a good part of the day in the garden, though often only blundering across the flowerbeds and even crashing through the shrubs to stand there with her muzzle pressed against the wall — just staring at the brickwork until such time as she was turned around and so could lumber off mechanically towards the subsequent obstruction.

I stroked her now for several minutes without obtaining much reaction.

"Perhaps Mr Dodd was right," said Junie, as I stood propped against the Aga with my ritual glass of Martini. "It might be kinder just to have her put to sleep."

"No. He wasn't right. Nothing about it would be right."

"Oh, Mum, we can't," cried Ella. "We can't!"

"In any case," I said, "it's very early days. We've got to give her her fair chance."

I went and stripped down to my shorts and carried the subject of this conversation to her bath. Normally, knowing all too well what lay ahead, she put up some resistance. But this evening she let herself be borne towards the bathroom without even a token splaying out of legs. After that, she simply stood in the warm water and neither made any attempt to escape nor raised any objection to the shower attachment. As I shampooed I sang to her, songs like *I'm gonna wash that man right outa my hair*, which didn't perhaps seem incredibly appropriate, unless the driver of the car were the man referred to, and *How much is that doggie in the window?*, which I hastened to point out didn't mean that we were looking for her replacement, it merely harked back to the time when *she* had been a doggie in the window, all huge black patch and fluffy white fur, climbing over and tumbling around her far less frolicsome companions. Now she stood there in rigid acceptance (trembling as usual and as usual disconcertingly whippetlike beneath the rinsed and flattened and cascading hair) but what was more normal — and therefore greatly reassuring: she afterwards ate with every appearance of enjoyment the handful of sweet biscuits that was always her reward for enduring bathtime, and also settled on the rug before the Aga to complete the drying-off process with an air at least of comprehension if not of actual contentment. She didn't even snap at the hairdryer.

The cleaning and disinfecting of the bath took nearly as long as the washing of the dog! At eight o' clock I needed to be at Ruth Minton's. Tonight the Seaside Players were to be reading and casting *The Deep Blue Sea*. For any other meeting I mightn't have bothered to turn up but this one would be crucial.

In recent years I'd played in two other Rattigans: had had a small part in *Separate Tables* and a larger one in *While*

The Sun Shines. Indeed, my roles were getting better all the time and I'd found so much satisfaction in performing them that — until tonight — this belated discovery of a real vocation had been turning, treacherously, into a probably silly but certainly very serious regret.

Yet now (it had suddenly come to me whilst I was bathing Susie) I didn't believe any longer in belatedness; nor — most definitely — in the harbouring of regrets.

"Supposing I were to apply to RADA?" I asked Junie at supper. "It's a dream, I know, madness even to mention it, but overlooking all of that for the moment, the possibly juvenile aspect, don't you consider I possess the talent? I mean — just maybe. And the looks?"

"Ha!" said Matt.

"Pipe down. I'm talking to your mother."

"The looks for the hunchback of Notre Dame," suggested Matt.

Ella, on the other hand, was more encouraging. "Don't listen to him, Daddy. I think that's a pretty cool idea."

"Children, your father's only joking," Junie announced, wearily.

"Half joking," I amended. "Remember, there's a thin basis of truth to almost every joke." I smiled at Ella, gave her a fond wink. I liked it when she called me Daddy, when she forgot to be acerbic. It was my own handling of her, obviously, which must so often be at fault; tonight, she'd been delighted with the bracelet, touchingly pleased it hadn't just come out of stock but had been chosen with great care at a jeweller's in the High Street. (All right, this was a fabrication but one which had given an immense amount of pleasure; whatever I did, I must on no account forget to prime Mavis.) And I resolved to try to cultivate Ella's friendship more assiduously than — I feared — had too often been the case.

"So how precisely would we live?" asked Junie.

"Why, very much as we do now. You yourself could run the shop." I was talking wholly off the top of my head but growing more and more convinced with every second. "I don't

76

know why we've never thought of that before."

"Well, I do. I do! You always told me you didn't approve of working wives. You always said it was the man who ought to be the breadwinner."

"Just like I always said it was the man who ought to decorate the house."

"Exactly."

"Then maybe I've been wrong. My God. Haven't I just been shown some pretty overwhelming evidence?"

"What! Can I quote you on that?" asked my son.

"*May* I quote you on that? My young Matthias, I hope I never mind admitting if I've been at fault. Old-fashioned — anachronistic — whatever. I'm not always all that bright. I make mistakes. Know I'm superficial. But I do the very best I can."

He was pretending to write it down; using his tablemat as a reporter's notepad. "What came after 'not all that bright'? What came before 'not all that bright'? I need to do you justice."

"You need to be a lot less cheeky. This is a meaningful discussion."

"Sam, are you really serious about all this?" Junie was staring at me as though I was someone who'd just wandered in off the street and helped himself to vegetables.

"Yes, indeed I am. About what — specifically?"

She spread her hands, a little helplessly. "Well… about wanting to go on the stage?"

"Cross my heart and hope to die."

There was a pause.

"I realise I may've been sounding a tad frivolous but even so — "

"Oh! In a minute he's going to tell us he was only joking," interrupted Matt, sadly. "I mean, about 'superficial' and all that stuff."

I raised an eyebrow at him. He'd clearly forgotten about yesterday's kiss on the back of my neck and what had given rise to that. Well, only to be expected, of course. Thoroughly normal. Tomorrow he'd remember it again; or ten years from tomorrow.

"But even so," I said. "You'd hardly have wanted me getting all intense and heavy about it. Would you?"

"Daddy, I think you've been sounding just fine."

"Thank you, darling. I appreciate that."

Junie began to chuckle.

The chuckle developed. She had to wipe her eyes. The children joined in; me, as well; puzzled though we all were.

"Mimsy and Pim," she said, "would have a fit! Only remember how they felt when you decided to leave the bank!"

"Is that why you're laughing?"

She nodded.

"Your mother and father," I observed gently, "have no say whatever in the way we run our lives."

Despite her own implicit criticism there was a slightly uncomfortable silence. I had often wished — in one respect, anyhow — that the loan they'd made us at the time we'd bought the house hadn't been converted to a gift the moment I could have started paying them back.

"It's none of Mimsy's business!" said Matt, hotly, apparently deciding that perhaps I did have the looks after all and unconsciously relegating his grandfather to the subordinate position which indeed he held.

"Now, stop it; that isn't respectful," said his mother. "All this is getting out of hand. To be honest," she said to me, "I'd probably quite enjoy managing the shop but I thought you were perfectly happy with things the way they were. It never occurred to me — "

"I am," I answered. I'd finished my meal and now I got up and went round behind her and kissed the crown of her head. "I'm as happy as anybody ever could be. I've got an excellent wife and two excellent children. What more could a man ask? It's just that occasionally one likes to dream, I suppose. To dream of doing something a little more colourful.

To dream of... "

"What?"

"I don't know. Of sailing into unmapped waters. Of spreading one's wings like a wandering albatross, or a sunbird, or a roc. Of realising perhaps a larger bit of one's potential."

"Trust our dad! Who else would ever spread his wings like a rock? Who else would even think of it?"

"R-o-c," I smiled. "As you very well appreciate, you little tyke." Matt had been all but weaned on the adventures of Sinbad.

"Yet getting back to the subject in hand...?" prompted Junie.

I gave a shrug. "Oh — as I said — I'm probably being adolescent. Stargazing. After all... out of every thousand expiring actors how many d'you suppose ever really get there?"

"Possibly," said Matt, "aspiring ones might stand a *fractionally* better chance."

"Why? What did I say? Oh, you're imagining things!" — when he'd explained. "I'll go and make the coffee."

Junie called after me. "But you could if you truly wanted to. If you thought there'd be the slightest possibility. I wouldn't try to stop you."

"Yes, go on, Dad, why don't you?" shouted Matt. "You old expiring actor, you! And anyway what's so wrong, I'd like to know, about being adolescent?"

"Bet you could, Daddy," added Ella. "You're by far the hunkiest dad in Deal. You should see the fathers of some of my friends."

I put my head back through the doorway.

"You're very sweet. All of you. We'll have to see. No promises, mind. I certainly don't mean to rush into anything. I plan to be incredibly circumspect."

Head withdrawn; head put back again.

"And, Matt, there is absolutely nothing wrong about being adolescent! Nothing! Don't you think it for a minute."

Junie followed me out into the kitchen. "Oh, by the way, Mimsy and Pim were heartbroken to hear about Susie's accident. But they're keeping their fingers crossed. And if there's anything they can do... "

"That's very kind," I murmured.

"And they thought you were totally wonderful yesterday. But they told me not to mention it."

I laughed. Junie went back to fetch some more things off the table; or possibly to encourage the children to do it. I looked at Susie lying on the rug. Supposing I *could* get into RADA? It wasn't feasible, of course... but just supposing? Not simply would it be a means of expanding my horizons: of maybe one day actually travelling a little, getting overseas: to New York perhaps — San Francisco — Sydney. It would also mean that, sooner than this (hey, what price autumn?), at least during termtime, I'd be able to stay partly in London: an end to any problem over being with Moira. (And indeed wouldn't that in itself represent an expansion to my horizons? And how!) It seemed too good to be true, a ready-made solution where as yet I'd hardly been on the lookout for one: thinking no further than that little house in Silver Street, which I now saw would have been hopelessly impractical. But this changed everything. Moira in the week; Junie and the children at weekends. The ingredients for paradise.

For paradise... Capten, art tha listenin' there below?

And — who knew — into the bargain I might even make a reputation?

There would always be the holidays, of course. But one could worry about those a bit later. *You mustn't cross your bridges, Sammy.* I could hear my father saying it now. *Don't ever burden today's strength with tomorrow's loads.*

Pretty good advice.

In the end I didn't even go to Ruth Minton's. The deep blue sea still beckoned but this was a deeper, bluer, wider, warmer, infinitely more inviting ocean than any that had ever lapped upon the shores of Deal or Dover or points further west along the coast. And to expand a little on that Rattigan metaphor — the sleeping prince had at long last woken; woken with knobs on. He was up in the crow's nest watching out for El Dorado: Prince Valiant — coasting through the Spanish Main; Prince Theseus — tracking through the golden maze (thinking on things pre-eminently possible). This risen prince wrote a lengthy letter to RADA; addressed it simply to The Secretary, Royal Academy of Dramatic Art, London; if it was meant to get there it would; and I knew for sure it was. I asked for information regarding grants, scholarships, auditions. I listed the plays I'd been in and let them have a recent photograph I liked; it made me look all of twenty-eight; together with five hundred words on why I thought I should be suitable. I knew full well I had to sell myself.

I enclosed copies of cuttings from the *East Kent Mercury*.

Then I walked down to the post office. Naturally there wasn't a collection till the morning yet it was comforting to think my fate was sealed, already winging into the unknown. Or at least — not to get *too* carried away, or highflown, or roc-like — that the envelope was.

(Though for Junie's sake, I certainly wanted to remain rocklike; as rocklike as ever.)

That night the count was up to nearly nine hundred...

Yow-w-w-w!

11

The following morning partial sanity returned — thank God, though, only partial. For the first moment I felt alarmed by what I'd done; but then I laughed and shrugged and thought oh what the hell. Cast your bread upon the waters... nothing ventured, nothing gained. All my life, I now believed, I'd played things far too safe. I was thirty-six. In another four years...! Thank God I'd woken up in time.

Ungrudging endorsement: the phone at the shop rang only a few minutes after I'd got there.

"Sam? Good morning. This is Moira. Moira Sheffield."

I had recognised her voice on the first syllable. Although my heart at once stepped up its action it didn't monkey with my pitch or phrasing. There'd been no time.

"Sweet heaven. I was thinking about you."

"Really? What were you thinking?"

"Oh, nothing good, I promise."

"My, that's a relief! How are you?" she asked.

"Fantastic. You?"

"Also pretty good. But listen, Sam. I've decided that after all Deal won't be seeing me next weekend, I — "

"Oh, *no!*"

I shouldn't have said that. It had been shocked out of me. I was cold with disappointment.

"No, wait: I was offered two tickets for Saturday for that new American musical that's been getting so much hype. I hadn't the chutzpah to turn them down. And the title seemed to clinch it: *Half a Farthing, Sam Sparrow?* Oh, such relevance! I was wandering if you'd like to come."

"My God."

She laughed. "Is that a yes or a no?"

"Exact translation: I should love to come. There's nothing that could give me greater pleasure... " Yet I was speaking with deliberation. My brain was trying frantically to get to grips. In my own mind the sentence wasn't finished but she didn't realise this.

"I'm so glad. I think the show should probably be fun. Despite the hype!"

"I haven't really caught the hype; just the hit tune — which is catchy as all get-out." (Strange lyric, though: 'You feel that you're on trial — and so you're in denial — you want to cry and run a mile — but still you lie and still you smile — and smile and smile and smile... ' Rather dopey.)

"Yes, hard to get off your mind, once it's there; we'll certainly drive each other crazy! Now what I also thought was this: is there any chance of your making a full weekend of it — coming to London on Friday night — getting your assistant (Liz tells me she thinks you've got an assistant) to be in charge on Saturday? There's plenty of room at the flat and I've already made some plans for things that we could do together — you said the other day you don't know London awfully well... " But then she faltered. "Or do you think I'm being presumptuous?"

"Presumptuous? Good heavens, no. It sounds out of this world. But... "

"Is it your grandmother? I was worried that there might be complications."

"Yes, may I ring you back? Say — in an hour? Will you be at home?"

She gave me her number. "See what you can manage, Sam." I promised her I would. We ended — a bit bathetically — talking about transport.

Forty minutes later I rang Junie.

"Darling, guess what! Guess who I've just heard from!"

"RADA. They've offered you a place."

"Not yet," I said, "although I admit they're being a little on the slow side."

"Then I give up," she said. "Who?"

"John Caterham."

"John Caterham! Good gracious! You mean the John

83

Caterham who was in our class at school?"

"As opposed to all the others that we know?"

"But how — why — where? I wouldn't even have thought he'd got the name of the shop. Where was he phoning from? Or do you mean it was a letter?"

"No, I spoke to him. He asked after you, of course. Sent his love. Couldn't believe our children are now old enough to be at the County High or that old Hinchcliff *still* hasn't retired."

"But what about his own children? Aren't they — ?"

"No, he married later than we did, remember."

"How many has he got?"

"Three. But listen, Junie, let me tell you why he phoned. He's still living in that place near Lincoln and they've got some important cricket fixture arranged for next Sunday but one of their best players has broken his leg and John's desperate for a good replacement. He asked if I could go up for the whole weekend and I said yes because although it's really a bit of a bind it does sound as if they're in a fix and I was quite flattered he should have thought of me. Mavis will look after the shop on Saturday but I said you might pop in and relieve her at lunchtime. Naturally John would have asked you and the kids but his wife's away at the moment — her mother isn't well — and they've got the workmen in and anyway what with its being Ted and Yvonne's anniversary celebration on Sunday... "

The gabble was to let her know it was a *fait accompli.* I had no fears she'd stand in my way but I hoped she wouldn't sound reproachful.

Which she didn't. Not at all. I should have known how she'd react.

"Darling, obviously you've got to go! It's like you're answering a May-Day signal and though we're going to miss you — of course we are — you could scarcely have refused. But just imagine! John Caterham! After all these years!"

So then, having first sent Mavis out for babas, I phoned the station about times of trains: as Moira owned a car we'd

84

both considered it unnecessary for me to drive — a point I would have fought for if I'd had to, since I shouldn't have wanted to leave Junie and the children dependent upon lifts. After that I rang back Moira.

And found she was engaged!

I counted in a determinedly disciplined fashion up to fifty; then tried again.

Walked round the shop and made myself breathe deeply; this time counted to sixty. My pulse rate had gone mad and even my bowels threatened treachery. My bladder, too. The patisserie wasn't far away and what if on my third attempt the line continued busy… ?

It didn't.

Merciful heaven. The delay couldn't have lasted more than two minutes; not in reality. I relaxed.

(Up to a point. I still needed to impress.)

"If I leave here mid-afternoon on Friday I should get to Victoria at six-forty-eight. This means, of course, I'll have a pretty long wait at Dover Priory; I hope you appreciate that."

"Oh, I do. I shall be at Victoria at six-forty-seven-and-a-half in a strenuous effort to compensate!"

"Thank you. To strike a more serious note, however, you don't have to come to meet me. I used to be a boy scout; could probably still find my compass."

"I'm glad to hear it. To strike an even more serious note, however, I should like to come to meet you."

"And to strike the most serious note of all, however, I was simply being polite. Have no wish whatever to spurn a sympathetic guide. On the contrary. I'll carry a white stick and tap my way along the platform like old Pew."

"You're better-looking than he was."

"That's a blessing. I can't believe I've only met you twice."

"It's going to be fun. I'm looking forward to it. Oh — and while I think of it. Will you bring your dinner jacket?"

"I… Yes, of course."

"We'll do the thing in style."

"You bet we will." I heard the bell above the shop door.

"Damn. I'm afraid I've got to go. Customers."

"It's all right, Mr G; only yours truly," called out Mavis, over the partition.

"See you Friday, then. Ciao."

"Ciao," she answered. I cursed the interruption but sensed it could be better like this. Left to my own desires I might have gone on talking for an hour. That would have been lovely but... but I wanted to play it cool. I was totally without experience of intrigue yet knew I had her interest and also knew, according to received wisdom, it would be safer at this stage to retain a little mystery, keep her guessing, not to wear my heart too openly upon my sleeve.

"You are an idiot, Mr G — it was only yours truly," Mavis repeated. She'd now opened the office door. "Sorry about that."

I tilted my chair back and hitched both thumbs into my trouser pockets. I was magnanimous. "Nay, lass, think now't on't."

She giggled and held up the paper bag. "I had to get meringues. They hadn't any babas."

"No sweat," I said. With Mavis I could play it cool.

But even with Mavis it was partly touch and go. I felt I could've let out a whoop; grinned idiotically; chortled uncontrollably. Felt I could've run a mile. (Literally). Could've jumped into the sea in all my clothes. Jumped into the sea without a stitch. Kicked a football (we had one), hurled a cricket ball (we had one), watched them either disappear above a rooftop or else re-descend to make the perfect header, present the perfect catch. I could've rung the bell on one of those things which test your strength at fairgrounds — and maybe broken the machine.

I merely sat there at my desk with the most active thing about me being my brain. "Want me to make the coffee?" asked Mavis.

"What?"

"Coffee?"

"Coffee? If you like. Up to you." Yes — sure. There were times when I could be remarkably chilled-out. "Hey, Mavis. I want you to tell me something. Frankly."

"Oh, Lord. I hate it when anyone says that."

"Does my hair need doing?"

"Is that it? The question which requires a home truth?"

"Haircuts are important things. You mustn't underestimate a haircut. And next weekend I aim to cut a dash."

She gazed at me, consideringly. At rare moments Mavis seemed to lose her breathiness. Her little girlishness. "A rugged or sophisticated dash?" she asked.

"Both."

"In cricket togs I'd be inclined to go for the more rugged one. I like you with long hair."

"In white flannels, yes. But what about evening dress?"

That perhaps was indiscreet. But all she said was: "My word, is there also going to be a dance? Well, Mr G — life is a compromise. You'd better play the match, then run off to the barber's as soon as stumps are drawn."

"I don't believe in compromise."

"Ah... I always said you must've led a magical existence."

"You did?"

"No — never."

"But how right you would've been! A *very* magical existence."

I sprang up.

"I shall go out for twenty minutes. You, my girl, can eat the two meringues. Make up for a lifetime of half measures."

While I was in the mood I went into the bank and by chance was able to get an interview with the manager. (No, not by chance; by charm — by the irresistible persuasiveness of someone convinced that life, let alone bank managers, could deny him nothing. From now on, I reminded myself, I would never not be in the mood.) Hal Smart had been a schoolfriend: no bad thing in a bank manager. Because we'd regularly had our arms around each other in the rugger scrum and larked together in the shower it meant I never felt trepidation about asking for a loan; Hal knew better than to condescend. (In fact if either of us felt superior it could well have been me: he'd run to fat and lost a lot of hair; no stranger would have considered us the same age.) This morning he readily agreed to my request; understood about the upkeep of old houses — owning one himself. We asked after each other's families and said, as we always did, we must all get together sometime. Then he walked me to the main door and slapped my back by way of farewell; an attention not every overdrawn client was likely to receive from his bank manager. "All the very best, Sam." I wanted to tell him I'd already got it. I strode away jauntily, with my shoulders squared and my hands in my trouser pockets, like a man who'd just staged an eminently successful hold-up and knew in these enlightened times that the censors were going to let him get away with it, enjoy the fruits of his inventiveness and daring.

From the bank to the hairdresser's; but only for the merest trim. (Okay, Mavis, I admit — a compromise!) I also had a manicure. It was good to have a svelte and pretty blonde holding your hand and telling you the latest chapter in the saga of her search for Mr Wonderful. I aimed to offer her some sound and sympathetic and worldly-wise advice.

Then finally — or almost finally — the men's outfitters; the snazziest in town. With more warning I could have had a dinner jacket made. The one I settled on, however (and I was assured that without fail the alterations could be carried out by Friday), looked extremely dashing. Even without the proper shirt or tie or shoes. I turned this way and that and was far more impressed than I revealed to the probably gay assistant. Why on earth had I ever waited so long? I was a toff. I was a man-about-town. I was the model off the cover of a Harrods catalogue.

I wrote the cheque in the same happy fashion I'd handed out tips at the hairdressers. With something of a flourish. I needn't even have done it until the alterations had been made.

But I'd been gone for nearly two hours; it didn't seem possible. "A long twenty minutes, Mr G." Though not in any spirit of complaint.

"I'm sorry. Have I made you late for lunch?"

"It doesn't matter. I did eat both meringues; and I telephoned to warn my ma."

"And by the way I've just got something for your ma. Thought a bottle of wine might cheer her up a bit. Encourage her to shimmy like her sister Kate."

"Or maybe shimmer like her uncle Sam. Bless you," said Mavis. "You are good."

12

"I've been thinking," I said. It was the same evening, while we sipped our Martinis. Poor Susie sat beside my chair with her head on my lap and we told ourselves she was steadily improving. After all, not yet forty-eight hours, for heaven's sake! I scratched between her ears and she seemed to be enjoying it for she had closed her eyes. But the old vitality was missing — for the moment — and although there were many things which she remembered, incontestably, we would still often find her with her nose against a wall, or against some other large blank area like the back of a settee or the front of a bookcase, merely standing and staring and placidly waiting. This obviously was worrying and Mr Dodd had said we should see how she was doing in another week. "That old defeatist," I'd declared. "He doesn't reckon for the power of love. You've got to be positive, haven't you, Suze? It's love that's going to pull you through."

"Hurray for love," said Junie. I don't know why that sounded out of character. It simply did.

Not too unlike her reply — a short while later — to that *I've been thinking* of mine.

"Well done," she said.

Though she was smiling.

I stared into my drink. It had been the lead-in to something quite important. "How are things? You seem a little tired."

"I am — a little. I think my period's due."

"Oh, hell. Already?"

"I don't mind really. The sooner it comes the sooner I get it over with."

"Yes, of course." I did my best to adjust to this. "You poor old thing. It isn't right. You have a lot to put up with, don't you?"

"Mmm, its unusual. Not many women get periods. Why me, I ask myself. Why me?"

I laughed. If she was acting a trifle oddly I reflected that, a, it was good to have a wife who could still surprise one after seventeen years, and that, b, it was mainly her period talking. (Which shouldn't have begun until the following weekend — blast it! Ah, the best laid schemes o' mice an' men an o' potential Casanovas...)

But at times of small reverses such as this I had always liked to remember Count Basie's basic philosophy. 'Life is a bitch and if it's not one damn thing then it's going to be something else.' I topped up our Martini — for the beautiful people. And when we sat down to supper I almost immediately got up to fetch four wineglasses and a bottle of *Graves* from the sideboard. (On the way I tousled Ella's hair. "Oh, *Dad!*" she said — and jerked away her head. "Oh, *Dad!*" I said, with the old familiar sense of disappointment.)

"What's that for?" asked Junie, surprised, indicating the bottle.

"Mum, don't stop him!" cried the children, in rare harmony.

"I'm going to put it in the fridge. So we can have it with our puds."

"Fine," she answered. "Good idea. I simply wondered why."

"In celebration," I called.

"What of?"

"Just things generally. Of life. Of the fact you're all so nice."

"That's very sweet," said Junie, once I'd returned.

"Oh, Pop," said Matt, "I've just remembered. I got my project back today."

"So soon?"

He lowered his head; gave a shamefaced smile. "I know I let you think the deadline was yesterday but I suppose I misled you a bit: most people handed theirs in two weeks ago. Sorry."

91

"Well, anyway. Thank you for coming clean about it. That's what really counts."

"Though perhaps it would have been even better not to tell such a fib in the first place," Junie said. Junie had this dreadful reverence for truth.

"At all events... What was the verdict?"

"Miss Martin seemed pleased with it." Matt's look of penitence had quickly faded. "Especially — you were right — with the thing I did on Theseus. The thing *you* did on Theseus. But she said I omitted the ending. Said he wasn't someone I should want to emulate in every way. I mean, leaving aside the killings or the executions or whatever you want to call them."

"Why? What was she on about, then?"

"Ariadne."

"What about Ariadne?"

"Well, you sort of gave me the impression they got married; lived happily-ever-after; all that kind of guff. One of the great love stories, I thought you said. She told me he turned out to be a louse. That he deserted her."

"She accused Theseus of deserting Ariadne?"

"Yes."

"Called him a louse? I think you must've got it all wrong."

"Dad! How can you dream up louse? Dream up desertion?"

"Then I'm sorry. *She* must have got it all wrong. You'll have to tell her."

"Well, I suppose it isn't so world-shakingly important." He shrugged.

"Of course it's important!"

"Then you tell her; I shan't."

"And don't think I won't. Next parents' evening? When's that?"

"You don't mean you're actually coming this time?"

"Try to stop me!"

"There's one in... I think it's a fortnight Thursday."

"Please make me an appointment!"

We all laughed; even me. "Action Man," observed Matt.

"Three cheers for Theresa Martin!" added his mother.

Action Man… I savoured that for a second or two. On one of the tables in the shop there was an Action Man stripped down to his black briefs. I often saluted him as I went past; or picked him up if vibrations had caused him to topple. "Glad you've noticed the resemblance," I remarked, modestly.

"Why don't you just phone her, Dad?" asked Ella.

"No, you shut up," said Matt. "He's coming to the parents' evening. They both are. Aren't you, Dad?"

"'Course I am."

"Promise?"

"Only the grave could stop me now. Honest."

"Honest Sam Groves," said Junie. "My husband the bookmaker."

"Funny you should say that." Though I hoped she hadn't got in mind a recent, far from funny incident.

"Why? Is that what you're thinking of setting up as?"

"Well, no. Not necessarily. But you remember I said earlier there's something I've been thinking about?" Yes, this was as good a time as any; the children could be in on it, as well. Right from the outset. "It's this. That RADA business last night. I don't believe it's going to come to anything. I don't see how it can; one's got to be realistic. One's got to be — "

"But, oh, you're not giving up the idea of being an actor, are you?" Ella exclaimed.

"You really shouldn't interrupt, darling," admonished Junie.

"If RADA auditioned me and decided to take me on, that would be wonderful, Ella. But what I'm saying is it isn't very likely. Yet supposing it was? We'd been talking about Mum being the one to look after the shop, hadn't we, getting out a bit more, meeting people, discovering — ?"

"Well, I can't say I'm all that disappointed," Junie cut in. "You don't have to worry you might be letting me down."

"You said you'd quite enjoy it."

"That's true but — "

"Junie, hold on. I went to see Hal Smart today."

93

"Hal? You mean, on business?"

"What other reason would I go to see him for?"

I paused. It had suddenly occurred to me how sad was that remark. Hal and I had once been very close. I'd actually had a crush on him. For practically the whole of my fifteenth year, during what had turned into an unexpectedly curative, even an almost carefree time, the two of us had been inseparable. 'They'll never prise apart young Groves and Smart,' some budding versifier had once scrawled across the blackboard, 'they're like apple and cloves, young Smart and Groves,' and I recalled how I'd secretly felt immensely proud to be half of such a brilliant couplet, a couplet which had seemed to me quite as inspired as any in the *Golden Treasury*, of which my grandmother had given me a copy on my last birthday. But now, some twenty-two years afterwards...

"Yes, of course on business," I said. No wonder I should be such an expert on the matter of life's little ironies.

Seeing Hal now could sometimes make me shiver in disbelief. And also in distaste.

"And... ?" Junie queried.

I looked at her.

"Darling, what were you leading up to?"

"Oh, yes. Sorry. I got sidetracked." Remembering a rider the nasty Evan Saunders had later added to that couplet — though only orally, thank God, it was never taken up. 'Apple and cloves, young Smart and Groves, right tasty tart, young Groves and Smart.' In some ways I'd minded it less at the time than I did today. At any rate it hadn't tarnished my then pride in the original.

I hastily reassembled my thoughts.

"Woolgathering," I smiled. "It's just that... Well, you know I never worry you about these things, Junie — not normally — but the shop isn't doing all that wonderfully at present. It's probably nothing very serious, of course: the usual pre-summer lull: and I suppose I should never have thought of taking Mavis on full-time... " It really went against the grain to sound so negative, required an actual effort of will, and — like Matt last Saturday — I had my fingers firmly crossed (though *I*, naturally, kept them well out of view). This helped a little: feeling like my son. Gilded youth! Gilded youth but in fact fewer than twenty-five years divided us; I must be careful not to forget that. My own golden future gleamed as brightly as... as brightly as the lightship from the Goodwin Sands.

"Oh, *Sam*... "Junie got up. She came and did to me what I had done to her the previous evening: stood behind my chair and put her arms about my neck and kissed the top of my head. "I knew you'd been behaving a little too cheerfully these past few days. Darling, I should have realised what it meant. I think you're *very* brave but I also think you're *very* foolish... " She bent and put her cheek against my own.

Unsurprisingly, all this solicitude brought the tears to my eyes; I had been known to weep at a commercial. Also, no less predictably, it brought a mocking reaction from our children. ("Oh, do they always have to carry on like this?" asked Matt. "At mealtimes, would you believe? Ashes, d'you think they actually *want* us to throw up: a way of saving on the food bills?") Junie went and sat down again while I told them — though with a tolerance roughly equal to their own — not to be so silly and to grow up; and was unsporting enough to remind them they hadn't yet received their wine.

"Darling, it's truly not so tragic as all that." I made a humorous performance out of dabbing at my eyes. "Especially since I've had a bit of a brainwave and it's all due to this thing about writing off to RADA; I don't think it would've occurred to me otherwise. We've got to try and make some extra money — right? And the job opportunities in Deal at the moment, like in any other small town in this country, are virtually non-existent and — "

"I could try to get a job at Marks & Spencer's," said Junie, "or British Home Stores or somewhere. Sam, you should have *told* me if we were getting into difficulties."

"No. That isn't your department. Nor is getting us out of them. It's very sweet of you, darling, but..." I gave a shrug.

"But what?" she persisted.

"But I could earn a far better wage in London, where there *are* jobs, than you could ever hope to do down here, where if there's anything at all it's most likely only part-time and very poorly paid. Besides, darling, you know me: I've never liked the idea of my wife going out to work."

"What would I be doing at the shop then? Getting a suntan?"

"That's different."

"How?"

"You'd be the owner. The wife of the owner. It's somehow not the same."

"Mr Spock would never understand," declared Matt, mournfully, shaking his head.

"Captain Kirk would."

"Well, I'm not too sure about this," said Junie. "I don't think I go for it. We're a family. When would we ever see you?"

"At weekends. I'd be home every Friday night; wouldn't leave again till Monday. You'd hardly notice I was gone."

"Is that what you honestly believe?"

"Obviously it's an arrangement none of us is really going to like. But if we look at it positively there may be some advantages. I mean — apart from all the extra money and the higher standard of living and the holidays abroad."

"We already have holidays abroad."

"Yes, but that's only because your parents pay so much towards them — and naturally have the major say in where we go. And that's nearly always to some part of France. But this way we could sometimes branch out: Italy, Greece, maybe even California. Just think of it, how good that would be for the children's education... "

Ella and Matt were instantly in favour of extra money, a higher standard of living and holidays abroad. Even Junie herself was invariably influenced by any question of the children's education.

"Also," I said, "think how special the weekends would be. Absence makes the heart grow fonder — so they say — not that in our case this would be any easy matter, not on my side. But a father coming home brings presents and a husband coming home takes his wife out to expensive restaurants on Saturday nights... "

"That's not fair," said Matt immediately.

"And his children."

"It is getting fairer," he allowed, reluctantly.

Then added: "So long as it can really be relied on." His tone had grown mournful again.

"Hey!" I said. "Matthias. What do you take me for? A welsher?"

"No — an expiring actor. The very hairs of your head are all numbered."

This too was a running gag between the pair of us. And not always wildly apt. But that's what made it funny. (Or anyway so we thought.)

"Oh, but you're being silly," protested Junie. "Presents! Expensive restaurants! You'll have two homes to run. Meals. Either train fares or petrol. You'll have a job just breaking even."

"What do you mean, two homes to run?"

"What do you think I mean, two homes to run?"

I recollected myself; spread my hands and gave a patient smile. "But you don't grasp the situation. My needs are simple. A cheap bedsitter with a gas ring. I don't care about the area — I shall always have my home to come back to." I laughed. "Darling, it almost sounds as though you doubt my potential earning capacity; as though you doubt my real worth."

"The only thing I doubt," she answered, "is the ability of other people to recognise your real worth; though since when has a person's earning capacity been any measure of a person's worth?"

Then she added: "And you know I don't mean to be brutal but what precisely would you say you're qualified for?"

97

"Pop, only imagine what she could do if she did mean to be brutal!" Matt shuddered. "Don't you find that scary?"

"Here, kids, I think you've got to help me a bit."

"We'd like to. But the trouble is — poor Ashes hasn't any imagination and you told me not to lie."

"No, no, it was your mother who told you that. You know my credo. Anything I can hope to get away with."

We had a jolly time. Between the four of us — though, to be honest, the women advanced far fewer suggestions than either Matt or me, whether sensible or silly — we came up with hotel work, reception work, clerical work, shop-, maintenance-, security-, gardening-, driving-, even garage work. Junie set out a couple of conditions.

She wouldn't have me going into security work and she wanted to be sure I held onto my Saturdays. Beyond that, she didn't think most of the other jobs, even in London, would pay enormous salaries but on the other hand she really didn't mind (she supposed) how much I might choose to lower myself — none of them did — provided it only happened a very long way from home.

"Yes, what do dustmen get?" asked Ella. "And roadsweepers? Or bus conductors?"

"Gravediggers?" Matt put in. "'Alas! poor Yorick.' Recitations on the side."

"There must be about a hundred things that Dad could do, when you really think about it."

I wasn't too happy about their concepts of demeaning oneself. But at least there weren't likely to be many road-sweepers, gravediggers or dustmen passing through our hall right now and it didn't seem the moment to get pompous and discuss ethics.

And we talked about my project, off and on, for the next two or three hours — with the children, without the children — round and round, finding a few fresh arguments but basically repeating ourselves.

"Well," Junie said at last, "you might as well give it a try.

If it doesn't work, it doesn't work. I suppose we haven't much to lose."

"No, not a thing," I answered, gaily.

13

Wednesday and Thursday represented in one sense quite the longest two days I could remember, even though, simultaneously, perhaps I wasn't wanting them to rush. Matt would have laughed at me and felt impatient but I kept saying to myself: this time is special, special — unrepeatable. So I passed the hours in a kind of sun-shot haze and imagined myself about to leave the quayside: the impatient traveller anxious to be properly under way but the home-loving man still appreciating his view from the ship's rail. All the people waiting on the dock to see me off seemed at their very nicest, whether they were relatives, acquaintances or total strangers, and I felt that every word I called back ought to be wise or humorous or in some way worth the uttering. Is it true; is it kind; is it necessary? Even when I spoke only to Susie, or to the rubber plant in the hall, or the yucca at the bend on the stairs, I tried to choose my sentences with care. With careful spontaneity. That seemed to be the order of the day.

And here's a small example of how everything works together if you're steering a true course: Junie's period didn't come — not on the Tuesday, nor the Wednesday, nor yet the Thursday. And even though I couldn't help myself at odd moments thinking about Moira (calamitous, I'd discovered, on one occasion earlier in the week) — even though on the Thursday morning, running late, I scarcely tried to discipline myself at all — the count shot up amazingly: nearly to two thousand, which represented a solid twenty-five minutes, possibly more. No one could feel hard-done-by at twenty-five minutes, or not feel hard-done-by at twenty-five minutes, even if it might occasionally provoke a stifled yawn. (Yet poor Junie: you couldn't blame her: a pair of teenage children — well, Matt was all but teenage — made up an exhausting package.)

But then — would you believe? — on Friday, when I'd decided I wanted in any case to begin this tremendous day in a state of chastity, Junie informed me her period had arrived during the night! It was almost enough to give you faith in a beneficent god — that is, if you were a little weaker and more malleable than you should have been.

Unfortunately, though, I didn't sleep well on the Thursday night. As a precautionary measure I'd wondered whether to ask the doctor for some Nitrazepam but though I'd lain awake for a long time during the small hours of Sunday morning (and been very glad to do so) since then, surely due to all that unaccustomed sexual activity, I'd had no trouble whatever over sleep — no, not even following the heady nonsense of the RADA episode. Indeed, all the greatest excitements of my life in recent years: playing Lord Goring, for instance, or else Freddie Eynsford-Hill; or taking part in the local tennis tournament organised every summer for charity: these had never once, so far as I remembered, left me short of sleep.

But that Thursday night felt endless and instead of relaxing I worried about it: I wouldn't look my best, my reactions would suffer, my conversation, my sexual performance, everything. I shouldn't be able to get through; I'd be a tedious, lifeless, disappointing lump.

The only thing maybe that stopped me from a full-scale panic, i.e. deciding to postpone the whole weekend on the grounds of someone's illness (whose?, not my grandmother's, we'd then have had Moira rushing down to help look after her), was the thought I might at least manage to doze on leaving Dover.

The reassurance in this idea, together with a mug of hot milk and some biscuits, which I should obviously have got up for a good deal earlier, mercifully did the trick... but by then it was already half-past-four. And all part of the same irony — we had gone to bed for once a little before ten; turned out our lights, probably, even before Matt and Ella would have turned out theirs. Fools that we were; or rather, of course — fool that I was!

Yet anyhow, although I overslept again (therefore we all did) and woke up feeling pretty grotty, this was nevertheless an improvement on the way I'd felt a few hours previously. I had to rush my bath and skimp my breakfast but I'd done most of my packing the night before, along with polishing my shoes.

Skimping breakfast, though — I imagine it was this — meant that my bowels didn't function properly for the first morning in I don't know how many; which had I been a little weaker and more malleable than I ought to have been, and ever had faith in a beneficent god, would have been almost enough to turn me sceptical at once.

Because if I didn't have a satisfactory movement after breakfast I seldom compensated for it later and the whole day could be one of bloated, if largely psychological, discomfort. And merely the thought of railway lavatories — whether on the stations or the trains themselves — was enough to make me feel unclean.

Hell and damnation.

However, I did find time to say goodbye to Susie. Since for the moment it didn't come to her automatically I had myself to roll her over in order to tickle her tummy. This wasn't easy but what made me persevere was that she still gave the impression of enjoying it: far more from the way in which her legs stretched out than from — these days — any soppily abandoned grin. It seemed to be worth it.

I told her: "I shan't be seeing you, old thing, till Monday night. Four whole days! How shall we survive? But here's your list of instructions, Suze. Kindly pay attention. Get into the open air a lot — when I come back I want to see those roses in your cheeks. Take your medicine like a good girl. Repeat over and over, 'I am getting better, I am getting better, I'm going to get well again for Master!' Right? Message received? Absolutely no cheating now because I'm going to set my spies on you; and, besides, we have an understanding, you and I. Don't we?"

I gave her a final pat and she struggled up to follow me out, lumberingly, towards the gate.

My farewell from the children hadn't been so affecting. While I was still upstairs Ella, probably reminded by her mother, had called from the front door, "Have a lovely time, Dad; see you Monday," but I'd barely had an instant to call back before I'd heard her running down the path; while Matt, who had gone off a few minutes later with the classmate who invariably collected him, had forgotten to say goodbye at all. This was completely usual but today I'd hoped he'd have remembered. I'd shouted down at what I thought was the last possible moment... and found that I'd misjudged it.

Junie was going to come into Treasure Island sometime during the morning because having baked a fruit cake for the Caterhams she'd decided belatedly to marzipan and ice it. It had struck her with John's wife away looking after a sick mother and leaving three young children possibly in need of cheering up that her cake could do with all the decoration available.

I myself got to the shop less than ten minutes after my normal time — though it was only my ingrained sense of punctuality which had made this seem necessary; and when Mavis arrived I suddenly wondered why I hadn't eaten my usual decent breakfast, driven along with the keys, then driven home again and bathed and dressed at leisure. It should have been the obvious solution and I couldn't understand why I hadn't thought of it.

Yet because I hadn't and attributed it to the fact of my unwonted tiredness I immediately felt tireder than ever. And instead of this weekend shaping up as the most wonderful in my experience I had premonitions it was going to rank among the most disastrous; perhaps actually *be* the most disastrous.

Again I thought of telephoning Moira, saying I myself was ill: some sort of stomach bug, nothing too serious but incapacitating and infectious; or was there some other minor ailment sounding more romantic? In any case I couldn't do it. Couldn't jeopardise this opportunity for happiness... no matter how doomed it might be coming to appear.

I had to go back to the outfitter's before noon. I'd been resolving half-heartedly that if by any chance the evening suit wasn't ready or the alterations just weren't right — then I *would* ring Moira. But not only was everything in order: when I tried the suit on it looked terrific; my lack of sleep had *not* affected my appearance! From that moment the whole downward trend of the day — hitherto irreversible — splendidly reversed itself.

I collected the patent leather pumps I'd bought at a nearby shoeshop on the Wednesday but decided not to pick up till this morning. My new dress shirt and cufflinks and black tie were in the bag with the dinner jacket. My wardrobe was complete.

Complete even down to the white walking stick I'd thought it might be fun to borrow... hadn't I spoken to Moira of tapping my way along the platform as helpless as blind Pew? (Not that he *had* been helpless, of course; which made the simile *much* more suitable.) I wondered if knowing we'd got one in stock had precipitated that particular piece of foolishness.

When I returned to the shop I found Junie had already been, with the cake for the Caterham family tied securely in a brown carton previously used by Messrs Holland & Barrett to transport roasted and salted pistachios but now thoughtfully provided with a strong loop by my wife. "And two messages," added Mavis. "The first: you've got to score a century and not bother to come home unless you do. And the second: she's decided to drive into Canterbury to try to find inspiration for your sister-in-law's anniversary present. We spoke about how hard it is wanting to buy something nice for the person who has everything."

We had been speaking about it all week, Junie and I — admittedly amongst one or two other things.

"She said there didn't seem much point in her waiting," Mavis continued, "since I hadn't any idea how long you'd be.

She only wanted to wish you luck and say she hoped you'd be a great success."

Of course it was as well I hadn't come strutting back into the shop swinging my purchases. The bags themselves looked glossily expensive: not the kind of thing in which I normally collected jumble. (Maybe another instance of my not having been thinking too clearly but not one this time that depressed me: I would have invented something, I would have got away with it, I could have got away with bloody murder!) Yet I was sorry to have missed her. It meant we hadn't said goodbye properly. And although I heard in this the murmurings of superstition I felt it was somehow wrong to be going off at such a time without both giving and receiving a hug — a kiss — a blessing — a brief restatement of our love. I tried to phone her: wondered if, with luck, she might have gone home for any reason before proceeding to Canterbury. But the telephone just rang and rang, bleakly, in the empty hall.

"No luck?" asked Mavis. "I didn't think she'd be going back."

Even so, after an interval of several minutes, I gave it another shot. She might have been in the garden or on the loo and the ring wasn't a loud one.

"No. Damn. Well, never mind."

"You're certainly a most devoted husband!"

"Thank you, Mavis. Since it isn't truly to my own credit I feel I can answer yes to that. Yes, I am."

"Well, it makes a nice change, Mr G, it really does. We should hang you up as an example."

"Hold me up is what I hope you mean."

She laughed. "Not that I believe you need much holding up. You're not the kind to go all limp." I wasn't sure whether or not that contained a *double entendre*. But either way the sentiment was pleasing.

At first I wondered if I couldn't leave the carton. I already had my holdall, plus two carrier bags, plus a white walking stick. But hiding it would have been risky. Customers often asked you for things you believed you might have seen *somewhere* and supposing Mavis should helpfully embark on a wholesale rummage... ? Or what was equally unlikely — yet at the same time equally possible — supposing Junie herself during the hour or so when she'd be filling in should venture out upon some fascinating voyage of discovery... ?!! I might be living dangerously but — oh my God! — I liked to think I wasn't actually posting clues.

Also, leaving Junie's cake would have seemed both callous and disloyal; not the proper way to be setting off on an adventure — especially in conjunction with the fact I hadn't said goodbye as I'd have chosen. It would almost have seemed I was leaving behind a part of *her*. And therefore, perhaps, by extension, a part of *me*.

I tried to phone again at three-fifteen but she had doubtless stopped in Canterbury for lunch.

I gave up then. My train was at three-forty-five and I wanted to take my time over walking to the station.

Indeed, I wanted to take my time over every aspect of these next three days. *See and appreciate. See and appreciate.* It should've been written across my forehead. In copperplate.

"I really hope you and Wendy will have a great time at... Herne Bay?" No. Mavis and her friend would be spending the holiday at Broadstairs...what would be left of the holiday. Had it occurred to me I'd have suggested we shut up shop from this evening. Oh, damn! How selfish could you get? But perhaps it wasn't too late? We could always put a notice on the door? Yet mercifully she salved my conscience.

"No, Mr G." With a vehement shake of the head. "Wend couldn't've got away before tomorrow afternoon. And Mum, too — I couldn't've left Mum alone for three whole nights. She's in enough of a hu-ha as it is. But she's not an invalid; and while I can do so I've got myself to think of. Haven't I? I tell her it will do her good."

"You're right, Mavis. Everyone has to think of himself occasionally."

106

"But you make sure you have a great time too. Knock 'em all for six. I mean — both on the cricket field *and* on the dance floor."

"Naturally," I said. "Oh, by the way, did you happen to mention the dance floor bit to Junie?"

"You're not trying to tell me she doesn't know?"

I paused, in the face of her astonishment. "If it's deception, it's only deception in a very tiny way. I just don't want to run the risk of making her feel… oh, I don't know what the word is."

"Jealous?"

"Well, sort of left out of things."

"Okay. It's as well you warned me."

"It wouldn't have mattered."

"You know something?" she said. "I sometimes think you're just too good to be true."

"So do I. Isn't it nauseating?"

Talking of warnings, I'd wondered whether I ought to warn John Caterham — or indeed his wife. (Every time I thought of her I had to remind myself that, no, she wasn't visiting her sick mother; at least, it would have been amazing if she were.) But the odds against Junie trying to contact me in Lincolnshire were so great I really didn't want to beg that kind of favour. John would instantly suppose our marriage was in trouble and I would mind about that. I had no wish for any wrong ideas to call up either sadness or self-congratulation in someone who'd once used to play for us, repeatedly, an old seventy-eight of his mother's: 'They tried to tell us we're too young… ' (That, maybe more than any other, had always been our tune: Junie's and mine.)

Yes, I believed in covering my tracks but why on earth should Junie ever seek to reach me? In the event of an emergency she had her whole family living practically within earshot.

No. There were risks and risks. You didn't want to get obsessive.

Obsession wasn't cool.

"Why on earth are you wanting that old thing?" asked Mavis, as she held the door. I had the stick along the top of my holdall.

"Oh. To play a joke on someone."

"That sounds hilarious. Boys together. Have fun."

Unexpectedly, while I was walking to the station, it was Mavis's mother whom I had in mind. Wishing there was only some way I could've let *her* have the cake. That would've been something, wouldn't it? Probably no one I knew could have made more use of Junie's thoughtful and festive morale-booster in a time of deprivation. Probably no one I knew was looking forward less cheerfully to the long weekend that lay ahead. It must be hell to be old and so much on your own.

But obviously — life being life — there was no way I could simply act on impulse.

More's the pity.

14

I abandoned all idea of tapping my way towards our meeting. It wasn't so much I lost my nerve as that it came to seem a bit juvenile. A faintly teasing echo: *That sounds hilarious*? At any rate I left the stick on the train. It would probably end up at some lost property office and people would wonder what had happened to the poor soul who'd had to stagger on without it.

And besides. What if Moira hadn't remembered the reference to blind Pew?

Or if she'd got there late? *Imagine!* Everyone stepping out of my way or wondering if they ought to offer help. I could hardly just have jettisoned the stick and given a sheepish little smile that asked for merry understanding.

So, yes, maybe it *had* been a case of lost nerve. I wasn't a fraud but people would have instantly suspected I was up to no good. You could hardly have blamed them.

Discretion... valour... He who learns to run away lives to fight another day.

But, anyhow, blindness was something I no longer had a need to worry about. (Thank God! I'd often attempted to imagine how it must feel; had frequently walked around the shop for shortish periods with my eyes closed.)

And Moira — most certainly — *was* there.

At first, though, I scarcely recognised her. I'd been expecting someone taller. And her hair was still red — of course — but somehow not the shade I had remembered. She wore less makeup, perhaps, didn't appear so... quite so glowing or vibrant. Or Technicolored. But then I realised what it was. It was simply the numbers of people jostling across my line of vision. As soon as I actually reached her — and she smiled — she immediately grew strong again, clear-cut and radiantly distinctive.

And she'd evidently had something of the same problem. "How ridiculous! I didn't see you. Despite your height. I'm getting too shortsighted."

Too shortsighted, I thought. Shortsighted itself was already too shortsighted. I've always said it, however: it's absurd the things that'll flash across your mind at moments of maximum tension.

But I merely set down all my luggage and extended my hand. She shook it for an instant, put her other hand across it, and then we both leant forward to kiss. Lightly on the lips. I had many times asked myself how it would be during these first moments. Now I had my answer. Apart from the *very* first of them it had been wholly spontaneous and natural and right.

"I was feeling slightly jittery," she laughed.

"*You*?"

"Well, weren't you, then — just a little?"

"Oh, maybe. Just a little." I definitely wasn't going to tell her the closer we'd got to Victoria the more time I'd spent in simply wondering whether, first, I could bear to use the lavatory on the train or whether, second, I could even be said to have any choice in the matter. It's only nerves, I'd told myself; stop panicking, it's only nerves. But then I'd remembered that perhaps it wasn't; from the minute I had tried on my dinner jacket I'd forgotten about that morning's constipation. So maybe, it seemed to me, it was going to be a question either of inevitable contamination aboard the train or of having to make straight for the men's cloakroom on reaching the station. ("Moira, just look after these an instant; gotta run; talk to you when I get back!") Either way, not the most propitious lead-in to a love affair. I shouldn't even have been thinking of such things. Moonlight, wine and roses would have made a better mix. And that was the period, too, during which I'd decided to dispense with the walking stick. Hadn't felt I could achieve the right insouciance.

But then the Fates had been kind again. With a good

twenty minutes still to go the old man who'd been sitting beside me all the way from Folkestone — yet without addressing one word to me — now began to fuss about the train being late. He had a very tight connection to make out of Liverpool Street. Suddenly he seemed more agitated than I was and in my efforts to reassure him my own agitation imperceptibly fell back. He appeared so soothed by what I said (naturally not realising this was a blatant case of the blind leading the blind) (ha ha!) that I was then able to start a simple conversation with the object of distracting him. I soon learnt he was going to stay with a married son near Cambridge but that he'd never got on with him so well as with his other boy, who was living in Vancouver and for the past seven years had been busily saving up to get him over there. Seven years! That struck me as rather pathetic — and of course a bit ironic — since it didn't appear this older son could really be going at it all that hard. But then, fair enough — judge not — I didn't know the situation. What I did get to know, however, was what the old man considered to be the greatest mistake of his life bar none. Thirty years earlier, he told me, his wife had been unfaithful and at that time he'd been unable to forgive it; had walked out and been prevented by his pride from ever going back; even before she'd died, he whispered, he had been the loneliest — the very loneliest — man in all existence. Now the only thing he waited for, apart from a month or two in Canada, and really even more than that if I was hoping to hear the honest truth... did I know what it was? It was to be able at last to rejoin her and try to make amends. "Many the time I've been tempted, you know, to go and do something silly. But it wouldn't just have been silly, it would've been *wrong* and might've put paid to whatever small chances I've got." He was a simple man and obviously misguided but I felt very sorry for him and casually enquired his name and whether he lived in Folkestone: I thought that one day Junie and I and the kids could drive over and take him on a picnic or out to tea or something. The name was Jack Bradley but he didn't have time to say where his home was; at that point we'd started to cross the Thames and he exclaimed he must be making his way up to the top of the train. I offered to help but he had only the one suitcase, which he'd kept the whole time on the table in front of us, so he was away, very agitated again, even before I could slide across the seat and manage to stand up, let alone collect together my own things. Anyhow, I had his name so it shouldn't be too difficult to track him down and arrange that outing; and I watched his beetling progress through the compartment with something that was already a bit like solid paternal affection. Or maybe filial. I hoped his journey to Liverpool Street would be an easy one.

And then I realised we'd arrived and that I actually felt reasonably calm about it.

"Oh, maybe. Just a little," I confessed, grinningly. I stooped to pick up my belongings.

"What shall I carry?" asked Moira.

"How about this? You'll never guess what it is! Not in a thousand years!"

"I think you've baked me a cake."

I stared at her. Am even prepared to believe I may have gaped.

"What's the matter?" she asked.

"I gave you a thousand years," I said. "It took you all of half a second."

"It isn't really a cake?"

"Cross my heart and hope to — "

"How extraordinary."

"Talk about kindred spirits! D'you think we're telepathic?"

"Clearly no other explanation..."

Though it immediately occurred to me this might have its problems. "Semi-telepathic," I amended.

"Yes, that could be another explanation," she agreed. We laughed — why had I ever had a second's worry? It was all going to be phenomenal from beginning to end. Good old Junie and her splendid cake. "It's certainly quite heavy," she added, weighing it consideringly in both hands rather than holding it by the loop. "I hope I haven't said the wrong thing. I hope it isn't a jam sponge."

I shook my head. "Not quite. But are you good at riddles?"

"I don't know. Try me."

"When would something that isn't quite a jam sponge — yet has strong affiliations — be likeliest to come between us?"

She pursed her lips in reflection; her pupils moved from side to side. "I'll tell you one thing. I may be telepathic but I'm not much good at riddles."

"So d'you give up?"

"I think I'll have to."

"When it makes the filling in a Victoria Sandwich!" I wished for a moment a second's worry *had* given me pause before I'd plunged headfirst into that one.

But the sheer and utter awfulness of the solution made us start to giggle; exactly like my children in facetious mood. Indeed Ella had recently told me I behaved like a retarded ten-year-old, which was a pretty cutting thing to say, as well as a sad one, because all she meant apparently was I often exclaimed, "Isn't this fun!" if we walked on the seafront licking an ice-cream or had races barefoot on wet sand or even just set off together to the hairdresser's, her and Matt and me. I extracted pleasure from the simple things, I'd answered, and in that lay the art of living. Cripes, she'd said, but since she couldn't come up with any more articulate riposte I hoped I might have made my point. Further to emphasise it — and also to annoy her — I took Matt's hand and we skipped side-by-side along the pavement, laughing hysterically and showing off like mad, despite what seemed a bumper crop of passers-by. 'The art of living', in fact, was one of those pet phrases I repeated to myself from time to time as a reminder that life was fleeting and we passed this way but once. By and large I considered I knew more than most about the art of living. Perhaps I was merely kidding myself but didn't believe so. Sometimes I'd asked various people if on the whole they were happy, only to be told, "Yes, suppose so, never really think about it... "

Cripes!

Now, though, in spite of all our laughter, Moira expressed a hope the level of our repartee might rise a little during the weekend. I answered it appeared to have no other option.

"I'm still not altogether sure I can believe you've gone and baked a cake."

"No?"

"No. So, now. In all truthfulness. We're making a fresh start," she cautioned. "Right?"

"Right."

"Is this a cake?"

"Yes."

"In all truthfulness, mind. You're not allowed to cheat."

"As though I would."

"All right. Is it a cake, then, which you've made yourself?"

"Do you mean — for myself?"

"No, I do not mean that. Stop being devious. I mean is it a cake which you yourself have made?"

"Oh. I see. Still in all truthfulness?"

She nodded. Intractable. Unrelenting.

"Then in that case," I said, "I can't honestly claim it is."

"Aha! At last. Now maybe we're getting to the heart of it." She fitted her finger through the loop and I thought of the little Dutch boy trying to stem the flood. "In other words you're telling me you've bought it."

"Really? I wasn't aware of that. I'm sorry. I didn't set out with the intention to deceive."

"In a moment I am going to scream," she said. Instead she simply smiled — quite broadly — and in the process looked enchanting. "All I'm asking is... please Sammy, dear Sammy, *kind* Sammy... "

"Ah, I understand: what makes Sammy run?" I interpolated, helpfully.

"No. I swear it. Nothing half so complex or so tangled. Purely — *who was it who baked the cake you say I'm holding?*"

114

It was a fair question; and it needed to be answered. But 'in *all* truthfulness' would have to come later. And come it would; indisputably. During the week I'd given a lot of thought to this. Naturally. Whatever else I was, I wasn't an idiot. For the next seventy-two hours or so, while we really got to know each other, I could carry on with the game: the fun and the frivolity. Or, rather, those were the accoutrements, the colouring on the box, eye-catching illustration on the lid; because the game itself was deadly serious. But until the final part of the weekend or, anyway, what I considered the best moment for the raising of it... until then the lid stayed firmly in position. Only the cellophane could be removed.

"My grandmother."

We continued to form a totally unheeding island round which swirled the inconvenienced sea of tourists and commuters.

"Well, that's incredible," said Moira. "What a fantastic person she must be."

"Like grandmother, like grandson," I admitted.

"Hmm. At least I'm willing to believe her influence could only have been beneficial."

"And after all. Who was the one who had to carry it? Spirit it over mountaintop and lug it down through vale and valley?"

"Through vale *and* valley? My, how you make light of it! But was it her idea or was it yours?"

"I cannot tell a lie. I can't. I can't. We're talking of the cake? It was mine."

"Really?"

I laughed. "No, of course not. It was hers."

She leant forward, reached up and gave me a kiss. Unfortunately I was still carrying the holdall and the two bags so I couldn't put my arms about her. "What was that for?"

"For being a good boy — finally — and telling me the truth."

"Oh gosh — oh gee — oh golly. I'm going to tell a lot more truth from now on, Miss."

115

"Then I'm very pleased with you, Sammy."

"So can I have another of those nice things to demonstrate you are?"

She gave me one. This time I dropped the baggage and held her very close.

After some fifteen or twenty seconds she pulled away. "I can see I shall have to be a whole lot firmer in future," she said. "You may not believe this but there are some who might even describe it as displaying guile and a distinct lack of sportsmanship. That manoeuvre of yours just now."

I looked chastened.

"So pick up your things, please; then follow behind and do your best to behave."

"I can't."

She must have realised I was now in earnest.

"Why? What's wrong?"

"I'm afraid you may have to wait a minute."

Suddenly she understood my predicament and started to laugh. More practically she bent down and herself handed me the three items. But she didn't comment on the situation. Clearly thought it might be better-bred to run with something safer.

"I just can't wait," she said, "to open up this tempting box." One expression of amusement immediately gave place to another. "Heavens! I sound like Pandora."

"Well, then, it's lucky I've got faith in you. You're the one who gives life, not destroys it."

"At any rate I'll try to leave you with a scraping of hope; a *generous* scraping of hope," she promised.

With which gracious assurance we started at last — but rather slowly — towards the station entrance.

15

Her car was parked in a side street near the Army & Navy. Someone had left a Morgan there too and I exclaimed excitedly. (Ella would have called this a further symptom of arrested development.) "Let's go and take a look!"

"Why not?"

"You know," I said, "when I was a young man — that is, an even younger man — the thing I wanted more than absolutely anything was a two-seater identical to this. I used to dream about owning one. Sometimes, I mean, really dream."

"But you still can't have wanted it enough."

I shook my head, however. "Believe me, it wasn't that. I may have been a dreamer but I had my practical side as well. And a Morgan just wouldn't have been the right size for a fam— ." I stopped short. I saw her look at me. I felt I was about to blush. "For a family outing each weekend with my grandparents."

I couldn't remember now what I had told her about my grandfather — who had died when I was three — or, indeed, if I had told her anything. Neither could she, apparently. She looked back at the car.

"You really are the sweetest person."

I honestly didn't wish to hoodwink her like that; to win her liking under false pretences.

"I was only wanting to impress you," I said, modestly. "I have this awful compulsion to present myself in the best possible light."

"No. You were all confused. I could see it slipped out unawares. You even went a little red." She paused; then indicated the Morgan. "Well, have you now feasted your eyes sufficiently?"

"No. I could never feast my eyes sufficiently. But life is

hard: force me, please, to tear myself away."

"Why?"

"Why what?"

"Why don't you take this and just get in?" She was holding out a key ring.

It had never occurred to me to ask what kind of car she had. Apart from Morgans themselves and certain other snappy sports jobs — and old crocks too, of course — I wasn't much interested in things like that. Nor, unsurprisingly, was Matt.

She said: "Validation of proverb? Everything comes to him who waits. Synchronicity."

"This car is *yours?*"

She nodded. "Though for the moment why not say it's yours?"

To facilitate my inspection of it I'd deposited my luggage by a railing. Now I actually picked her up and did a pirouette upon the pavement. It reminded me of last Sunday morning: *Hey, why so physical? He's acting pretty weird today.* I saw her face above me, laughingly responsive, with her red hair swinging and her slim arms wrapped about my shoulders; and she felt weightless — or extremely light. It must have been a full half-minute before, reluctantly, I set her down.

"Your own fault; you shouldn't give me these surprises! You see, it was either that or flinging my ten-gallon hat in the air or swinging my lasso or firing my repeater. Yee-hee-e-e-e! May I actually drive it?"

She now handed me the ring. "It's a miracle you didn't lose it! What if it had flown from my fingers and gone skimming down a grating: your dream of a lifetime?"

"I should've sat and cried."

"Then it's a good job I was holding on."

"My saviour. Will you marry me?"

It was a joke, of course, and she was joking too when she replied but it gave me an instant of faint queasiness amidst my giddy exultation.

"No. Don't think so. I'd rather go on liking you."

"Oh, very well. The right decision. Lets me off the hook."

Three minutes later I had (with difficulty) stowed the luggage and handed her into the passenger seat. I settled myself at the steering wheel but felt in no hurry to start up. I ran my hands over the instrument panel. "If my friends could only see me now."

"Sammy, get serious. Are they *ever* looking at any of the right moments? Say yes and you're deluding yourself. Heading for a fall."

"Oh, you know something?" I exclaimed. "We *are* kindred spirits!

"I think that's certainly possible."

"Yes! I knew it from the very minute you walked into the shop! Almost the very second!" I paused; savouring my intensity of happiness; sat holding the steering wheel like an eighteen-year-old who's just obtained his licence and is about to drive his first car out of the showroom: a gift from either the gods or from every kid's vision of the perfect daddy. "Didn't you know it, too?"

"Well, let's simply say I liked the look of you."

"Why?"

"You looked strong."

I sat there in a kind of virile silence.

"But at the same time vulnerable." This was uttered in a tone of near-apology. "An endearingly lost and boyish air. No, not lost, perhaps. Questing."

"Oh, that's all right. I don't object to that." Now I did at last turn the key and start carefully to manoeuvre my way out. I had to let up a little on the virility bit. "Perhaps you ought to be doing this? How could I live with myself if I were to scrape or damage something?" But she expressed full confidence and I soon felt as much at home behind this steering wheel as I ever did behind my own. More at home maybe: it was my natural, dreamt-of place: and presently all my instinctive caution had obediently done a bunk. "Thank God it isn't raining! A Morgan wouldn't be a Morgan without its roof drawn back. D'you think those clouds look threatening?"

119

"Yes."

"They wouldn't dare, though, would they?"

"In fact the forecast didn't sound too bad," she said.

I glanced back at the sky. "Just listen to her, please! And it."

Then she did the directing. Her flat was in West Hampstead, in a converted house off Mill Lane, and though she'd decided we'd go via Camden Town ("Land of the Dusty Old Gentlemen?") she told me there were several ways of getting there.

"Like to Rome?" I asked. "Or paradise?" This struck me as quite apposite.

"Well, I wouldn't say *all* roads lead to West End Green. I don't know about paradise."

I braked for a pedestrian crossing; though no one had yet reached the kerb.

"That may be one thing we haven't got in common," she said.

"What?"

"A belief in the afterlife."

It was plain she'd taken me more seriously than I'd intended. I was about to set her straight when she continued. "That was another impression I received in the shop: I mean, about your being religious."

"Why on earth?"

"I'm not sure. Or perhaps it was that evening. Some little thing you must have said... "

"But in fact — "

"And — a bit paradoxically — that was another part of the attraction you held for me. I envy those who can believe in God: their optimism, basic serenity. When not crossed with bigotry — clearly. Or with hypocrisy."

We were driving on again but I was hardly even aware of it.

"And that's the trouble, isn't it, Sammy? It's so often a case of 'Do as I say, not as I do.'" She paused. "But you appear to be the real thing. I'd say you're one of the best commercials

120

on the market."

I'd reverted to my virile silence; being at a complete loss what to do otherwise.

Finally I murmured, "Yet haven't you faced the possibility I could be sailing under false colours?"

Oh but what the heck? Lighten up, Samuel. We were then driving round Trafalgar Square and I gave a familiar wave to Nelson and his lions. "I feel like a king," I suddenly announced. "I bet everyone envies me. You — and the car — and the music… "

"Do you want some music? You could certainly have some."

I at once supplied my own. "'If they made me a king I'd still be a slave to you… '"

"You're a nutter. Albeit a nutter with a nice voice."

"Just one thing missing," I said.

"What's that?"

"I ought to be wearing my dinner jacket. Hey! Shall I hop out on the pavement and get changed? Then they *would* call me a swell and no mistake."

"*And* an exhibitionist. But would swell be better than king?"

"A royal swell. A swell royal. Whichever way you look at it…first-rate; and in a position to do heaps of good… For what more could anyone ask?" An idea occurred to me. "Hey! Let's not wait until tomorrow. Let's deck ourselves — respendently — tonight."

"Hey!" she said, mockingly. "Okay, then."

"Don't laugh at me. Can't help being happy. Gotta sing, gotta dance."

"I'm very glad."

"All this. It's funny to think one day we're going to die. And no one will remember we were ever here, celebrating the start of a bank holiday, having a good time. And when we're dead Trafalgar Square will still be every bit as busy and people will still be having a good time. It won't make any difference. There was a sad old fellow on the train this evening." I didn't know what had reminded me of him.

"Has anyone ever mentioned you have a mind like a butterfly?"

"Oh, yes, Junie for... Junie for one."

"And besides. What makes you think everybody's always having a good time? Sentimental old songster! Who's Junie?"

"Someone I used to know at school."

"Girlfriend?"

"Yes."

"All right. I won't be inquisitive. Well, whoever she is, she was spot on. Did she ever mention, also, there's a strain of melancholy that pervades even your happiness?"

"No. She never did."

"Because I really don't think you have to worry too much for a day or two. I mean, about being dead while the world goes on without you."

"But even so. Everyone should hold it at the back of their minds. That notion of mortality."

"Not a touch morbid: such a point of view?"

"I don't know why. All it does is heighten the pleasure of living. Makes you more aware; makes you more grateful."

"Ah, but there you are, you see. I've no one to feel grateful to."

"That's sad," I said — and for a moment truly meant it. *What*! Was I already so wholly immersed in the role she had assigned to me? Surely Ruth Minton didn't appreciate what a shining addition I made to The Seaside Players. That part of the shallow charmer in *The Deep Blue Sea* should so obviously have been cast my way.

"No one, right now, but you," she added.

The glow which I was in any case experiencing strengthened and spread. "Me? But why should you feel grateful to me?"

"Oh, I don't know. Maybe for bringing back a few *hey*!'s into my stale and staid existence; together with the prospect of some rather awful songs — "

"Madam, they are not awful songs! Beware! If you spurn the song you spurn the singer. 'If I were a carpenter and you

122

were a lady, would you marry me anyway, would you have my baby... ?'"

"No, not awful, then. Let's only say a mite dated."

"But things which are good don't date, they merely reflect their time. Besides, it only shows my tastes are wide-ranging; I like modern songs as well. 'You feel that you're on trial — and so you're in denial — you want to cry and run a mile — but still you lie and still you smile — and smile and smile and smile... ' Q.E.D. Ancient *and* modern."

She laughed. "Not altogether unsuitable, I suppose, for the proprietor of a junk... for the proprietor of Treasure Island."

"Isn't this where we came in? You were going to say — a junk shop."

"Yes. Why do some people never learn? But you know how I feel about junk shops. And their proprietors."

At any rate I knew she could make me literally expand with pleasure.

We were now going up Tottenham Court Road. Hundreds of people were milling on either pavement and I could practically have sworn most of them looked as though they were having a good time. But it was wrong to say I wasn't a realist. (Not that I saw anything bad in sometimes being a little sentimental.) I knew only too well there were bound to be those in the crowd in some way similar to Mavis's poor mum — not to mention all the dispossessed, the junkies and the alcoholics, the mentally unstable. If I were indeed a royal swell, or a swell royal, the first thing I would do would be to eradicate homelessness. I'd at least make damned sure of that.

And while I was about it Moira was wrong about something else. I wasn't worried about the world going on without me; just couldn't wholly credit it, that was all.

But wrong or not she was entirely wonderful. And how could I even say 'wrong' when these were certainly not points she would have stood by? How could I even say 'wrong' when she had provided a racing-green Morgan, a golden, auburn-haired presence and a setting for my own enhanced vitality which I secretly knew was attracting a good deal of attention? I was well aware I had never welcomed red lights or traffic jams with such winning yet apparently self-effacing benevolence. I felt like a film star. A stunningly approachable film star.

"The Short Happy Life of Francis Macomber," I said. "I'm sure they filmed that in the forties. My own will be a very *long* happy life but I suppose they'd call it still quite short at present. Born around noon last Saturday. Barely a week old. I think that at twelve tomorrow champagne corks should pop, Big Ben strike, cannon go off in Green Park. Something small to notify the masses. To commemorate our meeting; record my radiant, my radical renaissance."

'I feel that you expect too much," she warned. "I'd be thrilled to pieces if just Big Ben remembered."

I affected a sneer. (Hoped my loving public didn't misinterpret.)

"Like hearing your name on the radio, you mean?"

"Yes. Exactly. Ariadne Scrumpenhouser."

That was amazing. Really amazing. Really, really amazing.

Ariadne... !

It could hardly be coincidence? Something so fantastic, so extraordinary? There were even those who claimed there wasn't any such thing as coincidence.

But I didn't comment on it. I wanted for the moment just to hug it to myself. It was good enough for *The X Files* but even David Duchovny — to whom recently I'd warmed — would simply have to show some patience.

I observed instead, hearing my own words as from a distance, wrapped around in something of a dream:

"Yes, you're right. Of course you are. A tribute from Big Ben would make a fine endorsement. Would look impressive in my diary, too! As well worth preserving as — well, as driving an open-roofed Morgan with a princess by my side. I shall now entitle this journal *The Long and Happy Life of Samson Groves*. Hemingway will eat his heart out. Or turn in his grave. Whichever comes to him more naturally. Any views on such a subject, Miss Scrumpenhouser... ?"

"The lights have turned to green and we're being hooted. If you're not very careful, Mr Groves, they'll have changed again to red — and you will not be popular." Her hand was on my arm and perhaps already she had given me a nudge.

"... Or may I call you Ariadne?"

16

Her apartment was splendid; what else would you expect? Yet I could see why at times she'd want to get away from it. I was sure there were advantages to having the upper storey but it was the lower floor which — though in all likelihood equally cramped — had the use of a garden; or, rather, of a strip of concreted back yard, for the house was a mid-terraced one. However, I suppressed comparisons with our own former rectory in Deal and admired it, Moira's flat, with all the sincerity which I could muster.

"If you're not already at the top of your profession you damned well ought to be."

"Roughly halfway up, I'd say, but getting there." She looked about her. "It's deceptive, isn't it? From the outside you'd never believe there could be all this room."

"No. No, you wouldn't." My sincerity took a nose dive.

She laughed. "You don't agree, though, do you?"

I faltered. "Am I that hopeless a liar?"

"But thank you, anyway, for trying. And I can see your point. You in your ten-gallon hat. In Kent you've evidently more space to swing that lasso."

"Yes. Don't fence me in. Et cetera. You know, sometimes I feel I wouldn't have minded being a cowboy. To sit tall in the saddle and gallop off into the sunset. The stranger who passes through and leaves things better than he found them."

"What an incurable romantic!"

"Yep, ma'am. Sure is a lonely trail."

Though *realistically,* I thought, it was maybe quite a crowded one: the Shane character irresistibly drawn on to pastures new but always hoping he would be remembered, lovingly remembered, as someone who had made a difference. The wayfarer. The good Samaritan. (Almost the

Christ figure.) The fellow who had left his mark.

"I'm wondering, is it trail or trial?" smiled Moira. "However... Let's take a look at your granny's cake." She was about to take her kitchen scissors to the string but I stopped her just in time.

The cake was a beauty. Standing on a silver board and encircled by a wide and frilly golden band it was decorated with literally scores of Smarties which had bled slightly and looked like the picture on a packet of mixed seeds — except that white icing maybe formed an unexpected base for cottage garden flowers; it produced an impression of snow arriving in the midst of summer.

"I'm going to ring her!" declared Moira.

But luckily I had foreseen that. "She's a little hard of hearing; she'd much prefer a letter."

"It looks like a photo out of *Good Housekeeping*."

"And as though it was meant to keep us going half a lifetime!" I stood and gazed at it in shining and unabashed pride.

There was more. When I tore at the sides of the box, because the square cake board made such a tight fit it would have been impossible to prise it out, we found wedged beneath the board a container of frozen pea soup, two jars of homemade jam and a meat pie wrapped in silver foil, all very neatly and even prettily labelled. Thank God, while Moira was exclaiming over and examining the first of these finds, I spied an envelope which I rapidly palmed, crumpled and pushed into my sleeve: the scratchiest handkerchief ever. With this done I flushed cold at the narrowness of my escape.

You'd think this might have killed off the prickings of guilt which had quickly succeeded my pride but I still had to keep reminding myself that the Caterham children were *not* motherless, not even temporarily, and were no doubt regularly nourished on home cooking. It didn't help a lot. Naturally.

127

Apparently Moira's conscience was also causing trouble.

"All these things," she said, "and I hadn't even planned to be feeding you at home. Apart from breakfast when I might have stirred myself sufficiently to rustle up some fruit juice and croissants and coffee... "

I had to make an effort. I peered into the broken box still lying on the table. "Wot! No cornflakes?"

"You see, I thought it might be more fun to eat out. Though it goes without saying, doesn't it? Exclusively Dutch."

"Fine. Except rid yourself of those last few syllables."

"No," she said. "When times are good I think I probably earn more than you. Or is that tactless?"

"Yes, it's tactless. You are *always* being tactless."

"And times are good."

"Well, there I'm in agreement with you. Total. Times were never better."

"Then let's have a glass of something. We'll drink to that. Before leaving."

"Where are we off to?"

"There's a place by the Heath. I've reserved a table. Hoped you wouldn't see that as a liberty."

"Don't know. All depends, Miss Scrumpenhouser. Am I going to be allowed to foot the bill?"

"I really can't see why you should."

"I'd like to — isn't that enough? Besides. You're giving me a roof over my head; not to mention the use of a lovely car, the fulfilment of a dream. And live each day as though your last, I always say. I came prepared to splurge."

"The roof and the car," she persisted, "are just thrown in. I used the word 'liberty'; I also believe in equality and fraternity."

"I don't."

She laughed. "You're so bull-headed, aren't you?" (I nodded; that's what Junie always said.) "All right, I may give in tonight but only on condition you won't be living tomorrow as though your last. Nor Sunday, come to that. Nor Monday."

"It's difficult."

"Why?"

"Live each bank holiday as though your last, I always say. You can't demolish all my sayings at one go."

"Good grief," she exclaimed.

"Meaning what?"

"I think I'm only just beginning to realise what I've taken on."

I didn't tell her but I liked the sound of that; I rather cared for the idea of being taken on.

"And by the way," I suggested, "let's put off the glad rags till tomorrow. You see, I don't like everything to come at once. I've got a dark grey suit in my holdall."

"Perfect," she said.

"Perhaps I'd better go and shake out the creases."

"Yes; or give it a quick press if it needs it; I've got a steam iron."

I hoped my expression didn't register the slight degree of shock that took place just behind it. Junie would never have said a thing like that. She would simply have got out the ironing board and asked me to bring her the suit. At home we had a steam iron too; I wasn't even sure how the damn thing worked.

"No. Just point me in the direction of a clothes hanger if you will; before you point me in the direction of that drink."

While I hung up the dinner jacket as well as the grey suit I felt an almost nostalgic wave of warmth, of gratitude, even of… well, yes, homesickness. Five-past-eight. I wondered if they'd finished supper yet. I thought the chances were they had. Right now she'd probably be standing at the kitchen sink. Listening to *Friday Night is Music Night* as she did the washing up.

The telephone rang.

I caught hold of myself. This was ridiculous. There may well have been occasions when Monsieur Gauguin had thought extremely fondly of Madame Gauguin after he'd upped and flitted to the South Seas in quest of freedom and fulfilment. But that was an escapade which had lasted him a lifetime, not merely one weekend. On the other hand, of course, I hoped mine was going to last a lifetime, too; even if only a lifetime of Mondays to Fridays. So in someone taking his first steps into totally uncharted territory, aiming to set free, as he did so, both himself and those he was pledged always to look after, a qualm or two was not perhaps unnatural. Even Theseus had shed a few manly tears on first being parted from his mother.

I heard Moira's laughter in the sitting room.

I hadn't been going to open Junie's letter. Correspondence intended for someone else — even a picture postcard — ought to be inviolable.

But there were mitigating factors. Had I been present at the time of writing I'd not only have been freely shown her letter; I'd have been earnestly requested to pass it as okay.

Also, she might have asked questions in it to which she really wanted answers; have made little jokes she might expect our friend to comment on; everybody's interests demanded that I know.

I took it to the bathroom when I went to change.

Dear John,

What ages since we met! Isn't life full of surprises! Sam says that's what makes it worth living but I'm not always so sure. But *this* one is so nice!

Now you must come and stay with us, now you're back in touch. We have plenty of room. It will be good to meet your wife and little ones. I'm sorry, I must have forgotten her name. I'm sorry that her mother isn't well.

Thought these few things might come in handy. The pie and the soup have already been frozen so you shouldn't refreeze them. Whatever you do make sure the pie is *well and truly* heated before you eat it. Never take chances, I say! Not with food. Maybe living is different. (Sam will explain.)

I wasn't sure if you'd prefer a chocolate or a fruit cake but my lot like this recipe best and I thought it would go further.

Ella is 15 and Matt will be 13 next week. A man now, says Sam!

We also have a dog — poor Susie — she's just had a very nasty accident. It would finish Sam off if she was put to sleep. We shall have to keep our fingers crossed.

We shall keep our fingers crossed about your mother-in-law too.

And with the builders in! My goodness, have you got your hands full! I hope it's going to lead to something nice.

Well, that's all for now then, just wanted to say a very quick hello! I'm sure you and Sam will have a real old 'get-together', I look forward to hearing all about it when Sam comes home. Hope yours will be the winning team, and hope we will *all* have a real old 'get-together' soon, before too many blue moons have passed.

Must close now. Much love to you and your wife and three children — *three,* gracious, how ever do you cope?

From your very old friend,

Junie.

P.S. 'They used to tell us we're too young, too young to really be in love!!!' I'm sure you must remember.

It was in fact a typical Junie letter. Somehow on paper she always sounded a bit less educated but at school she had generally just laughed over her literary shortcomings; it was only now she tended to worry and even to agonise about them. (Particularly when having to write a note to school.) I addressed her fondly whilst sitting on the edge of the bath and restoring her smoothed-over letter to its smoothed-over envelope:

"Whatever happened to Baby June?"

And I got back the smiling and time-honoured response. "Oh, something rather horrible."

"Ah... poor crazy mixed-up kid!"

I put the folded envelope into a back pocket of my jeans wondering how I'd dispose of it. Scarcely any problem. Something which *was,* however: this looming question of four Caterham Christian names. Perhaps I'd need to go to Somerset House on Monday. Or whatever they called it these days.

Except I didn't have any dates of birth. Damn!

And come to that, I didn't even know if John had three kids. Why had I given him *three?* An unconscious attempt to be magnanimous?

Yet our 'real old get-together' en masse, it seemed to me, wasn't a difficulty... we didn't even get to see the Smarts! But if by some ironic twist of fate it ever did take place then I'd have to feed the Caterhams a suitably amusing story as to why I had required an alibi. And anyway that risk of false conclusions would have become completely obsolete when they'd be witnessing at first hand how very lovingly we dealt with one another. My wife and I. There wasn't any need to fret. (Except, sweet Lord, that problem of those kids!)

Moira had finished on the phone. I passed on the directions concerning pie and soup as though I'd only just remembered. In fact I considered them expendable but this again smacked of betrayal. "No, not fussing at all!" refuted Moira, on my dear dead granny's behalf. Dear? I suppose so; but in truth a bit repressive; I shouldn't be too sorry soon to have to kill her off. Anyway, I apologised for being a forgetful dunce. Moira answered, with a nod towards my dark suit, pink shirt and silk chequered tie, "Oh, I forgive you. You can't be beautiful *and* brainy."

"You seem to manage it."

"Thank you."

She looked gorgeous in her dark green; more *soignée* than ever with her hair up. I had forgotten (no, I had never known, exactly) the thrill of being the escort of a strikingly attractive woman. They say that in appearance two lovers, two potential lovers, will nearly always gravitate towards their equal. I considered that this evening I had more than found my equal. And although the ability to turn heads might not be your partner's most impressive feature it still felt agreeable to find out it was there.

Oh, my God, yes. It felt wonderful.

17

We returned to the flat around twelve-thirty. It still hadn't rained; we hadn't been prevented from driving with the roof down. "The luck of the Irish," she'd remarked.

"No. Sod all to do with the Irish. I've found a talisman."

Despite this I was feeling nervous as we got out of the car; I imagine we both were. But the whole evening, of course, had been shot through with apprehension. Pleasurable apprehension. Which happened to be the name of a horse I'd once backed — Pleasurable Apprehension — during my short-lived gambling days. Short-lived because I'd seldom won anything worth having and had had the sense, finally, to see the pursuit for what it was: a mug's game. Indeed, only a few weeks ago I'd had to deliver a homily to Matt on the follies of hoping to get rich quick and of relying on luck to pull you through. It had been necessary to play the heavy father, extolling the virtues of a down-to-earth outlook and diligence in work and duty. We had just received his school report.

"In a moment," Ella had said to Matt sympathetically, very much copying his own way of putting things but probably not consciously, "in a moment, I bet, he's going to throw in that bit about searching for the bluebird of happiness." We'd been sitting over supper at the time; our only real communication, during any normal week, took place at the supper table.

"He's going to do no such thing," I retorted, in some anger. "Mind your own business, Ella. The bluebird of happiness is completely irrelevant at this juncture."

"Isn't it true, then?" she muttered sulkily. "Does that mean I can stop having to keep my eyes skinned every time I set foot outside our crappy old back door?"

"Don't you know yet what 'irrelevant' means?"

"Ella — kindly watch your language," Junie ordered. She gave a sigh. "And I do wish, Sam, you wouldn't always pick on mealtimes to start this kind of conversation. It takes me hours to prepare something I hope we'll all enjoy and then I find I end with indigestion."

"You?" I said. "You never suffered from indigestion in your life!"

"Well, I must say! You've a short memory. Perhaps you're forgetting I've twice been pregnant?"

"Apart from then."

She made a vaguely conciliatory gesture. "All right. That may have been true once. It certainly isn't now."

"Change of life?" asked Ella, dispassionately curious.

"At thirty-five-years old?"

"Thirty-five and ten months?" offered Matt, slyly; understandably in favour of prolonging this or any other distraction.

"No, it is *not* the change of life!" said Junie. "The change of something, maybe, but not that."

She turned towards me in the same half-humorous manner: "And, Sam, I know you have this enviable talent for blocking out whatever you don't want to hear but you do always pick on mealtimes and I only wish, I really do wish — "

I shouted. I felt the rush of blood. My complexion possibly went puce.

"Have you all quite finished? Well, have you? I thought I was trying to make a serious point. Perhaps nobody noticed. Does nobody but me think Matt's future is important? Think it shouldn't be brushed aside with talk of people being born lucky and having the confidence to take risks or get away with bloody murder even if they haven't got degrees? Well, I'm sick and tired of everyone ganging up on me. You can all do what you like, see if I care, I wash my hands of it! I'm off! Good riddance to the lot of you!"

And throwing down my napkin I'd walked out; leaving a trio of extremely startled faces. I too had felt pretty startled:

134

once I was up and running I'd found it incredibly hard to stop. All of it so unexpected. I'd had a pleasant day at work; been feeling quite relaxed on my return. Even when Junie had shown me the report I'd had no premonition things were going to change. None whatsoever. I later made a secret vow. Never again should I fail to see the danger signals; never again should I fail to heed their warning. Never; never.

"What are you thinking?" Moira asked.

"Remembering a racehorse out of my guilt-ridden past."

"Tell me."

"Pleasurable Anticipation." I laughed. Good grief; not apprehension at all. Why should I have thought...?

We walked upstairs and into the sitting room.

"Nightcap?" she enquired.

"Please. Another whisky."

"Just help yourself," she said, over her shoulder, as she went to draw the curtains. I felt surprise: had failed to notice they hadn't been drawn earlier; so much for my awareness. They were floor-length, of dark blue velvet, almost black. She paused before pulling them across. "The other night there was a glorious moon. I wish there'd been a glorious moon tonight."

I know it was corny but forgetting all about my whisky (though maybe not about helping myself) I went and stood behind her and put my arms around her waist. Then counselled her in a supposedly Austrian accent. "Oh, don't let's ask for the moon. We have the stars!"

In fact the moment had arrived. No more procrastination. No more apprehension. Apprehension was *not*, nor ever could be, pleasurable.

And Moira leant against me with a sigh. Gave a soft laugh. "Her line," she said; "not his."

"Don't care." I could afford to be extravagant. I rested my chin on her head. My hands moved upwards to her breasts.

"And besides. We don't even have that many stars."

I said: "Then we'll just need to provide a few of our own!" Oh, dear. "In any case, Miss Scrumpenhouser, this is surely not a time to be pedantic."

"You're right. But remember the view of them we had last Saturday? I think you rarely see anything like that in London... " But she was talking only out of nervousness — which made me feel even more loving — and I knew that what would soon be happening between us was going to match the splendour seen in any sky; excel the sunset floating on a golden sea, the moonglow falling through the Apennines, the rainbow basketing some lovely bay. In short, it was going to be beyond description. Beyond compare. Beyond everything. She turned in my arms and pressed her body against mine and lifted her face up for a lingering kiss.

And... oh, my God.

I came.

The man who could ram his wife about two thousand times.

A marathon entrant who couldn't even make it to the starting post.

It could have been disaster. I thought at first it was. But I was seeing it through my own eyes, not through hers. Moira was marvellous. "It's no big deal, my love. It only means you haven't been in practice. That's something we can easily set right."

We stood together in the bath and showered. I'd never held any woman's naked body other than Junie's, and from even seventeen years ago, when we'd been newlyweds, I could remember nothing like this. Nothing remotely like this. While I only kissed and soaped her Moira had two orgasms. The readiness of her responses was intoxicating. By the time we'd turned off the good clean water — warm and soft and full of absolution — and gently dried each other down, my penis was again, thank God, weightily tumescent.

When we presently got to bed (crisp white linen and a snow-white duvet which had soon slipped to the floor) she asked if there was anything I fancied in particular. I said I'd love to have her ride me; to use me as her strong-winged horse. "All the way to Banbury Cross?" she queried, and

136

I replied, "Great Scott, no, who wants to go to Banbury Cross? I mean halfway round the world and back: over valleys and forests and above the Barrier Reef... "

"Good heavens. A poetical Pegasus."

"And one who's stamping at his stable door. All ready to bear you off to Samarkand or far Cathay; to the Hanging Gardens of Babylon; or along the route that Sinbad took."

"And to think I was about to settle for a sleepy little market town near Oxford; and merely a one-way ticket, at that!"

Then she descended lightly onto my outstretched legs and bore down slowly to the very root of me. I cupped my hands around her breasts and she glistened as she rose and fell, gasping with every downward lunge and looking more rapt and disbelieving by the instant. We came together, after possibly less than three minutes, but it felt like the first orgasm in the whole of history finally to break the pleasure barrier. We shuddered and juddered and shook, and she opened her eyes at last, and smiled at me, loving and peaceful and unguarded, then sank with her breasts against my chest and I held her very tightly and we lay in silence with my cock still feeling large inside her.

It was I who ended the silence. "Well, we embarked upon a voyage to Australia but hardly left the docks at Tilbury." Then scared she might have misconstrued my meaning — "Yet I never realised Tilbury had so much to recommend it. Like, let's see, the pyramids and the Pantheon and Durham Cathedral and the Golden Gate Bridge."

"I could willingly," she said, "spend the rest of my life in Tibury." She lifted her head a short way and planted lazy kisses on the tip of my chin and at the base of my throat, teeth gently pulling at the clusters of coiled tendrils she discovered there. Then breaking my embrace she raised herself on both arms and with her own red-and-golden hair, a little damp still from the shower, draping her charms as if she were a mermaid from some movie, gazed down and said: "And shall I tell you how it felt? Like a thousand shooting stars splattering against a backcloth of black velvet. That's how it felt." And if her choice of simile was maybe unwittingly influenced by my prophecy in front of the window — well, who cared? It was a compliment to be treasured and kept fresh for ever. Not even a compliment; better than that. A remark.

But next time, I joyously reflected, we should get a long way further than Tilbury. She'd have a thousand stars exploding inside her at every second; but still we'd sail on, fly on — roll and pitch and swoop and soar. Tilbury was great; but only a beginning. I dreamt of ecstacy drawn out an hour, mind-blowing, toe-curling ... ecstacy verging on torment.

An hour? Well, then, perhaps not totally guaranteed: not the next time. "But anyway," I said, "I think we're getting there."

"Sammy, you ask too much of yourself. Or you ask too much of life. I happen to think we well and truly arrived."

She laughed.

"Or is it God that you expect too much of?"

We arrived again — this time far across the North Sea, even a good way into Eastern Europe — before we finally turned out the lamp and fell exhausted into sleep.

And actually I had been chanting silently throughout: as good a method as any of trying to distract myself: Okay, then... get in on this act, get in on this act, get in on this act! And, as I say, he took us into Yugoslavia. The *former* Yugoslavia. By which I felt quite gratified. But mine was the power. Definitely. And mine was the glory. (I didn't mind about the kingdom.) No way would I let him do me out of either one of those.

But thanks, mate. All the blooming same. Good on you, cobber.

18

I was awoken to find the sun streaming in at the window and a tray containing a glass of grapefruit juice, a bowl of muesli, a boiled egg, warm rolls and butter — and a pot of black coffee. Moira herself looked remarkably fresh and chipper in a sunny yellow housecoat. She sat on the edge of the bed.

"But I can't possibly eat all this."

"You've got to," she said. "Got to keep your strength up."

"And what about you?"

"But I've already had mine. I've been up since ten. Now I shall simply sit and enjoy watching you. Perhaps I'll drink some more coffee." She stroked the hairs on my arm. "Nearly twelve o'clock," she smiled. "Happy first anniversary! And don't the years go rolling by?"

The instant effect of this was to strengthen the erection with which I'd woken.

"I love you, don't you know?" I said it huskily.

"Thank you, Sammy. Eat your breakfast."

"But that's the real truth." It was on the tip of my tongue to start the day with my confession; this struck me as completely the right moment and gut instinct drove me on, said that I should never feel more calm. "Moira, there's something I must tell you."

"Yes, darling?"

But I hadn't worked it out; and at all costs must be careful to avoid clumsiness. I couldn't bear the thought of that sanguine smile being blasted off her face.

"I'd like to make love to you before I have my breakfast."

"Well, you can't," she said. "Your egg will spoil and your rolls and coffee will get cold. Besides, I might have other plans."

"Like what?"

"Like your making love to me *after* you've had your breakfast."

"So... ? Couldn't we find some way of possibly reconciling those two aims? If we really set our minds to it?"

"And you hadn't forgotten either: I mentioned on the phone having one or two other plans for your delectation?"

"No, I hadn't forgotten," I answered, wearily; feeling deflation going on beneath the duvet. "But I might've hoped you had."

"Well, maybe it's a bit late anyway for catching a boat down to Greenwich," she consoled me. "Or for lunching at the Zoo. Or driving out to Richmond." She ignored all my punctuating nods of vigorous agreement. "But I'd also wondered if you'd like to wander round the Portobello or the National Gallery or Harrods. Whether you'd like to row on the Serpentine; or gaze at the crown jewels. Visit some bookshops. Be taken on a guided tour of all the lesser-known landmarks." She sipped reproachfully at her coffee. (A car backfired. "See!" I said. "There go the cannon in Green Park.") "I really can't believe that in place of so many interesting and variegated alternatives the only thing you want is to get laid."

"How can I convince you?"

But not in any attempt to do this I then ran to have a pee and wash my hands; returned to bed and decapitated my egg.

"And, anyway, why does it all need to be packed into one weekend? You're so neurotic, Moira. What have you got against weekdays?"

Then I told her of my plans to look for work in London.

I shortly wished I hadn't. It led to unforeseen questioning. (Which shouldn't have been unforeseen: so cotton-picking obvious.) What was going to happen to my grandmother? Was it kind — or even safe — to leave her alone in a large house for five full days a week? And what would happen to the shop? Did I mean to sell up?

"I thought it might actually please you, the notion of our

being able to spend more time together." I didn't say: of my being able to move in here, cramped though it is, on a semi-permanent basis. This one did *not* strike me as completely the right moment.

"Of course it would please me. But mightn't it be better just to leave it for a while? Who knows... when people get to that age... ? And Sammy. Don't you dare turn all pathetic on me!"

There was justice in that: I realised I must've been sounding aggrieved.

"Wot! Me? Pathetic?"

I drained my second cup of coffee. "Anyhow. My assistant would have taken care of the shop. And as for Gran... well, naturally I wouldn't've left her unattended. Naturally I'd have looked for someone who — "

"It would have needed to be someone terribly congenial."

It wasn't worth discussing. (Another reason why I should've spoken earlier. Detail was piling up on detail. Each one so needlessly adding to the detritus to be removed; substantiating an intent to deceive which simply wasn't there. I was a dolt but never mind. I wouldn't let it spoil our day.)

In any case that second cup of coffee had produced some welcome intimations.

I again handed Moira the tray. "Call of nature," I said. "That was a smashing breakfast."

"I'll go and wash the dishes."

"Quite right. A woman's role."

In the bathroom I began to sing. Despite that brief moment of disharmony I thought even the few things which hadn't gone right yesterday were now busily correcting themselves. On Thursday night I'd slept badly but last night I'd slept so well I couldn't remember either dreaming or turning over. Yesterday I'd been constipated; today's evacuation left me purified and clean. All was absolutely for the best, in the best of all possible worlds. And the best of all possible worlds was in Solent Road, West Hampstead.

I cleaned and flossed my teeth and spent hardly five minutes under the shower. I took longer than that over shaving and splashing myself in cologne.

Moira was still in the kitchen, watering some plants on the sill. There were nets at the window. I switched off the jabber on Radio 4; got rid of the milk bottle; then drew her in close. After ten seconds or so I started to unbutton her housecoat.

"Mmm. You smell nice," she said.

"It's called My Scintillating Future."

"As distinct from Your Guilt-Ridden Past?"

I laughed. I pressed her buttocks to me and she leant back from the waist and ran her hands across my chest. "Here! What was that song I heard you singing a short time ago?" She pinched at one of my nipples.

"What song?"

"'If I am fancy-free and love to wander... '"

"Was I really singing that?"

"You were. I turned on the radio to drown you out."

"No, I think you must've misheard. I was singing, 'If I had a talking picture of you-oo... ' 'If' was right. Even 'If I'. It was a fairly understandable mistake. Please don't blame yourself."

Remorsefully, she licked and soothed the red mark she had made — and which I had taken like a man, without wincing. But not all *that* remorsefully. "Nobody could ever accuse *you* of being stuck in the sixties, could they? Or do I mean the fifties? Or the twenties? What can we do? I suppose it must be Granny's influence. Or Kipling's."

I sighed. "Haven't we had that conversation before? Anyway, I don't think this is Granny's influence. *Or* Kipling's."

To illustrate my meaning I lifted her off the floor. She threw her arms about my neck and twined her legs around my bottom. She kissed me long and hard — inhaling sharply upon penetration. Between us we moved her back and forth, gently at first, then with mounting acceleration. It was

142

murder on the biceps but nowhere else was the sensation remotely one of pain.

I needed another shower.

Moira took hers separately. "I warn you: we shan't be in any fit state to go to the theatre!"

"You wanna bet? That's another five or six hours away."

We compromised. We made love only once more before then, and that was after five o'clock, before we started getting ready. And even then it was nothing too adventurous or demanding: just the plain old missionary. To a count of under four hundred. Not good. Not bad. Incredible.

We would save the Goldfingering till later.

Meanwhile we followed one of Moira's earlier suggestions. ("I get the feeling I should humour you," I said.) We went rowing on the lake: not the Serpentine but the one in Regent's Park since it was nearer and there was somewhere nice, in Queen Mary's Garden, to have tea. The weather wasn't perfect for boating — perfect boating weather meant shirtless and a suntan rather than T-shirt and a jumper — and in some ways I'd have preferred to hire a skiff and feel that I was really showing my paces, working hard and skimming across the surface like a skier or a bird; but all the same it was pleasant just to idle round the contours of the lake and round a central, wooded island, even resting on the oars and briefly drifting… at those times when a watery sun tried to reproduce the brilliance I'd awoken to at noon.

"I enjoy rowing. I enjoy any form of physical exercise — the harder the better, really — anything that makes you feel your muscles are working. At Oxford or at Cambridge I'd have been a rowing blue."

"Do they have rowing blues at London?"

"Why do you ask that?"

"I was only thinking," she said. "If you're serious about coming to live up here why not apply to London University?" I had told her last night over dinner I'd never been to university and how much I regretted it. "I'm sure you'd get a loan and that somehow or other we could — one could —

manage to pay it back."

Before she'd changed it, she had definitely said 'we'.

I stopped rowing. I wouldn't comment on that… I couldn't, of course… but *God!* The glory of the woman!

"That's an inspired and magnificent idea," I answered, slowly.

"Better than taking on some mediocre job — because these days, without a degree, you're not going to find anything else. And it would certainly be a good way of fulfilling yourself."

"You know," I said, "it's utterly extraordinary how my world has opened up in just one week. Suddenly there seems no limit to all the good ways there are of fulfilling myself."

"I'm glad." She was leaning over and trailing her hand in the water. "In fact I feel it could really be the making of you," she said. "Though I hope that doesn't sound patronising."

I paused. "There's something solid about that phrase. 'The making of Sam Groves'. It has a ring to it. And even if it were patronising (which it most emphatically is; how could you doubt it for a single instant?) let me tell you here and now: I know no one I'd prefer to patronise me than you."

It was time for us to return to the boathouse; we'd had more than our full hour. As I prepared to hand Moira onto the landing stage a father and his three children were waiting to take our places. They had with them a large shaggy-haired white dog which jumped into the boat even before the two of us had properly left it and made everybody laugh. "Jimmy can sometimes be a little overeager!" the man apologised.

"Jimmy reminded me of Susie," Moira said, as we walked away. "How is she — your little black-eyed Susan?"

As yet Moira knew nothing of the accident. I told her what had happened but kept talking of Susie as though she were my own dog and not that of our neighbours.

"I still feel so very bad about it."

"Well, it wasn't exactly *your* fault!" She'd been holding my arm and now hugged it to her sympathetically.

"Wasn't it? I should've had her on the lead. Some people are such *garbage!*" In fact I still couldn't believe there were human beings capable of running down a dog — rat, pigeon, hedgehog, anything — and not stopping to ascertain the state the animal was in: if only with a view to maybe having to kill the poor thing off completely. "Scum!" I added. "Bastards!"

"Hear, hear!" she said; yet seemed surprised at the pent-up rage with which I'd expressed what she agreed with. "But anyway, Sammy, you haven't a single thing to reproach yourself for. Not the least thing in the world."

"I read quite recently," I said, "about two men who gouged out a pony's eyes with an old nail."

"Dear God!"

"I think they got three months. Time off for good behaviour... "

But happily we were interrupted. A football crossed our path and simultaneously we heard a cry: "Can you send it back, mister?" It broke our mood completely. I thought: I'll show those kids a thing or two. I should of course have looked a charlie if my kick hadn't fully connected but fortunately the ball went soaring in a hugely gratifying arc and covered the requisite thirty-yard distance as though it had a built-in homing device. The six or seven boys were patently impressed. "Here, mister! You want to come and join in?"; and I could have been most seriously tempted. "Another time!" I called back, with a wave. "But thanks." They seemed like a bunch of good kids. Totally unbidden, it crossed my mind, No need for you to get in on *that* act. Was there? Eh, old sport?

What price glory now?

What price glory, indeed? "Superman!" said Moira. "I too was quite impressed."

"And so you were intended to be. And so you damned well should be. Just call me Alan Shearer."

"You ought to be a father."

"Yes... well."

145

"You're as good with children as you are with dogs."

"I hoped you were going to say with women."

"Yes, even there you're not bad. Clearly an all-rounder. All things to all people. In short — insufferable."

For a while we walked without talking. I turned my head a couple of times to look back at the football.

"Why *don't* you go and join in?"

"It's already after four." In fact I'd just glanced at my watch with such a possibility in mind. "You know you're dying for that cup of tea. I am, too."

Besides, supposing I hadn't managed to live up to that intial impression? It was years since I'd played soccer. And people were often impressed by me at first but I felt their high opinion rarely lasted. I sometimes said such very foolish things. What went on in my heart (I hoped) was worthier than what came out of my mouth. And even what went on in my heart, perhaps, wasn't always worth so very much. But anyway I engaged in a constant struggle to increase its value. And that might get me somewhere.

I smiled. "One of the most underrated secrets in life is knowing when to leave the party."

I'm not sure she was listening. "Would you like to be a father?" she enquired.

It was an awkward question and one I hadn't reckoned would come up, not carrying as it did, as I felt certain it did, the implication that Moira's childbearing days were rapidly running out and perhaps... Some two years ago I'd allowed Junie to talk me into having a vasectomy. Apart from the obvious loss-of-manhood thing I'd never had good reason to regret it. Until now.

I shrugged.

I thought I detected a flicker of disappointment. I hated the thought of causing Moira any disappointment. I put my arm about her waist and gave a cautious squeeze. To my relief, she then put hers round mine. It was a long time since I'd walked like that with anyone.

I myself had felt a flicker of disappointment... or of something. Earlier. That father with his three children on the landing stage... presumably they'd all been his. He had looked lusty and attractive. I knew I had experienced envy of some kind. As usual — hastily suppressed.

"Oh, anyway, I didn't finish telling you," I said. "About Susie. It's nearly a whole week since it happened and she's making progress every day. You wouldn't believe how much better she's got. It's a miracle, Moira. It really is a little miracle."

"That's wonderful," she answered. My relief was compounded by the lack of any flatness in her tone. "And for you that's not just some worn-out and meaningless old cliché, is it? You truly do believe in miracles."

I gave another small shrug — as if perhaps this was something one ought to feel a bit ashamed of.

"And you love that dog as though she were your own."

19

I'd bought the Goldfingering at a haberdasher's in Abbey Road, on our way to Regent's Park. I'd hardly known it could exist: a London shop that surely hadn't changed in over fifty years. Impulsively I'd stopped the car; there was a parking space a few yards down the road. Maybe if there hadn't been I'd simply have smiled and driven on and thought, "Oh, what the hell, perhaps some other day," but the parking space *was* there and the combination of that and the haberdashery had seemed a charming gift too timely to refuse. I'd asked Moira whether she would mind waiting.

"Not in the least. But what are you after?"

"A lifeline."

"Oh? Is that all?"

The shop had a polished mahogany counter and a wall fitted with small drawers that would have made young Arthur Kipps, or even H.G. himself, feel instantly at home. Not seeing any kind of railway overhead I still half-expected to discover a chute for change-bearing cylinders tucked away in some corner. Half-expected to be served by somebody sweet and venerable and wearing a choker.

But at least I wasn't let down in the one respect that mattered. The young woman with the sniff knew immediately which drawer to go to.

In fact, I hadn't imagined for one moment that she wouldn't. I remembered Moira had only brought me this way because she'd wanted to show me the studios where the Beatles had recorded. But I also remembered — for the second time in far less than twenty-four hours — that apparently some people claimed there was no such thing as coincidence. Or chance.

It made me think again about *The X Files*.

The truth is out there!

As I walked back to the car Moira must have seen I'd been successful. I sat in the driving seat and handed her the paper bag. Inside... the ball of Goldfingering.

"The last they had. I might've bought a second but I think the one should be enough."

"Oh, you honestly do believe so?"

"Yes. By the way I didn't realise it was called that. Did you? They also showed me a hank of gold Lurex wool but I thought the thread was more appropriate."

"I am likely to scream before long."

"You do repeat yourself."

"Maybe I'm driven to it. Something in my genes."

"Or — much more likely perhaps — something in mine." But heaven help me I meant no innuendo. "I am sorry: I know you think I'm only playing with you. Yet that's what this is all about in one way. Games."

"Games? What kind of games?"

"I'm not certain 'games' is actually the right word. You remember the myth of Theseus and the Minotaur? Well again, you see, the truth happens to be out there." Naturally I had to send that up a bit. "In its entirety."

"No. Remind me. The Minotaur... ?"

"Well. Where to begin? The Minotaur had the body of a man but the head of a bull. He was a pitiful hybrid who's always received an extremely poor press. For being merely the victim of his own natural dictates, I suppose. No more inherently evil than a crocodile. But he caused a vast amount of suffering. Unconsidered suffering."

"And so Theseus... Theseus, did you say?... set out to... To what? Kill him? Reform him? Show him the error of his ways?"

"No, that would have been sweet; really sweet. Bible lessons — cautionary tales — Just-So Stories. But alas I don't think reformation was ever quite on his agenda. I'm afraid to have to tell you he was doomed from the beginning."

"Who was? Theseus?"

"No, not Theseus! The Minotaur!"

"Sorry. Got muddled."

"My fault. Didn't mean to snap. Any mix-up and it's me."

"At all events. Our hero slays this sad, pathetic beast?"

"Assisted by a beautiful princess who remains at the entrance to the maze. You see, the creature lives in this maze; a melancholy place; practically impossible to get out of."

"But she couldn't have been much help if she remained there at the entrance. Or did you say she had long arms? Extendable? Twistable round corners?"

"No. Stop it! This is serious. It's my own progression I'm attempting to describe. The princess stands there clutching the thread which Theseus has attached to himself and without which he'd be lost. Utterly lost."

I already was lost. Our giggles in that parked car reminded me of when Junie and I — not quite a week ago — had rolled about in bed.

Moira was the first to compose herself. There were passers-by and (for once!) I think she was more aware of them than I was.

She waited until no one could have overheard. "The thread! I do believe I'm beginning to see daylight. Tell me: how — or where — has he attached this thread?"

"Aha," I said. "Perhaps we'll have to work on that tonight." No doubt — if I hadn't been groping for my handkerchief — I should have coyly glanced away.

"Mmm. Well, I hope it's good and strong."

"Of course it is. It's golden and enchanted."

"I fear I may have got confused again. Are we talking of the thread or the thing it will be tied to? But before you answer that — you haven't told me yet the name of the beautiful princess. Was she Titian-haired and quite amazingly captivating? And did she capture all men's hearts?"

"She did! She did! Well, she certainly did mine."

"And the name... ?"

I had intended this to hit its mark; and hit its mark it clearly did.

"You do not mean — of the royal house of Scrumpen-houser!"

"The very same. Is there any other?"

"It's odd I should've known my name was Ariadne."

"Odd you should've known I have been waiting for you all my life. For you and excitement and the spur to good. Odd you should have known that one day you would lead me to the light. Back to the light. Out of the heart of darkness."

20

After we'd made love and showered we put on our regalia. Moira wore something silky, lavender and long; with a sash in deep lilac. I whistled at her. "Cor!"

"Like it?"

"Now I can honestly understand why you had to get up two hours earlier than me." My hands were on her shoulders. "I want you to know, kid, I think you made good use of all that time."

"Thank you," she said. "But if only I'd realised what a picture *you* were going to make I feel I would have taken longer."

"Course you would. Course you would."

We were in the kitchen.

"Now stop being an ass. Sit down; do something useful. Like open the wine, maybe — then light the candles?"

I obeyed her to the letter.

"This is only going to be a snack," she said. "We'll be having our main meal after the show. On me," she added; "and no arguments — you understand? I want this to be my evening."

I decided we should have to see about that.

We ate some of Junie's soup, and some of Junie's steak-and-kidney pie, and some of Junie's cake. Apart from the half-bottle of Bordeaux, medium white, and the strong black coffee from Colombia, it was a homely little repast; and I was hungrier than I'd realised — having had nothing since breakfast apart from just a cup of tea and a Penguin. Now I ate a second piece of cake. But as I picked the Smarties off the top — I particularly liked the coffee and orange ones, because they really did have quite a flavour of coffee and orange — it suddenly struck me this was as close as I would ever get to actually taking the food from the mouths of children. (Whether three or only one; we knew there was at least one.) It was a little disconcerting.

That second slice of cake, even though it was fairly thin, could have given me indigestion.

Which would have been a rich revenge. I never suffered from indigestion.

(Except following those rare bouts of compulsive eating. But if Junie was changing was there some fear that maybe I was changing too? We had always been extraordinarily sympathetic.)

We left the flat later than we'd meant: it was after half-past-six. Moira had wanted to be at the theatre some fifteen minutes early, because she said she always liked to watch the audience arrive; but I myself considered privately it might do the audience more good to watch us arrive. The latest weather forecast had again been more or less all right for the short term: mainly mild and dry in the south: and personally it didn't worry me too much if there *were* going to be dramatic changes from around midnight; this evening was to be the high point.

"Not," I'd said to Moira, "that I can understand your having so much trust in all those dinky little weather men. You're a very gullible young woman."

"They don't usually let me down."

"How could they – in that dress?"

"Thank you, darling. On the other hand I wish occasionally they would. I'd been thinking we might be able to drive out into the country tomorrow — have lunch at an olde worlde pub I know, where there are tables on a lawn sloping down to the river."

"Sounds idyllic. But never mind: if we can't do that I'll take you for a ride elsewhere. To Banbury Cross and Tilbury Docks and all points west."

"East."

"Who's the pilot? I'll take you to the Never-Land, where there are mermaids and fairies and lagoons — and Red Indians and pirates" — my voice, with each new item, grew darker and more threatening — "and a crocodile with a great sense of timing patiently awaiting his chance... *to gobble you all up!*"

I pounced, and she shivered, theatrically. "Isn't that the place where all the Lost Boys go?" she enquired, innocently.

"Yes," I answered; matching innocence with innocence. "There was Nibs and Tootles. And there was Slightly. And... ah, yes, that's right... there was one called Curly, too." I nodded, reminiscently.

She looked at me with suspicion.

"Is it at all possible you could be having me on?"

"Now what purpose can you believe there'd be in that? Begorra."

The uncertainty turned swiftly to respect. "But how on earth d'you ever remember such very way-out things?"

"It's the downside, I suppose, of being so intellectual. Are you impressed? And I promise you it's not for nothing I've been referred to in my time as... Old Memorybags!"

She shook her head. "But anyhow. Enough of all this nonsense. I don't know why I'm laughing; I'm beginning to have some very serious doubts concerning you." She kissed my cheek. "Give me two minutes in the bathroom and then we're on our way."

I myself was fully ready; Moira had retied my tie before she'd sat down. "I'll wait for you by the car," I said.

Once outside, I glanced at my watch. It gave both time and date. Twenty-three minutes to seven on the third of May. It felt like a caption to write beneath a photograph.

And at twenty-three minutes to seven on the third of May there was an elderly woman standing at her front gate on the opposite side of the road talking to an elderly man on the pavement. There were two little Minnie Mouses walking gingerly towards me in ankle socks and grown-up shoes. There was a young man sitting on his parked motorbike while his girlfriend hurried down her path to join him. It was nice to know I would be noticed. First time ever in my dinner jacket out in the street. An occasion. I sauntered unselfconsciously around the car, fiddling casually with this and that. I propped myself against the pavement side of it — ankles crossed — and studied my fingernails. I began to whistle. The hit tune from tonight's show.

And I *was* noticed; no doubt about it. And when Moira came swishing out of the house and I was standing there gallantly holding open the car door I was still noticed; but now we both were; which made it even better. My consort had arrived. The old people opposite and the two small girls were giving us frank stares. The motorbike pair was being a bit more cagey. I felt it wasn't too soon for the jungle drums to be already beating out their message down the street. Net curtains should be twitching; flatmates shrilly summoned to the window. By now the fashion photographers could well be on their way.

Yet even if they weren't they'd soon be able to catch up. We blazed a golden trail; made a royal progress. Pedestrians weren't actually lining the route but I saw many who literally came to a standstill to gaze after us. I saw the occupants of other cars, too, eyeing us with reverence. And at one set of traffic lights — we seemed to catch so many that were red — I'd swear that half the passengers on a double-decker must have defected to our side to get a better view. When we arrived down West we had to proceed even more slowly and I began to be afraid we might miss the overture or even the rising of the curtain and have to find our seats in darkness; but we were lucky again with our parking (God, were we lucky: a turning just off Oxford Circus!) and by using the subway under Regent Street and cutting a dash into Argyll Street — apologetic, laughing, hand-in-hand — we made it to the theatre with almost as much as five minutes to spare. Perfect timing! Maybe the last lap of the journey had even added an extra lustre: the gaiety which sparkles in relief. As we moved across the thick pile of the foyer, amidst other late arrivals, then on into the auditorium (down one side, along by the orchestra pit, back up the middle aisle: I hadn't realised our seats were on the gangway) I knew I walked with a back even straighter than usual and with a smile which in an understated way was encompassing the world. We weren't the only ones in evening dress — this, after all, was just the third night of the run — but I doubted that few of those couples, if any, shared in the more natural advantages Moira and I possessed or were so gleamingly and irresistibly in love. From *that*, perhaps, unravelled the greatest skein of enchantment which any golden hero could acquire.

Golden hero... Golden heroine.

And then the show began. That too was magical. Of course. We were all in the right receptive mood: a company of strangers forever to be linked by the forging of an evening's memory, a shipload of voyagers soon to disperse to different corners of the globe but with whom we'd merged in an unrepeatable experience. (Essentially unrepeatable. Like when I'd heard on the radio recently an audience clapping sixty years ago during a concert at Carnegie Hall: I'd been as respectful of the onceness of that applause as I was of the onceness of both Benny Goodman and Gene Krupa who'd occasioned it.) And how amused we all were at the absurdity of people not realising when they were well off; at their selfish fears of growing old and missing out; at their readiness to chase rainbows, to fall so desperately in love with love... all of it quite patently pathetic although our laughter remained tolerantly benign. Added to this the songs were jaunty and many of the lyrics gave you something to think about: i.e. live for the moment since you don't know what's to come. Likewise, be true to yourself, "and it must follow, as the night the day, thou canst not then be false to any man." Not that this last bit actually came from *Half a Farthing, Sam Sparrow?* Or even featured in it. Though something else from the same play very well could have done: "there's a special providence in the fall of a sparrow"; and a further something else — though from the Bible, not the Bard — unquestionably *should* have done: those two or three verses in St Matthew not so long ago learned by my son, and tested by my son's father, because Miss Martin had invented an exercise on namesakes. "Are not two sparrows sold for a farthing? and one of them shall not fall on the ground without your Father. The very hairs of your head are all numbered. Fear ye not therefore, ye are of more value than many sparrows." Now *that* would have made a wonderfully memorable lyric. Plenty of bounce! Plenty of pazazz! I couldn't understand its omission. Because if you're going to choose a particular title surely you've got to acknowledge and pay credit to your sources. However... allowing for that one small yet stupidly niggling reservation: not a big price for such a satirical and spectacular entertainment...the show provided a truly marvellous evening in the theatre.

A marvellous evening out of it, as well. Moira and I left the car where it was and nearly floated off down Regent Street, as if contained in our own little bubble, like the one which the good fairy always used for transport in and out of Oz. The Munchkins invariably went, "Ahh... ," when they saw her coming in to land.

"Where shall I get it to dissolve?" I asked. "And please note I say 'dissolve'. Not 'burst'."

"Tonight I feel there's nothing that could make our bubble burst."

"No," I said, "nothing. Moira... "

"You can dissolve it at the Ritz," she said.

"The Ritz!"

"We're having dinner at the Ritz."

"My God," I remarked. (A little premature, perhaps, to enquire about my national Boss-of-the-Year award?) "How much higher can we possibly go?"

"That's something we'll have to find out, isn't it?"

"'Up, up and away in my beautiful balloon... '"

"Wouldn't it be nice," she smiled, wistfully, "to be able to travel round the world in a balloon?"

I promised myself I would surprise her this summer with a flight in a balloon. Maybe not transworld or even trans-

157

Atlantic but at least trans-Thames. That was something Junie would never have wanted: any kind of a balloon trip. But Matt would. Matt would! And was there any reason why he and Moira shouldn't in some way soon meet and get to be real friends… and then… ?

"We could drift across oceans and meadows and over mountain peaks and cities… ," she said.

"You sound like me!" I cried. "You sound just like me! I think I must have influenced you!"

"I think you must."

"A good influence?"

"Undoubtedly a good influence. And we could sip champagne and eat biscuits with Stilton or — better still — with caviar."

"I've never eaten caviar."

That night we ate caviar.

We drank champagne, as well.

We lived like lords and ladies. Like film stars. Like sultans and rajahs. Like swashbuckling adventurers. I felt like Errol Flynn — like Errol Flynn as Robin Hood awaiting execution — dashingly irrepressible. I wasn't sure how, or why, this transition should have taken place: from royalty to rascal: but I suppose I must have felt there was room within me to express varying personalities, given the right stimuli: like a sailor with a wife in every port and a different face to present to each one. That's why I knew I had it in me to become an actor. I looked about that splendid dining room for any show-biz celebrity and if I'd seen one should most likely have trolled over and besought guidance — heaven helps those who help themselves. The theatre was where I really longed to be. Rather than the shop, the office, even university.

But the Ritz that night was short on show-biz celebrities. It didn't matter.

"All the world's a stage… " I can't remember now if there was any run-up to this small confidence or if I even let Moira know to whom I was referring: "They have their exits and their entrances, and one man in his time plays many parts."

I *can* remember, though, remarking that if I'd written that particular passage I might have improved on it a bit. "It isn't logical. Entrances should come *before* exits — well, obviously." I saw myself at that moment right at the cutting edge of scholarship. "Do you love me?" I asked.

"Yes," she said. "I think I do."

"I feel I ought to tell you," I told her... carefully... "that I am not altogether very lovable."

"And I feel I ought to tell you that perhaps you're not altogether the best judge of that."

"Will you be my judge?" I then asked, earnestly.

"In this case, yes, certainly," she smiled. "With pleasure." She put on her white cap. "I pronounce you very lovable."

Anyone who can place a damask napkin on her head in the middle of the Ritz dining room — even for just a second or two — has to be a fairly decent judge.

I felt very safe being in the hands of such a fairly decent judge.

"But you haven't all the facts." I knew there were many things I ought to say; and that I'd never have a better opportunity for doing so. I tried to gather in my widely rambling, in-the-playground thoughts. I swallowed some more wine.

"Give me all the facts," she invited. She gazed at me now with unguarded devotion. She leant her elbows on the table and put her face between her hands. "I don't know if I can reverse the verdict but you'd better acquaint me with the evidence."

"Well, you see, Your Honour, it's like this." What was it like, though? Exactly? I made a truly heroic attempt to consider what it *was* like. Exactly. "I'm really, you see, a married man. And I've been a married man for many married years. And I've got a daughter of fifteen called Ella and a son of Matt called twelve. And my grandmother didn't even make that cake, although I told you that she did, because my grandmother is dead and no longer does the cooking. And Susie doesn't belong to any of the neighbours

159

— she belongs to me — well, to us, that is, to me and Junie and Susie and Matt. And I love you very much and I'm very sorry that I made up stories."

21

In the car I told her in great detail of my plans: London from Monday to Friday, Deal for the weekends. ("But you'd hardly notice I was gone.") I had the impression that all the right words were coming to me, that I spoke with unusual eloquence and persuasiveness, was really getting through to her, letting her know all about my childhood and my frustrations and mistakes. And all about the compensations I'd found along the way. I remember at one point I related to her the plot of *The Captain's Paradise*: how Alec Guinness, as the captain of a steamer plying between Gibraltar and Tangier, has a very domesticated kind of wife in one port and a very exotic and sensual kind in the other: the seemingly perfect situation. (In spite of its containing risks. As when the two women, each unaware of the existence of a counterpart, strike up a conversation in a store in Tangier at a moment when he himself is hurrying there to keep a rendezvous with one of them... ! The suspensefulness could still make me laugh, even now.) Seemingly perfect, I should say, until Celia Johnson unexpectedly begins to change — she's the quiet, domesticated one — grows tired of always being at home and wants to go out dancing; while Yvonne de Carlo — who's the sultry one — starts wanting to stay in and cook delicious suppers...which also struck me as a pretty fair solution so there must have been some reason why he hadn't just adapted and why he'd somehow ended up before a firing squad (I'm sure there hadn't been a murder) though as the film was comedy one naturally knew he wasn't going to get shot; I think he must have bribed somebody... In any case I told Moira, quite honestly, I wasn't certain about that, which led me on to reassure her that until our meeting on the beach I had never told a single lie to anyone... well, never a whopper at least; there were always going to be the very small ones, weren't there, and nobody's name had ever been George Washington other than George Washington's and anybody else who'd either been named after him or coincidentally been called George when their parents had already happened to be a Mr and Mrs Washington... and, anyway, I hadn't really meant to deceive her, it had just sort of grown — "O what a wangled web we weave, when first we practice to deceive!" — and it was only because I had liked the look of her so much and had wanted to make myself interesting because I had liked the look of her so much (so in a manner of speaking it was she who was to blame: she shouldn't have bewitched and enthralled me like Cleopatra enwitching and bethralling Antony)... It suddenly occurred to me she hadn't said a great deal through all of this — or indeed, perhaps, hadn't said anything at all through all of this — but this was obviously because she couldn't concentrate both on the driving and on thinking over the various convincing arguments I'd put forward; not as well, I mean, as being expected actually to reply to all the various convincing arguments I'd put forward.

Besides, I knew at the moment she was probably feeling angry with me (and had a perfect right to be feeling angry with me). I began to suspect that my growing awareness of there being a distance between us wasn't solely due to the fact of her concentration; and I understood this — it was natural — any woman (even the kind of woman Moira was: an angel: "there were angels dining at the Ritz") could certainly have been expected to feel angry with me.

Very angry.

Even Junie. Perhaps even Junie.

So then I began to apologise and to hope I hadn't ruined her evening because until I had started to get everything off my chest it had been the very happiest evening of my whole life, the very happiest *two* evenings of my whole life, with the very happiest night and day dividing them. But the chest-baring had been necessary — as of course I knew she realised — though I greatly wished it hadn't. And I

162

appreciated, too, the way that, apart from a single glass of champagne, she had stuck to only fruit juice or spring water throughout the entire evening, even at the theatre bar during the interval (though she'd also had a glass of the Bordeaux before we'd started out), which was a sacrifice which like the similar one the night before I hadn't at all taken for granted. By rights it should have been my turn tonight to make the sacrifice and I was really a cad not to have insisted. I very much regretted that. And I was still apologising as I followed her up the stairs to her flat; and was alarmed suddenly to find there were tears running down my face. All right, I was a beast, I knew it and I hated it, bestial through and through, but I was going to make it up to her; I would eliminate the beast if that was the very last thing I did; and only weak men cried. I tried to wipe away the tears and pretended it was just a piece of grit and told her that mentioning Celia Johnson had made me think of *Brief Encounter*, about this woman with a dull but happy marriage who gets a similar bit of grit in her eye while waiting for her train and then has it removed — in the station refreshment room — by a nice-looking doctor who the following week walks into the overcrowded Kardomah restaurant where she happens to be having lunch... But it wasn't at all a funny film like *The Captain's Paradise* and it would depend on whether she wanted a laugh or a cry as to which I'd recommend if they chanced to be showing simultaneously, say on BBC 2 and Channel 4, and she hadn't got a video recorder.

Which she hadn't.

And neither had I.

Or neither had we.

But perhaps she'd already seen *Brief Encounter*? Perhaps it would have been surprising if she hadn't. Perhaps she'd already seen *The Captain's Paradise*? Perhaps the courteous thing would have been to find out.

Belatedly, I tried to find out.

Asked the question. But no good. I couldn't wait to hear the answer.

Had to rush off to be sick.

My God but it was sudden. Yet at least I'd made it home; at least I'd made it to the loo. At least I hadn't spewed up in the car. Thank heaven for small mercies. No; for *huge* mercies. Oh, my God! Imagine! Supposing I'd spewed up in the car!

I hoped she couldn't hear me. I knew damn well she could. The tears really did fall then, while I knelt and encompassed the cool china and disgorged throatfuls of splashing brown vomit and retched and retched as though my final hour had practically arrived. It distantly occurred to me that my dinner-suited arms embracing the white lavatory bowl looked like a thick black border reaching round an envelope of mourning.

What I obviously needed was sleep: lots and lots of sleep; and then it might come right once more. Somehow come right once more. But not tonight. There was no way I could take her riding round the world again tonight: neither on a cockhorse, nor up in a balloon, nor even under sail. Just the thought of any kind of undulation was enough to make me heave.

And heave and heave and heave.

22

Oddly, I woke again around eleven-fifty. Alone in the bed. But before I realised either of these things I had remembered all the throwing up; remembered it with a cringing in my gut, a shrivelling in my crotch. Oh, God. Oh, God. *Oh, God*! But I couldn't remember anything that followed.

My last recollection was of being on my knees; in my dinner jacket; with my arms around the bowl. I couldn't even recall undressing or brushing my teeth or leaving the bathroom. Strain as I might I couldn't even recall having flushed the lavatory. I *must* have flushed the lavatory. Whatever else I had done, or had not done, during the whole course of the previous evening — during the whole course of my previous life — I must, please God, dear God, I must have flushed that lavatory.

I had been on my knees — yes — I could remember that. Now I tried to will myself into a recollection of the act of getting up from them. I couldn't. Couldn't. Had I simply passed out? There on the bathroom floor?

Yet I was certainly undressed.

Except for the boxers. I flexed my feet. And except for the socks.

That was it then. If I'd undressed myself I'd never have left on my boxer shorts and socks. I never had. It would have felt... oh, I don't know... it would have felt strangely indecent.

Oh, Moira.

Moira.

Where are you?

She must be in the kitchen. Drinking tea. Reading the newspaper. And yet... the depth of the silence... I heard the thrumming of the fridge; a far-off conversation in the street.

No radio. No stirrings on a wooden chair. I pushed aside the duvet; slid my legs across the bed; forced myself to find the floor.

Extreme mortification, a desperate desire to take at least that first step along the road to recovery, to atonement, kept my hangover to some extent at bay: quivering before me at arm's length, at finger's length, while I stumbled, collided, lurched towards the door. Sudden contact with even mud-coloured daylight — via the undrawn curtains in the kitchen — felt stingingly offensive.

But she wasn't there. She wasn't in the sitting room. She wasn't in the bathroom.

I stooped painfully; raised both the lid and seat of the lavatory. Everything was fresh, sweet-smelling; the water tinted blue. (Well, surprise! Had I just expected her to leave it?) More painfully I examined the exterior of the porcelain, the fluffy rug around its base. But then I remembered that yesterday the rug had been the glowing shade of thick honey. Today it was dull brown.

My evening suit lay folded on a stool. My shirt perhaps was with it but I didn't want to look.

I urinated; washed my hands; washed out my mouth. Made my way back to the bed. Lay down on it, closed my eyes, tried to think calmly. Tried to retrieve my memory, gain with it some measure of reassurance.

Half an hour went by. I couldn't stay like that; knew I had to be showered and shaved and smelling of toothpaste and Cool Water (My Scintillating Future!) by the time that she returned. I should be clean and penitent and dignified. Not rough-skinned, sour-breathed, rheumy-eyed. No whining; no weakness. The situation wasn't lost.

Respect recoverable? That was the issue. The *sine qua non*. Without respect you lost value. Well, of course. Precious transmuted back to base. Second-class citizen. In the eyes of those who had recast you...doomed always to remain one. No appeal; no redress. You might as well be dead.

But even so. The primary move to forestall this looming

tragedy required willpower. Severance from inertia.

Yet soon proved worth it. Abundantly worth it. I felt so much better afterwards I now believed that I could drink a cup of sweet tea and perhaps manage a piece of toast. Balance and sanity and hope were dribbling back.

Wearing a set of entirely clean clothes — apart from my jeans and they were still well-pressed — I felt not merely freshened up but smart. Though that was only physical. For my spiritual cleansing I had urgent need of Moira.

Where was she?

I drew back the curtains at the bedroom window and looked out as far along the street as possible. Morgan absent. But even as I looked there came a sudden sharp pattering on the glass. Well, good, I thought. At least the rain might hasten her return.

Back in the kitchen I came across her note. A sheet of blue stationery near the breadboard on the worktop. I was surprised to think I'd earlier overlooked it.

It said:

Sam — Have gone out for the day. Paracetemol in bathroom cabinet. Suit is sponged but needs dry-cleaning. Doorkey on table in hall. Please drop it through letterbox. Thank you.

Moira.

I turned it over in case there was a message on the back: "P. S. I love you. Everything will work out." I'd even sat down before I'd turned it over; briefly speculating on what little variations might await me there.

It was the coldest note I think I'd ever seen between two friends. Junie would never have written me a note like that. Forget the punctuation.

I started to analyse it. The word 'Paracetemol' leapt out at me. Her ballpoint had evidently run dry and after taking a new one she'd had to retrace several of the letters.

What also leapt out at me, associatively, were thoughts of suicide.

I put down the note and contemplated suicide.

Did so practically as a distraction.

I imagined trying actually to kill myself. Imagined giving the appearance of trying actually to kill myself. How many tablets would they consider reasonably convincing? And, then again, was four o'clock or nine o'clock more likely to be the hour of her return?

Yet I'd heard you should never use Paracetemol. You might initially recover but just as you were getting accustomed to being alive again — and maybe even feeling fairly thankful for it — you inescapably succumbed to liver failure; I hoped you could appreciate the irony. Aspirin, it seemed, were a whole lot kinder to the struggling liver.

But aspirin. My father had done it with aspirin. For twenty years or more I'd seen my father as a wimp: despite those rules which he'd laid down for my manly education and presumably always tried to live by himself. (Live by himself? He hadn't managed *that* for very long, had he? All of two whole days! And 'by himself'… so where had that left me?) "Sorry, Dad. Like father like son. When it came to it I couldn't climb to any greater heights than you!" Cruel: my own lack of open-hearted empathy — and cruel also, his revenge for it: reminder of a week ago.

But then my 'Sorry, Dad' had been a mocking one. Just now… I wasn't quite so sure. Or at least if I was mocking him I was also mocking me.

In any case the concept of even attempted suicide was totally untenable. Tomorrow Junie'd be expecting me home for supper. At suppertime tomorrow I could still be in some hospital. In no fit state even to telephone.

And from now on Junie had to be my first priority. Come what may. She had to be protected. Absolutely.

But she always had been, of course. In the whole of our seventeen years this was the only time I'd ever left my post. I had needed a holiday. That holiday was over.

However, the idea of suicide itself — the real thing, not just a cry for help — could suddenly sound like a holiday: some layout in a brochure showing leafy trees and running water and a deckchair set in dappled shade. A deckchair always readily available. And just the notion of this, coming as it did with a promise things need never get too bad again, whether in thirty years' time with cancer, or whether just tomorrow, with heartbreak, conveyed such an impression of tranquillity you were immediately tempted to get off your butt, run to the telephone and ask for details.

Yet get thee behind me, Satan. I did get off my butt, though only to put water in the kettle and take a glance into Moira's washing machine. I suppose I must have been alerted by the small red light: still on, despite its cycle being completed. Yes, there was the honey-coloured rug. All floppy and lonesome. Endearingly bearish.

Oh, and I did switch on the radio. As always, tuned in to either Radio 3 or 4: at present a church service or some recording of a hymn: "Dear Lord and Father of mankind, forgive our foolish ways..." I rapidly switched it off.

Returned to my chair at the table and to yet another reading of that graceless note.

So overwhelmingly devoid of charity. So overwhelmingly — And then, of course, it hit me.

Hit me with the same sharpness I had myself applied to switching off the radio.

I must have been blind. So blind and so stupid. So insensitive. I'd missed such very obvious pointers. As soon as I saw one I saw umpteen.

Five of them. Christ! They could scarcely have been more glaring had they been handed to me personally on Mount Sinai.

(i) The use of my name. Well, that was friendly enough. 'Dear' would have turned it into a formality; and 'Dearest' or 'Darling' was currently more than I deserved. While — self-evidently — 'Sammy' carried undertones of childishness; conferred on me the status, almost, of a pupil.

(ii) She had anticipated my hangover and hinted at a remedy; not merely hinted at but provided; could one deny this was considerate? In fact I didn't see what more she could possibly have done.

169

(iii) And she had actually sponged my dinner suit. Frankly up till now I hadn't given that sufficient weight; had even taken it for granted. However, being by this time clearer-headed and better able to read between the lines, I could begin to appreciate the meaning behind the gesture — its symbolism — its standing as an act of love. She hadn't been able to write 'love' at the end of the letter but — if only subconsciously — she had incorporated that very message in her text.

And (iv) in the light of all this those two words above her signature of course acquired a new significance. Like I say, she hadn't managed to write 'love' or 'my darling' — that would have been giving back too much, too quickly — and after all, being only human and very much a woman, she had naturally wanted to make me sweat a little. But she *had* been able to write 'Thank you'. It was incredible I should have missed the softening of that *Thank you*. The comprehensiveness of it. Effusion. Profligacy.

And furthermore (v) she had used a sheet of top quality writing paper. If she simply hadn't cared she would have done what I did all the time at home: have used the back of an old envelope or a piece torn from a message pad. So was that or was it not indicative? Was that — or was it not — a clincher?

Weren't they all clinchers?

These discoveries, all my detective work, had proved efficacious. I suddenly felt hungry; not just for a slice of dry toast but for several slices, spread with honey. The kettle had switched itself off, yet as it returned to the boil I realised I was whistling. Already on the way back. Well along the way back. "'When you're up to your neck in hot water be like a kettle and sing... '" What on earth had I been getting so uptight about? Nothing so terrible had happened. Nothing irreversible. I'd got a little drunk and I'd got a little sick. It happened to probably thousands every single day the sun rose.

Oh, and I had told her about Junie, of course. But the

170

incidence of husbands falling for the charms of an outsider — or in my own special case for the charms of an angel — was practically as high in this modern age as that of drunkenness. If nobody was harmed thereby it was simply a means of liberating your true self; loosening the constrictions; looking deep into your psyche. Thus it became an experience which could open up a whole web of gleaming opportunity. For now we see through a glass, brightly. Strap on your winged sandals. Take up your mighty sword. On such a full sea are we now afloat.

Also I'd told her I could be regarded as virtually a free agent. During four whole days a week.

And during four whole nights a week. I hoped I had sufficiently emphasised that. Not that I believed it needed emphasising.

So now we could make a new beginning; as from this very night; a new beginning even better than the old because it would be completely honest, free of all necessity to tread with care and to crane around corners.

I always drew as much strength from the thought of new beginnings as I did from the contemplation of old successes.

Tomorrow would be the first day of the rest of my life.

(Tomorrow in this case because today was practically over the hill by now and — besides — I had the feeling that perhaps I did need a bit of a breathing space. There was never any point in rushing at things.)

And tomorrow, too, I'd make a start upon my diary. (Thank God, in fact, I hadn't done so before this. How all things work together for good — to them that are forever thankful! Not only would I have needed to put in details I was now rather glad I didn't need to put in but tomorrow was the first bank holiday in May and therefore the proper and recognised time to celebrate the coming of the spring! What better day on which to make a new beginning? Could I honestly regard that just as chance?) Diaries didn't normally have titles of course but... *The Long Happy Life of Samson Luckyfellow Groves*. One up on *The Diary of a Nobody*, perhaps!

He saw! And he appreciated!
And he flew!
(Like a roc.)
Tombstone inscription?

23

I decided to go home. This time I'd play it really cool. The iceman cometh. I would take her at her word — ostensible word — and by doing so cause *her* to sweat a little. There would be irony in that. Moira was an angel but perhaps even she could benefit from a period of uncertainty.

I would telephone tomorrow.

The journey wasn't perfect. Despite my renewed optimism it was debilitating to see again Victoria Station and remember all our foolishness. It didn't help that the place was so much emptier than on Friday, exhibiting a degree of lassitude, a feeling of Sunday afternoon aimlessness which was maybe exacerbated by the long weekend but not by any means, I now discovered, a deadness endemic only to small provincial towns. Something livelier might have supported me. Nor did it help that I'd got very wet waiting at bus stops on the Finchley Road — or else walking between them, constantly looking back — and now felt chilly and bedraggled; nor that I found myself with nearly two hours to kill before the next train — and knew even that was going to be a slow one, stopping at every piddling little station. I bought a paper which I couldn't work up any interest in and sat over a cup of coffee so noxious I couldn't take more than just a sip or two for fear of bringing back my queasiness. My queasiness... This time, though in one sense I was travelling lighter than before (since I had neither cardboard box nor carrier bags: my bundled evening clothes, wrapped round the patent leather pumps, were stuffed inside the holdall on top of my cricketing whites) — this time, though I was physically less encumbered, I couldn't truly feel it in my bones that I was travelling towards the sunrise, no matter how I worked to keep my spirits up. I wondered whether, after all, I should have left some note: a debate as to whether strong manly silences could ever be worth more than correct social behaviour — and one that kept intruding, more or less insistently, between me and whatever article I tried to read. I hated to appear ungrateful. Or as though — smallmindedly — I nursed a grievance.

It grew less insistent while I was reading something I'd forgotten I would find: the review of *Half a Farthing, Sam Sparrow?* In other circumstances I might well have felt indignant; but now I didn't seem to care that much; could even derive mild satisfaction out of the complaints of the reviewer. Along with other things, he'd panned a number of the lyrics. Called them facile and pretentious claptrap. That struck me as mildly tautologous but I told him that *he* had done sufficient carping for the two of us.

My dilemma over the note was vying with another doubt. The meat pie and the soup; we'd eaten only about a quarter of each. So what would Moira do with the remainder? Suddenly I realised I didn't know her well enough to feel even remotely sure. I only knew I utterly loathed the thought of any insult to Junie; and also utterly loathed the thought of any waste... which was attributable, I suppose, to my upbringing, with its constant consideration of all those starving children in India. (And the most apalling loss of anything I could presently imagine was to throw down the drain — almost literally — that chestful of exquisite treasures from the Ritz. How could I have done it? And Moira's gift to me! — how must she have felt? That dinner had cost her... well, it made me squirm, it really made me shudder, to think how much that dinner must have cost her. I wished I could have been the one to pay. Talk about pearls before swine! Talk about manna, or stardust, turned to ashes!) Well, Moira might get rid of the pie and the pea soup. Yet at least I felt certain she wouldn't throw away the cake. I mean, she just *couldn't*. All the care and consideration which had gone into the production of that cake; to bin it would have been like burying a friend — like burying him alive, still wearing his smile and his pompommed hat. In fact,

I felt certain that before long we'd again be eating that cake together. Or anyway I tried to. At heart I believed it but really to feel it I had to repeat it firmly several times and once I even repeated it out loud. Thankfully the train wasn't full.

At some point, staring through the window at a blurry landscape, I once more attempted to whistle.

Yet with all this rain now lashing against the glass even the zippiest tune no longer carried much conviction.

At Dover Priory I had a further long wait. But count your blessings, I told myself, severely. At least there's no one working on the line. At least I and those five others aren't going to be shunted onto some wet and trundling godforsaken bus.

But I didn't notice any bluebirds over the white cliffs. All those predicted for us, mainly by Vera Lynn, with such patriotic fervour, some sixteen or seventeen years before my birth, had almost certainly become extinct by this time — or else been driven well away.

The hard thing was, however, I knew there'd been a glut in the vicinity even as recently as last Friday. Forty-eight hours ago! The sky had been awash.

I tried to convince myself they'd be back. *Were* back. It was only because I was so very tired all of a sudden. I couldn't see them through the rain.

The five others on the platform were all young and laughing and together. College students? I felt I'd have given a lot to be one of them. Out with my friends; going off somewhere nice. All bouncy and naive and pleased to play the fool.

I finally got home about nine. The house was dark; car not there. I'd forgotten. Junie and the children would still be at Jalna (The Dovecote). Celebrating. Happy. The festivities only now, maybe, beginning to wind down.

I went into the larder without even taking off my raincoat and started to eat. I wasn't particularly hungry but — I wanted food. I ate handfuls of Harvest Crunch and tore open a packet of biscuits. I moved to the fridge and found

175

cooked drumsticks; devoured all four. There were three pineapple rings on a saucer and a triangle of blue cheese. I followed these with a flavourless tomato. Once, I'd have given the tomato a perfunctory wipe, at least.

I returned to the hall, threw my raincoat over a chair, picked up my holdall from the mat. I was walking heavily up the stairs when something occurred to me in retrospect; weirdly delayed-action retrospect. I was at once deflected from the thought of sleep.

I ran back to the kitchen. Susie's basket wasn't there.

Wasn't there in any part of it.

Bewilderedly, I made headlong for the dining room, stood in the centre and scrutinised the base of every wall — as though the business of locating a dog's basket, even with the light on, would require swivelling feet, untypically sharp eyesight, an attention to detail.

Nor was it underneath the table.

I half-ran, half-strode, into the sitting room... the TV room... conservatory. Kitchen again. Larder and the outside loo. If possible, my pace sped up; panic escalated. Blindly back to hall. As I whirled round, surveying every corner, I must have caught the brolly stand. Which clattered onto varnished floorboards, cannoned into Junie's piano. I raced upstairs and into every bedroom, even the couple rarely used — one smelling now of paint and boobytrapped with decorating clutter. I fell on my knees and looked beneath the beds. Looked inside the bathroom. The lavatory. Stood on a ladder and shone our emergency torch around the attic.

Giddiness shook hands with paranoia.

I headed for the telephone.

Picked up the other end by Pim.

"Get Junie," I commanded. Neither greeted him nor told him who I was.

He started to mumble something but I cut across it with a question. "Listen — is Susie there? I just can't find her basket. I've searched through every room in the house and cannot find her basket. Is Susie with you? Is she there?"

He didn't answer. "Oh, for God's sake," I was going to say, "can't you understand plain English?" But then I heard the receiver being put down and I broke wind instead. That wasn't very pleasant, either, but I seemed to be past minding.

After what felt like at least five minutes I finally heard Junie's voice in the background — along with other voices, or maybe only one other voice, I wasn't sure. A man's voice. Jake's? Oh, probably the whole family was now filing into the hallway, taking seats. But I couldn't catch the words.

"Hello!" I said. "Hello-hello-hello! What the hell is going on there? Will somebody pick up the phone!"

And somebody did.

"And where have you been since last Friday?"

But it certainly wasn't Junie.

"What?"

"This is Mrs Fletcher speaking. You've been off somewhere with a woman — haven't you, Groves? And I mean to tell you how I feel about it. I'm afraid there aren't words strong enough to tell you how I feel about it. There! Did you hear me? You were never one of us. I've always known you were a mealy-mouthed hypocrite, thinking all the time you were taking everybody in, pretending to be so much holier than the rest of us, pretending even butter wouldn't melt — "

"Fuck off," I said. "I want to hear about my dog."

"Oh, you do, do you? Well, your dog is dead. Your dog has been put down. Dead," she repeated.

Then she severed the connection.

24

I immediately rang back.

The number was engaged.

If they'd left off the receiver I should have to charge right round — *now*, while my adrenalin was still racing, the small supply of it I had. At least the dizziness had gone but I'd need to husband that adrenalin. I was fighting for my life and I wanted all the energy there was.

Almost at the gate I remembered I hadn't got a car. Damn it, then — a bike. But on my way to the back porch to collect Matt's two things happened. Firstly it occurred to me it might be wiser to wait till Junie and the kids came home; my own territory — no heckling from the grandstand. And secondly... the telephone rang. That might be Junie now.

It wasn't.

"Hello, Sam. This is Jake... I've been deputised," he said, "to let you know the lie of the land. In fact I volunteered. I thought you'd rather have me do it than... well, than any of the girls, let's say. You know what all these Fletchers can be like. I gather you said something slightly naughty to Mama."

"How the hell did it all happen, Jake?"

"Apparently Junie tried to reach you in Lincoln. Spoke to some woman whom she didn't know and who didn't seem to know her either. Or about her. Or about you."

"Oh, God."

"Sammy," he said, "in some ways you're an astute and even erudite fellow. Yet if only you could've been a fraction more astute over the plotting of all this... ! You idiot. You might always have come to me if you'd wanted sound practical advice. Either to me or — I suspect — to Robert. But as it is, old lad, you've landed in the shit. It's going to be a long time, too, before you manage to climb out of it in *this* neck of the woods. If indeed you ever do."

"I couldn't care less," I said. "It's only Junie that matters. Junie and the children. And as soon as I... Do the children know about it?" I asked.

"Do the children know about it?" he repeated. "Whose children are we talking of? Some that live outside the county? Or I should have said — the country? Sam, you really are the weirdest mix."

"How've they seemed?"

"It's hard to say. Matt's been mainly very quiet. Ella... well, Ella's been fairly brassy; getting it out of her system, I think is what it's called. They'll be okay. I've been trying to make them see — the family at large, I mean, not simply your two children — that this sort of thing isn't really such a big deal. And just so long as you're not aiming to skip off again (because if you are, old chum, your days are numbered and the end is nigh) and just so long as you're willing to dance attendance for a year or six I reckon they'll all come round in the end. All of them. Even Junie."

"*Even* Junie?"

There was a slight pause. "Why does that surprise you?"

I gave a non-committal grunt; contented myself with informing him tersely of the one requirement: to prise my wife loose from the five thousand tentacles of my wife's interfering mother.

"No, but it isn't quite so simple. Perhaps you don't realise: she's taken this extremely hard. A girl of hidden depths, is Junie. Not that I have to tell *you* that, of course."

"If you want to do me a favour, Jake, you'll just get her to come home as quickly as you can."

"But that's why I rang. To say neither she nor the children will be coming home tonight. They slept here last night, too. She's even spoken about... To be honest, you've both of you taken me more than a little by surprise."

"Spoken about what?"

"About not coming home at all. I mean, not while you're there."

"Nonsense," I said. "Give me ten minutes alone with her. That's all it needs."

"Well, I certainly hope so, Sam."

We went on talking but not to any purpose. Tiredness redescended. I picked up the umbrella stand and went wearily to bed. Let tomorrow take care of itself, play any little joke it felt like. But why had she had to take it out on Susie? Why, why, why? What harm had poor old Susie ever done her?

Already down to my underpants I ran downstairs again. Discovered that as well as the basket — and its blankets and its cushions — Junie seemed to have disposed of the collar and lead; the much-chewed rubber ball and bone; even the packet of Bob Martins. The insecticidal shampoo. The brush. Large bag of biscuits. Junie had seldom fed her out of tins.

I felt inclined to search the dustbin for a souvenir. But... what on earth was the point? At least we had the snapshots.

I decided I must look for snapshots.

If only to keep me from further depredations on the larder. Tomorrow my thinking was going to need to be sharp and quick and unclogged.

I found two: amongst the quantities of snapshots we hadn't yet got round to sorting: two of Susie on her own. Probably taken by me. One showed the splayed paws, the dipped trunk, the pricked-up ears... all eager for the pitched ball. The other, the characteristic tilt of the head: someone out of camera had been telling her to stay and speaking to her of engrossing possibilities. Both the pictures smacked of melty-eyed devotion.

I studied them. I tore them savagely across.

Four pieces. Eight. Hurled them at the ceiling. Let them lie where they had fallen: carpet, coffee table, shelves.

Then I whipped off my underpants. But after half a minute's frenzied abuse... well, anyway, who was I trying to punish?

I left them where they were. Along with the cumbersome confetti. Trailed back up to bed.

The house felt cold, unwelcoming. Only the second time I'd slept in it alone, without a wife, or children, or a dog. That other occasion, more than fifteen years ago: Junie giving birth to Ella. (And I'd been twenty-one. Just twenty-one!) My grandmother hadn't as yet sold up or moved in with us.

Slept in it? I may have done, that first time. But now? Despite my father I had turned into a crybaby. (To spite my father I had turned into a crybaby?) At first I brushed away the tears but then permitted them to channel unimpeded to the pillow.

Those tears weren't just for me. Partly I cried for Junie, who had picked up a telephone in a fault-free world and had it sucked away in an earthquake. Partly I cried for Ella and Matt, who whether loud and cynical or mainly silent were now having to negotiate a quicksand which the best damned dad on record had unthinkingly led them to the brink of. Partly I cried for Moira, who had given me the keys to her Morgan and who had done her best to make this such a memorable weekend. And partly for Susie whom also I had failed; as badly as any living creature could be failed.

I even cried for my parents: for the cancer in the body and the cancer in the soul and for the legacy of weakness which had shown itself as strength. And this time I really did cry for my father. I knew in my heart he'd made a much better husband than ever I had; and probably, too, a much better human being. Well, if he hadn't at least... poor suffering devil, not simply for two days but for long anxious month following long anxious month, the tightly smiling face, the apparently hopeful disposition... well, if he hadn't, heaven help him! God help him.

So in the end, of course, it was mostly for myself I cried. Cried because I no longer seemed to understand so many of the things which had once appeared straightforward. Because I'd started out with such an abundance of blessings and finished up with... what had I finished up with? And because I didn't know how I was going to restore stability and trust, when trust was much the same thing as respect.

Or even restore the will to carry on.

Adventure?

Excitement?

Give me an income tax return. So long as I could live with self-assessment.

181

25

Early next day I walked to Jalna. All my adrenalin had drained off. Also, my stomach was troubling me... no earth-shattering surprise. I'd needed to prevent myself, by exercising willpower I scarcely knew I had, from setting foot inside the kitchen. That put the kibosh on a cup of tea.

The journey took an hour and twenty minutes. (It wasn't right without a dog; without the feel of all that keen companionship on the end of a leash.) I arrived there shortly after ten. I had chosen not to cycle, supposing a walk might better clarify my thoughts, expel my sluggishness, provide me with a plan of what I had to say.

Give me more time.

In all but the last I'd been mistaken.

It was Pim who came to the door. I was grateful for that; intended to apologise for my appalling brusqueness on the phone. Indeed, I experienced an uncustomary rush of warm affection — a sort of fellow feeling perhaps, as though in the past I had never been quite fair to him; underrated, patronised him. Not understood his problems. Nor even made any attempt to.

Suffering produces strange bedfellows.

I don't think he realised he was suffering. Or cared much whether I was.

"Oh," he said, after a pause. "It's you. We didn't think you'd have the nerve to show your face."

That rush of affection instantly dried up. Wasn't there some quotation about the weak feeling they had come into their own when they chanced on anyone yet weaker than themselves? "Wrong, then, weren't you? I want to see Junie," I announced.

In a way it wasn't a bad beginning.

"Junie's still in bed."

"And the children, please? I'd like to see the children."

"Gone to Folkestone for the day with Debbie and Robert and some of the others. To help to take their mind off matters."

"In this weather?"

"There are worse things than a bit of rain."

He was starting to win points: two to my one: we weren't even level pegging.

I brushed past him. I knew which bedroom she'd be in; we had several times stayed overnight.

On the staircase I met Junie's mother. Also known as Mrs Fletcher. She drew in close to the bannister and looked the other way. But my back felt her watching me intently as — with a wholly spurious reassumption of authority and decisiveness — I pushed open the door to the blue room.

Ted and Yvonne were in there, naked, on the bed. And making love.

Ted jerked his head round: justifiably startled. But minimised our blushes with aplomb. "Junie's down the landing, Sam. They've put her in the pink room."

"Thank you," I mumbled. "Sorry."

My mother-in-law was still standing halfway down the stairs. Before she turned I thought I saw the traces of a smile.

"Bitch," I told her, quietly. I don't suppose she heard.

I passed three other bedrooms on that floor. It struck me as ironic: that Junie should now be in the pink. Blue was evidently more suited to a man and wife together.

She was sitting up in bed, with an untouched breakfast tray straddling her legs; like the sort you get in hospital, except that it was wood.

"Hello," I said.

She appeared to be studying a pair of kipper fillets; her expression as wooden as the tray.

"How are you, Junie?"

"Did I hear you knock?"

"No," I answered, humbly; and attempted a smile. "But you should have done. I just caught Ted and Yvonne making the most of the twins being taken off their hands."

Yet it didn't evoke even a glimmer of amusement. "And ye gods! *Still* you don't learn?"

"And I forgot to wish them happy anniversary. Ought I to return?"

I paused.

"Junie, I've come to take you home."

"Have you? What a pity! I shan't be going home."

"But why not? This is silly, darling. This is all so silly."

"Well, maybe it is. Perhaps you should've thought of that before."

"I know. So what can I do to prove to you I'm sorry?"

"Oh? Sorry? Sorry, are you?"

"You'll never know how much, Junie. Never. But actions speak louder than words, of course. What can I do?"

"Suffer," she said.

I still couldn't believe it; not quite. Naturally we'd quarrelled before — countless times — over the period of the twenty-odd years we'd been boy- and girlfriend as well as husband and wife; but Junie had always seemed so... well, temperate... and her anger had chiefly revealed itself through cool detachment; any shouting or acrimony had come exclusively from me. She'd been sulky — hurt — bewildered. She had never been vindictive.

I'd been standing by the closed door. Now I took a few paces into the room and slumped onto an upright chair with seat upholstered in pink velvet. The chair looked fragile but I didn't care. (I hadn't very far to fall.) The room being smallish I hadn't wanted to intimidate her by getting up too close.

I suppose there were other ways of being intimidating. "Why did you phone John Caterham? Were you spying on me?" I hadn't meant to add that last bit; or make any of it sound accusatory.

In any case she wasn't cowed.

"All this time," she said, disdainfully. "And you still don't know me better than that!"

184

"No, I'm sorry; it didn't come out right." As though there were some way it might have come out right — that unnecessary rider. "Why, then?"

"Simply because we hadn't said goodbye." She gave a hollow laugh. "And believe it or not I felt unhappy about that."

"Yes, so did I. But you phoned me at John Caterham's just to say goodbye?"

"And to wish you luck."

There was an air of unreality about her tone. That didn't matter. At least she was talking.

At least we both were.

"And you didn't feel Mavis could be trusted to pass the message on?"

"When were we last apart?" she said. "To me it seemed important."

"Me, too. But why couldn't you just have waited? In the shop? You knew I wasn't likely to be long."

"I felt silly." We were extraordinarily alike. I remembered thinking it seemed almost superstitious: my attempting to telephone her at the house.

"I tried to phone you at the house."

"I know you did. I rang 1471. I missed you by about an hour." For a moment we appeared — very nearly — to be back in harmony: discussing things in common. "I'd wondered what you wanted. In fact, that was a big part of it: my deciding to telephone you later. That was the instant when it first occurred to me. Otherwise I mightn't ever have come up with it."

Dear God. Dear God.

"You could've rung back Mavis."

In any case all this was way beside the point. Though being way beside the point was possibly the lesser of two evils.

"And anyhow, after I'd mentioned it," she added, "it wasn't only myself, was it?"

"How d'you mean?"

"Matt hadn't said goodbye to you either."

"Matt?"

"And then it was him who spurred me on. Wouldn't give me a minute's peace. Straight after supper — oh, for the dozenth time. I said, 'They might still be eating, darling, I expect Daddy may only just have got there,' but he said, 'Oh, come on, Mum, you said eight, it's after eight, no one's going to mind.' He wanted to tell you something about his latest project — wanted to tell you before he told me because he said you'd appreciate the humour more and, besides, he needed your advice. And he was standing right there by the telephone, all ready to grab it, when that woman answered... "

Matt...

"And I felt such a fool," she said. "She thought I had the wrong number; thought I must be talking about different Caterhams. And she sounded as though I were being all quaint and muddle-headed."

"So what happened?" I asked.

"What happened? What d'you think happened? I told her I wanted the John Caterham who used to live in Deal in Kent (naturally it hadn't got me anywhere mentioning *your* name?) and then of course she had to go and get him. 'My goodness, if it isn't little Junie Fletcher! I mean, Groves! How *are* you? Don't tell me you're still living in that same drear place, the pair of you! And how's good old Sam?' But even then I couldn't take it in; I was so *slow*, so trusting; still thought there must've been some extraordinary yet basically simple mistake. But then I remembered how you'd forgotten to leave me the number — and you don't normally forget such things — even though the Caterhams' address hadn't been transferred into our last couple of address books; and how we'd only managed to get through at all because Matt had softsoaped Directory Enquiries; and then it suddenly crossed my mind but how *could* John Caterham have known about the name of the shop... And I couldn't talk and I was crying and Matt had to take the receiver and he just blurted out, 'Sorry, goodbye, yes sorry, wrong number!', and they must have thought I was so strange — and rude — and must've sat there talking about it all through the rest of the evening… "

She was crying again now and I got up a little helplessly and started to put an arm around her shoulders but she shook it off convulsively and I found myself taking a step backward in dismay.

"It was me they'd have thought strange — and stupid — and… and quite beyond words." Indeed I felt surprised they hadn't dialled 1471 themselves and then phoned back to tell her so. I felt if they'd been nice they'd have done that. John had certainly been nice before he'd moved away from Deal. Could fifteen years have altered him that much?

"And now you have the nerve to tell me I was spying on you!" She wiped her eyes and blew her nose, explosively.

I'm sorry about that, Junie, I really am. About that and about everything. It was the very first time, I promise. I truly am so sorry."

"Yes! Of course you are! Because you got found out!"

"How can I try to put things right?"

"Suffer!" she said again. But this time she went further. "Suffer like you've made me suffer. And Matt. And Ella. Suffer till it really hurts."

And she looked me in the face as she said it.

I didn't tell her that all she needed was to look a bit more closely.

I sat down again. Couldn't she guess how I was suffering? What did I have to do? I wanted to be contrite, yes, but not self-pitying. What woman could possibly look up to any man who felt self-pity? Kipling had done more than set before me an ideal, he'd handed me a lifeline: an achievable solution to every problem fate could ever throw across my path. If I'd happened on that poem just one year earlier I mightn't have run away and cried, face downwards in the grass, in the park, at the death of my poor mother.

I mightn't have got out on that windowsill and contemplated suicide.

187

I still remembered how I'd used to test myself at school: deliberately ignore my homework to invite punishment; deliberately (once) knock my wicket with the bat; deliberately (once) muff a catch I knew I could have caught — a lost opportunity which had deprived us of even a draw and thus heaped opprobrium on my head in place of adulation. Only Hal Smart had known; and not even Hal Smart had fully understood. But there'd been scores of small ways in which I'd aimed to prove I had no breaking point — that adversity could always leave me smiling. Scores? No; hundreds. Maybe thousands. At rock bottom I knew I hadn't stopped.

How could people scoff at Kipling? Even such a brief reminder as this could make me feel less battered; give me back at least the *idea* of feeling gratitude at finding myself tested.

Give me back at least the *idea* of tackling life one moment at a time. Remind me that every step which carried me a little further from the abyss symbolised a victory; was one more swastika notched up below the cockpit. "So when *will* you be coming home?" I asked.

"Certainly not today."

"Tomorrow?"

"I've given you everything," she said. "All these years I've given you everything. Everything and everything and everything. I haven't any more to give."

She was working herself up. Fresh sobs, I could have coped with — even welcomed. Hysteria was something else again.

"What more?" she said. "What more could you expect?"

"Nothing, Junie. Absolutely nothing."

"Sex? Was it that? I gave you all the sex you ever asked for. Did I ever say I had a headache when it wasn't true?"

At the right time we might both have smiled at that one.

"No. Never." Yet I couldn't resist adding: "Though you seldom seemed to enjoy it very much."

"And I suppose *she* does?"

I shrugged. But it appeared she was seriously intending me to answer.

"That isn't the same." I mumbled it.

"Why? Because she isn't fat, like me? Because she isn't old like me? Because she isn't thoroughly worn out at the end of an average day with looking after two teenagers and a house and a demanding husband?"

"As a matter of fact," I said, "you're younger than she is. Over three years younger."

"Is it this woman, then, who came into the shop? The one who's going to buy a house here?"

I had to stare. Just like I'd had to stare at Moira on the station. "How could you possibly know that?"

She didn't answer but I saw the look of satisfaction.

"In any case," I said, "I don't suppose she's going to buy it now."

"Why? Has she tired of you already?"

I hesitated; then gave a nod. *That* was a victory, if ever there'd been one. It took a lot of effort. It took a lot of courage.

"So has she discovered yet you're not that good in bed? Can't she bring herself to tell you how magnificent and strong you are, even when you feed her all the proper lines?"

"What?"

"I said, can't she bring herself to — ?"

I got up and made towards the door; was already opening it when she began to state her terms.

"If I come back there'll have to be some changes made." Much emphasis upon the 'if'.

I wasn't even going to answer. I simply stood there at the door and looked out on the landing: cream paint, red carpet, polished balustrade — all of it immaculate.

But then I thought of Matt having the receiver thrust into his hands and not knowing what to say; the two of them, not knowing what to say.

"Changes? What sort of changes?" I couldn't keep pace with all the changes there'd already been.

It was surprising she had heard me.

"No more talk of sloping off to Lincolnshire for the weekends. Or of sloping off anywhere. No more talk of disappearing up to London for a job. No more talk of any brilliant future on the stage. No more strutting round the house like some big he-man having to support the poor admiring little woman who can't — I don't know — can't even... "

Perhaps she was struggling to find some exalted metaphor or at least some way of avoiding anticlimax. None of it sounded like Junie. Surely she couldn't actually have been *meaning* any of it — with the exception of that curfew, that confined-to-camp? I half wondered if she had sections of script Sellotaped to her breakfast tray, worked on by her mother and maybe one or two of her sisters all day yesterday: an anniversary entertainment, perfect for wet weather. (No, why leave out *any* of the sisters or any of the sisters' husbands? I'd already had a taste of how Pim felt. Perhaps even Jake had had a hand in it? Was there anyone anywhere who at some level didn't relish the downfall of a hero? Indeed you had to look no further than Miss Martin at the school.)

"I don't understand. What should I have done? How could I have tried any harder than I did? What should I have done?"

"You haven't listened to a word I've said."

"But what have you said? And why didn't you tell me if things weren't... weren't the way you wanted them?"

There was a brief silence.

"Wouldn't you like to turn round?" she said. "How can I talk to you like that?" Her tone sounded gentler; practically like Junie's. "Why don't you just close the door and come and sit down again?"

I thought about it; then did as she suggested.

"Why didn't I tell you? Because we never communicated. We got out of the habit."

"And what does that mean?" That must have been — almost — the craziest thing I'd heard today. Up till about a week ago I'd always told her everything. I'd naturally assumed it was the same with her.

"And also because… I thought you couldn't help being how you were. But that was stupid. If no one tries to make us face up to ourselves — well, how're we ever going to change? Besides, all of this, it didn't happen overnight. Believe me, Sam, it's been a very gradual process."

What had? All of what? I sometimes wished she could have paid a bit more attention to her English at the County High.

But there was no doubt she was softening. For the moment I wasn't all that interested in any of the whys and wherefores. I didn't underestimate the shock she'd had. She'd been driven to retaliate. That was fair enough. I could even understand — just — how she could have let herself get back at me through Susie. And what was past was past; for both of us; it was the here and now that mattered.

Yet all the same. It did niggle. I wished I could have been clearer as to where I'd been at fault; apart from that one very obvious instance. Apparently — if I'd followed her correctly — she'd felt over-protected. How could *anyone* feel over-protected? Unless it was some child complaining he got sent to bed too early or wasn't allowed to climb trees or walk along high walls — that would make sense, obviously. But otherwise… ? I wasn't possessive or anything; I didn't place a check upon her movements. It was a woman's role to be protected. It was a man's role to protect. God in heaven. What wouldn't I have given, sometimes, to acquire myself a strong protector?

To have had a father whom I could have hugged.

"I think you ought to go. I feel so tired," she said.

Her? Tired? Lying there in the kind of bed the princess got — minus the pea, of course — and being waited on, and cosseted, and told she had to rest; and no doubt having it endlessly brought home to her what a victim she was and how woefully unappreciated.

While I… I hadn't even had a cup of tea.

"All right." I stood up. "So when will you be coming home?"

"I don't know. I shall have to think."

I hovered for an instant. I had over an hour's walk ahead of me. Our car was in the drive; I wondered if I'd be allowed to take it.

"There's something else perhaps you ought to consider." I found I couldn't ask about the car. "I know you always gave a lot but I did things for you as well."

"Sam – nobody's denying that." She yawned.

"Right." I turned towards the door; turned back again. "Do you feel then it may be tomorrow? Or more likely Wednesday? Or not until Thursday, perhaps?"

"I told you, I've not made up my mind."

"The children ought to be at school."

"Would you think they can't get there from Jalna?"

"The Dovecote." I believe that this was meant to be humorous.

"No; I'll give you a phone call," she told me, with finality.

"I see. This week?"

She gave a shrug.

"Next week?" I really hadn't meant to carry it right through. "Sometime?" I asked. "Never?"

She didn't say anything. Her face resettled in a mask of obstinacy. (God, how I knew — and hated — that look of placid enmity!)

"Anyway, I hear Ella and Matt are in Folkestone. Give them my love will you."

"I don't suppose they'll want it. They know how much it's worth."

"And tell them I'm sorry."

"What good d'you feel that's going to do?"

"And please — please — come home before Matt's birthday."

"Gracious," she said. "I can't believe this. Are you deaf?"

"All right, then. Only one last thing. What was it he needed my advice about; what's it on — his latest project?"

"I don't think you've any right to know." She relented,

slightly. "Besides. When I finally remembered to ask he just said, 'Oh, forget it, Mum. It doesn't matter.'"

"Oh, Christ." But still I hesitated — again, with my fingers round the doorknob. How could I leave it there like that? I had to make one last attempt.

So… I forced myself to think of nothing but the kind and gentle Junie, the lovingly considerate wife, who… It was a stupid thing for my stupid mind to seize upon but I still had that letter folded in the pocket of my jeans, the one she'd written to accompany the food. As I stood there by the door it made me think of notes being slyly passed from desk to desk; of my being chased along the High Street clutching her school hat, laughing, dodging in and out of irritable pedestrians, contriving to remain always just one yard ahead, despite being winded by that laughter; of our first, shy, inexperienced kiss behind some bookshelves in the public library.

"Oh, this is all so silly," I repeated. "This is all so silly. Can't you see? I love you, Junie Moon!"

My back was still towards her but I heard the quick catch in her throat and experienced an instant surge of gratitude.

"Oh, for fuck's sake," she cried. "Why don't you grow up? And damn you! Damn you! What ever happened to my cake?"

26

Then something wholly unexpected. Walking home I knew I didn't want her back. I would never quite trust her again; never be quite sure what she was thinking.

It was as sudden and as final and as simple as that. I didn't want her back.

I wanted Matt and Ella — yes, certainly I wanted Matt and Ella — but apparently I didn't want even them sufficiently.

I started packing: two expandable suitcases filled principally with clothes. I had a bath and shaved; washed my hair and used conditioner. I wrote out a list of do's and don'ts and dates and monetary details for Junie — "I'll let you have my address, of course, as soon as I've found one" — and left it on top of the piano, weighted down by a splendid conch shell which one of the children had brought home from the beach. (Yes... it had been Ella: "Can you hear the sea in it, Daddy? Hold it up to your ear — no, not to your *nose,* you silly thing! — and listen very carefully. Can you hear it now, Daddy?" My eyes filled brimmingly.) But I didn't eat anything; was almost afraid to; decided I would buy a sandwich on the train.

So last night oughtn't there to have been at least a tremor of foreknowledge: *this could be the last time you'll ever see the kitchen?* Not even so explicit but... some gentle intimation that my days were numbered? (Where had I quite recently heard that phrase?)

After all, this was the house in which close to half my lifetime had been spent.

But I refused to behave as if my present departure was in any way different to my many thousands of other departures.

I couldn't afford to.

And for the second time in twenty-four hours I pushed a doorkey through a letterbox; heard it fall and... yes, on this occasion... felt a flooding of relief. I approached the main road with eyes looking straight ahead but on reaching the corner allowed myself a backward glance. Mistakenly. I remembered the cheerful kindnesses of neighbours and the hospitality of friends.

I also remembered I'd left yesterday's underpants on the carpet in the middle of the sitting room.

("Please give me something to remember you by... ")

I hadn't got my diary.

Who cared?

Grow up, she'd said. My story wasn't that important.

I supposed she'd always send it on. If I asked her very nicely. Diplomatically. Remembered to enclose the postage.

Arriving at the station I had half an hour to kill. I left my cases in the ticket office and went to draw some money out of Cashpoint. Lingering by the bank I suddenly envisaged Hal more as a boy than as a banker and briefly experienced a vast resurgence of affection; after all, one had no idea why people changed and — exposed to whatever influences had shaped Hal — or John — or *Junie*? — mightn't I myself have been a different person? (Oh God. Oh Mum; oh Gran. Oh someone. What *did* happen to all those fine eternal ties of youth?) Then I did what I'd intended not to... I stared for several minutes through the window of Treasure Island. While I gazed I wondered idly what sort of few days Mavis was enjoying with her woman friend; and what sort of few days Mavis's mother was enjoying without her errant daughter. I resolved to ring early next morning to offer what I could in the way of reassurance. (Too late for preparation: at the very least Mavis would have gone without her lunchtime break on Saturday.) Poor old thing — poor loyal and generous-hearted old thing — and just when her finances had so really and truly seemed to be looking up!

From where I stood I could see Action Man watchful on his table. Turning away I felt almost as if this was yet another friend who'd soon be receding now far into my past.

I bought a book for my journey from a souvenir shop on the front. Commiserated with the owner on his disappointing day. These commiserations were genuine: I knew what he'd be going through. Without such direct knowledge I also empathised with the hero of the paperback I'd chanced upon: a book still holding my attention when I reached Victoria... when I reached West Hampstead. Mangam's wife and children had been blown up by the Mafia and he himself was on the run — though girding his loins, naturally, for the long and tough fight back. *His* loss, *his* problems, made my own appear negligible.

His outlook affected me, as well. I was stirred by his integrity, his persistence, and even by the set of his shoulders and his cleancut jaw — both depicted on the somewhat lurid cover. *Exterminating Jack Mangam.*

He reminded me I ought never to lose sight of the fact that you had to accept, accept positively, whatever life dumped on you. More difficult — whatever life dumped on those you loved. Though in this case that happened to be death. But Mangam had a faith and was able to convince himself his wife and children were now better off — incomparably. Now happier — incomparably.

This seemed glib but at least it helped him cope with his bereavement. Mine, too, was a little like bereavement. I tried to convince myself bereavement would be good for all of us. Me, my wife, my children. In fact I wasn't thinking so much about me. My wife, my children, might be better off, grow strong from the experience, learn of the realities of life. Grow yet more loving, each to the other. (Particularly the children; Junie was already pretty loving, towards them.) Matt would soon become a man.

It was right for all of them ... I mean, right for all of us. I knew I'd made the only possible decision.

Besides... 'The art of living', I reminded myself; reminded me and Mangam. 'The art of living'. All things work together for good to them that see a bright side to their troubles.

I'd been wondering what I'd do if Moira wasn't there. But the Morgan was: parked in more or less its usual place: two boys wistfully examining it. I wanted to let slip I'd driven it myself and authoritatively answer any shyly awe-struck questions they might have. But I imagined Moira fairly frequently came to her window on a spot check.

Before I rang the bell I stood my cases carefully out of sight.

Certainly she seemed quite taken back; it was hard to know if she were pleased. For an instant I felt she might be, because there was perhaps the start of a smile and the flicker of something joyful in her eyes, but then, if so, the smile stopped dead, the eyes grew dull, and when I made to kiss her she hastily averted her face — which reminded me of Junie roughly eight hours earlier. "I thought that you'd gone back to Deal."

"Moira, I've got to explain things."

"Why? So far as I'm concerned there's nothing to explain."

I said: "No, you're wrong. There's everything."

"Look, Sammy," she answered, "it was fun. In many ways it was fun. We had a good time. Let's leave it at that. I don't want any explanations. And I don't hold any grudges."

"But mayn't I even come in?"

"No. I don't think so. What point?"

"I've left my wife," I said. "We're getting a divorce."

For a moment she appeared to be studying the two boys studying her motorcar. They began reluctantly to move away.

"And what do you want me to say to that? How sorry I am? How surprised I am? What?"

"I want you to ask me up. I think you owe me that much — no matter what the flaws in my behaviour. There are things I have to tell you."

She sighed.

"All right. I can give you half an hour. But I'm expecting somebody at seven."

"What sort of somebody?" I asked it sharply and without thinking.

"That isn't your business!"

"No, I know it's not. I'm sorry. I meant... is it a man?"

"Yes. Since you ask." But then she unbent a little. It must have been my look of disillusion — pain. "A friend. Somebody I've known for years. Not what you're thinking."

I nodded. "Thank you, that's kind. I've got two cases here. May I leave them just inside the door?"

She raised an eyebrow. "So what're your plans?"

I had known, of course, exactly what my plans were. But naturally I couldn't tell her. Not here on the doorstep. Not in the face of such a welcome.

I had my pride. Whatever else I didn't have — I had my pride.

"I'm not too sure as yet."

She didn't comment. I followed her upstairs. We sat, decorously, in the sitting room: she on the edge of a chair, I on a corner of the sofa. She got up again when she offered me a drink but after she'd handed it to me didn't, as I'd been hoping, come to join me on the couch.

"Good luck," I said.

"Cheers."

But there was no meaning to it. I remembered how she'd writhed against me by that window. We'd had thirty hours of complete happiness. But nearly one-and-a-half times as much had now elapsed since those had ended.

"What time did you get back last night?" I enquired. Conversationally.

"Late afternoon. Five? Six? I don't know. Why?"

I didn't ask her where she'd gone; didn't want to hear what I had missed.

"Thank you for sponging down my suit."

She shrugged.

"I'm dreadfully sorry about that. All of that."

"It happens," she said.

"Never to me. Never before to me. That's what makes me so ashamed."

"Then you'd better just chalk it up to experience," she

advised — in the same discouragingly detached tone.

"But the timing!" She simply pulled a face. "And then the rug — and the mess — and all the rest of it." I couldn't, I couldn't, make any mention... ? "Tell me — just tell me — break it to me gently: had I flushed the loo?" (*Whatever else I had done, or had not done, during the whole course of my previous existence...* I remembered the chagrin of it; it had been so nearly like a prayer.)

"Yes, of course." She answered me quite briskly.

Thank you. Oh, thank you. For that I really owe you.

"But how in heaven's name did you manage to get me on the bed?"

"You weren't out cold. You managed to cooperate; up to a point."

"You should have left me on the floor. Or — at any rate — here on this couch."

"I slept on the couch."

"Oh."

It was a peculiar kind of reminiscence; we could as easily have been talking of the weather. (No. In the past we'd talked about *that* less impersonally. In the past? All of two days ago.) I suppose I'd been hoping for a sense of camaraderie to arise out of the ashes of even such details as formed the prelude to a hangover. I suppose I'd been thinking of a phrase I'd lately found consolatory. I take this man *in sickness and in health...*

"What was it you felt you needed to explain?"

"Mainly that I love you; and that I want to marry you."

"No," she said. "Impossible."

I had expected difficulties. I'd anticipated the necessity for a whole new period of courtship and the gradual reworking of my cause; but the coldness of that word of hers, the certainty that lay behind it, had essentially pulled the rug out from under me while I was still groping for the carpet tacks.

"Listen. You can't say that. We had so much going for us; we *have* so much going for us. I know you liked me; I think

199

you said you loved me. You told me I was the sweetest, kindest... " I sheered away from that one. "You even asked whether I wanted children and I'm sure there was more to that than showed above the surface. We shared dozens of the same interests. And apart from all this we had the best sex imaginable. If any two bodies were ever made for one another... " I was inspired by my own words: jumped up from the sofa, moved behind her chair and roughly cupped and squeezed her breasts. Enragedly she tore my hands away and let out a quick-breathed exclamation. "Don't you dare ever do that again or else... "

"Or else what?" Stunned I went on standing there. Abruptly she got up and crossed behind the sofa. It was like a game of chess: the king and queen divided by their lines of pawns: obstructed and protected. We stared at one another furiously. "Or else what?" I repeated. Bull-headedly.

"You'll get a kneeing in the balls: hard and crippling and delivered with delight." It should have sounded comic. It didn't. It was a statement which reached out a long way past comedy.

"Unless I do it with permission?"

"Which is something you are *never* going to get." She added, after a pause, and a good deal more calmly, "Believe me, Sam. You must. It will make it so much easier for us both."

"I feel completely miserable," I said.

"I'm sorry about that. I really am. But... Well, you did bring it on yourself, you know."

"Is that supposed to make it better? For two pins I would jump out of that window."

"It will pass," she answered, wearily. "I promise it will pass."

There was another pause. "You can sit down again; I shan't try anything. May I freshen up my glass?"

We exchanged places: Moira on the sofa, myself on the chair.

"Didn't you like me then? I mean — a lot? Wasn't I someone... rather special to you?"

She ran a finger round the base of her sherry glass. "Yes. Everything you said just now was true. Absolutely true. With the exception of one sentence. You said that we had so much going for us — which I, too, thought we had. But then at once you changed the tense; and that's where you went wrong."

"But I don't understand. Why? I'm a free man now — or very shortly shall be. Moira, I know that I deceived you but — "

"No buts."

"Darling, I only did it out of love. I love you — with my whole heart."

"I'm sorry," she said.

That, too, seemed utterly final. We both sat very quiet.

"Listen, Sam. I want to tell you something. Ten years ago I was married." (It was strange: I had totally forgotten she'd been married.) "When I met Zach I was twenty-nine, perhaps old enough to have known better, but I fell in love with him in a way I'd never thought possible for me; possible or even desirable. And it *wasn't* desirable: no, it was painful: he was Mr Wonderful incarnate and I was Little Miss Fairly Ordinary, gooey-eyed and quite unsure of myself, with hardly a thought that didn't revolve around this man or an opinion that couldn't be changed by him; hardly an hour — especially if we were apart — when I wasn't worrying tormentedly over some silly little thing I'd either said or had not said. In brief, there was no one in the world like him; never had been; never could be." She smiled. "And I had always looked upon myself as something of a feminist. Still do, of course."

"What was he like?" I asked, a little dully; but the important thing was at all costs to keep our dialogue from lapsing. Her expected visitor might have been merely a pretext but I didn't want her growing mindful of the time.

"Astonishingly like you," she said. "You could easily be brothers. I suppose that's not surprising. Don't they say people continue falling for the same type?"

She had fallen for me. Well, she had said so much already but her reiteration of it, even if unwitting, was of comfort. And this comfort was by no means snatched away by what she told me next.

"Like you," she said, "he was kind and demonstrative and witty. Basically good-humoured and usually fine company. Everybody liked him. Fairly intelligent, fairly well-educated, practical about the house. So with all that going for him — plus his physical attractiveness — I'm not surprised, even now, I should have thought him Mr Wonderful."

I was growing more interested in him by the minute. And identifying, in a way. "What was he like in bed?"

"Not as good as you."

Did you hear *that*, Junie? The atmosphere was changing; my whole mood was changing; everything she said — well, almost everything she said — reinforced the notion I hadn't really lost her; that if I could prove master of this situation my chances of salvation were turning into certainties. I shouldn't be able to move back in this evening, I realised, nor would it be wise even to hint at it but by the end of the month my address could very well be Solent Road and my future thoroughly assured. Hell, no, by the end of the month? By the end of the week, more like.

To all intents and purposes... by the end of tonight.

As confidence returned, all trace of tiredness disappeared.

"Was that why things went sour? Was he at heart a homosexual?"

"Oh, no. Oh, no. At least, I don't think so. And our sex life was... well, fine; I mustn't give the wrong impression. And even if it hadn't been... " She gave another shrug. I felt a little disappointed.

"Wouldn't that have mattered much?"

"No, not really. Good sex is lovely; but so long as I'd known he still loved me — no — I don't think it would have mattered all that much."

"So, then. What did go wrong?"

She hesitated. Her answer, when it came, was nearly

202

toneless. But it produced a similar effect to that which you'd experience if you were standing under a warm shower and the water suddenly turned cold.

"He was a liar," she said.

27

"You mean," I asked, "he didn't really love you?"

"Oh, I think he loved me — in his way. Probably as much as he was capable of loving anybody. But after we'd been married two years I was on the top of a bus one evening and saw him standing in a doorway kissing someone. I confronted him as soon as he got home. He denied it — absolutely; said how could I behave this way, couldn't I simply take his word for it and hadn't I been as happy with him, then,as he'd been with me? And didn't I know there were probably hundreds of fair-haired young men wandering round London in a yellow jacket and green trousers? Oh, you should've heard him. It was only after I said I'd actually got off the bus and followed the pair of them that he finally owned up. But swore it meant nothing. He'd merely slipped during a moment of weakness — we all had moments of weakness — if not why hadn't I had it out with him right there upon the spot? In any case, it was me he loved. Oh, easy to say, I answered; although in fact I think I believed him. And *then* can you guess what he came up with? He declared he could furnish me with proof. In other words — while we'd been married he'd had four other equally brief affairs and the one thing he'd learned from each was just how special I was by comparison!"

Although I kept my face from showing it — and was certainly not proud of what I felt — I was almost *enjoying* the stupidity of Moira's husband.

"But you said he was intelligent." I remarked quietly, with a grave, condoling look.

"I said *fairly* intelligent. He had a degree in mathematics. Was a qualified optician. Some of the views he held were… a little unthought-out; but he wasn't an idiot. What he was, perhaps, was ingenuous."

I frowned slightly.

She said, "He really believed I'd feel so flattered by the lessons he'd learned, and so reassured about the lack of meaning to this present little escapade, I'd overlook the fact he'd been unfaithful; five times unfaithful. That I'd be impressed by his honesty. By his wish to confess. I'd know him for a reformed character; one who'd never lie to me again. He fully believed I'd be willing, on account of all this, merely to murmur, There there, my darling, come to Momma, come to Momma, do."

"Which of course you weren't?"

"Which of course I was." She smiled. She'd clearly derived pleasure from leading me on to form one expectation but from then altogether confounding it. That was good. I saw it as part of a pattern. *Impossible*, she had said. Impossible would turn out, in the end, to be distinctly possible.

I didn't begrudge her the desire to play.

"After all," she said, "you don't fall out of love in just a single evening."

This was another clue that she was offering me. It could be either conscious or unconscious.

"And it was also very feasible," I said, "he was being perfectly sincere — your husband? I'm sure he could have meant to reform."

I wanted to demonstrate my sense of fairness, even though I recognised my gesture as being shallow. Obviously; since I already knew the ending.

"You think so, Sam?" She pursed her lips and nodded once or twice. "That's what I myself thought at the time. But since then I've never been quite sure."

It didn't cost me much to be magnanimous. I wasn't like some — like my father-in-law, for instance — who clearly believed in kicking a man when he was down.

"I feel certain he intended to turn over a new leaf. He was simply weak, that's all. Why won't you give him the benefit of the doubt?"

"Yes, perhaps you're right." She gave in very gracefully and though I realised it wasn't what you'd call a major victory I felt disproportionately elated. I, too, was a shaper of opinions. Helped myself to another shot of whisky without even asking.

"So you'll understand how I felt on finding out *only six weeks later* he was still lying to me? That he had another woman? Or maybe the same one; but by then it didn't seem to matter."

"But what I *can't* understand — never will — is how he could just chuck away something so incredibly precious."

"Then join the club," she suggested, bitterly. "Because you're right — it was precious: the way I felt about him; everything I thought we had between us; those two years of — apparently — almost perfect happiness. Good heavens, did we have fantastic times! Good heavens, did I love him! And good heavens — wouldn't I have done practically anything he asked!"

Believe it or not I sat there feeling jealous. Feeling jealous of this man who'd so messed up his life. Must now be frittering away his days in an agony of cruelly belated appreciation. *And for what? Dear God! For what?* A man who was, effectively, in hell.

Feeling jealous of my predecessor.

Oh, great! So much for empathy! So much for magnanimity!

"But all the same," she said, in a voice from which the bitterness had now receded, "I suppose you can sympathise, in a way. He was a pathological liar. Lied about everything. Simply couldn't help himself. At least," she pulled a wry expression, "such was the view of the psychiatrist."

"He went to a psychiatrist?"

"No. I did." She paused. "But a while later. After we'd split up. And after I'd spent most of my leisure time — and some of my working time, as well — sitting round like a zombie but managing to sort out absolutely nothing. I asked my doctor for some pills. He sent me on for counselling."

"Oh God! How awful!" I yearned to sit beside her and take her in my arms; but didn't yet know if I dared. I tried to inject all the compassion I felt capable of, all the compassion I wished I'd been able to show her at the time, into the mediums of my voice and eyes and body language. "A nightmare! To be married to a pathological liar — yet one who was obviously so very plausible! You can't ever have been sure of anything! I can't imagine how you coped."

"Well, as I say... finally I didn't. I went to pieces."

"For how long?"

"Six months?"

"But then you were over him?"

"Over him? I suppose so. Though you can't go through a thing like that without its changing you. And, of course, I don't mean for the better."

"Perhaps there you should let others be the judge?" The phrase set up unfortunate resonances; I wished I hadn't used it.

"Balls," she said. Now she did bring up her wrist and check the time. "Good heavens! I'm afraid I must be asking you to leave."

I made to get up but then, as if seeming to notice there was still some Scotch in my tumbler, sat back to finish it. "Yet you can't let one miserably unstable relationship disillusion you for the rest of your life."

I suddenly remembered something.

"No wonder you described yourself as cynical that evening on the beach!"

"And no wonder I'd now describe myself as being so fully justified!"

The stridency was unexpected. But brief. It reached its climax in her next three words.

"Oh, you fool! Perhaps it wasn't your fault any more than it was Zach's. But if only you had told me you were married! You could've found some way to tell me also, very casually..." But she didn't finish her sentence.

I was astounded. I was so astounded that for a moment I actually wondered if I'd heard her properly.

"But I'm not... ! I'm not like Zach! I'm not a... pathological liar!"

207

I could only hope my evident state of incredulity might at least be working in my favour.

"It was the one time — absolutely the one and only time! I swear it, Moira! You've just got to believe that!"

"Oh, you fool," she repeated; but now in a tone far less impassioned, a tone almost loving — it was still going to work out. "I took to you immediately. For the first time in years I found myself aroused. Not simply by your looks; by something that went deeper; I tried to tell you in the car. And then, after we'd met you on the beach that evening and we'd all been to the pub and you'd charmed the barmaid into bringing Susie a bowl of watered beer and even a bag of crisps she wouldn't let us pay for, I was already… yes, already… For the first time since Zach… and when I'd never believed it could happen to me again. You were kind and old-fashioned and dependable. And fun. I kept Liz up for a couple of hours after we got home, talking, almost exclusively, about you. I hardly slept that night, I was so full of dreams."

"I hardly slept that night, either."

"It was history repeating itself. The same old maelstrom. The same old burgeoning belief there was no other man on earth quite like you."

"And I had absolutely the same feeling! I'd already fallen in love too! In the shop. On the beach. I had to act so quickly. I hadn't time to think. What else would you expect of me?"

"You could have told the truth! Said you were trapped in a bad marriage! You could have told us in the pub, or told me on the phone, given me the facts, allowed me to make up my own mind as to the possibility or not of our having any future… "

"I was going to tell you in the pub. I really was going to. I'd decided about that right from the beginning."

"Had you?"

"God's honour. I know it mayn't sound like very much, since I'm not… " I stopped, awkwardly.

"Not what?" she asked.

"But I was scared I'd lose you. Can't you understand that? And then, after you'd telephoned — you gave me such a glimpse of paradise — I couldn't jeopardise the whole weekend — I... But I was going to tell you at the end of the weekend, I was going to make a full confession, and — "

I stopped again, abruptly. "But, hell, I *did* tell you, didn't I? I *did* make a full confession. That's what this is all about. Isn't it? There's the proof I no longer meant to take you in!" My voice rose: vindicated and triumphant.

"You were drunk," she said. "In vino veritas."

"But that doesn't make one jot of difference. It merely hastened the process."

"Because you knew it could only be a question of time before I found you out."

It seemed to me she was shifting her ground. (My goddess was shifting her ground?)

"Exactly! How could I have ever hoped to keep anything so big under wraps?"

"Maybe Zach had been your mentor?"

"Forget Zach! I am not Zach! I am nothing like Zach!"

"Besides." In place of conceding my advantage she simply altered the direction of her serve. "I used to love *The Waltons*. This must've been my punishment. I fell for someone who was so good to his granny and whose granny was so good to him — "

"No, you didn't," I said, angrily. "What on earth had you heard about my granny when you walked out of Treasure Island that first morning?"

She stood up. "By the way, you'd better take the cake with you. I couldn't give it to the dustmen and I don't think Oxfam would be interested."

"Then won't you even believe it was the very happiest period of my life: those moments which I spent with you last Friday night and Saturday?"

"I don't suppose your wife would be precisely over the moon to hear you say that."

"No. Listen. There's a difference. I was only nineteen when we married. I knew nothing about anything. Certainly not about love. I knew nothing about love. I may have thought

I did but... " Suddenly I went to her and took her by the shoulders. "I'm not sure how much of this is getting through."

"Not very much, I'm afraid. I feel sorry for you, Sam, but I don't imagine I could ever trust you. Not again. I'm sorry if that's blunt."

She made an attempt to pull away but my fingers simultaneously strengthened their hold. "You have *got* to believe me!" I repeated. "I feel desperate. Desperate. I don't know what I'll do."

Somehow she broke free. "Now no more caveman stuff — you promised. I'll go and get that cake."

"I couldn't carry it. I already have two cases."

"Where are you going?"

"I don't know," I answered, bleakly. It didn't matter. "Earl's Court? South Ken? Isn't that renowned bedsitter-land?"

"Or there's Kilburn," she said; "which is a good deal closer. Cheap and grotty. Or Hampstead: smart but pricey." She glanced at her watch again. "Though after seven o'clock on a Bank Holiday evening... You may have to go into a hotel for tonight."

"No, I think I'll try Kilburn. Cheap and grotty fits in with how I feel."

"Are you playing at being pathetic?"

"Pathetic? That's a bit of a far cry, isn't it, from strong and... from strong and vulnerable?"

I turned my head away. It was true that in the first place I had been making something of a bid for sympathy. But the moistness which filled my eyes just then was genuine and I didn't want her to see it.

"Oh, Sammy... ," she sighed. It was the last thing she should have said — I mean, depending on your point of view. Quite suddenly I was shaking, so racked with sobs that at first I couldn't draw breath. She stepped forward and took me in her arms and for perhaps a minute I just cried myself out while holding on to her.

"Please take a chance on me," I said. "You don't know how very much I love you."

Then the doorbell rang.

28

She remained downstairs for several minutes. I could hear the sound of both their voices but nothing of what either of them said. When she came back she seemed relaxed. "I didn't tell you earlier but that in fact was Zach. I still see him from time to time, either here or at a restaurant. I can't help feeling fond of him." She added: "Come into the kitchen and I'll scramble you some eggs."

"Did he mind being sent away?"

"A little. But I didn't feel this was quite the moment for the pair of you to meet."

"May I go and wash my face?"

"Of course."

"I didn't mean to do that to you, you know."

"I know."

"I always used to feel contempt for men who cried."

"You're just a sexist pig!" But she gave me the sort of smile I hadn't seen since Saturday.

While we were eating she said: "What did you mean, Sam, when you told me swearing on God's name mightn't sound like very much since you weren't — since you weren't what? A person who believed in God?"

I hesitated; looked down at the cloth. I fully recognised my answer could be one of critical importance. The supreme irony: I almost prayed again. This time for guidance.

I said: "I know I led you to believe I was someone who had faith in God. I... Well, that also... "

"What?"

I'd had it all planned out. It had come to me in toto. I had received my guidance.

"That also was a lie," I'd been about to say; "I think perhaps the last. Except — no — one further sin of omission: I never brought up the fact I've had a vasectomy."

I'd meant to impress her with my honesty.

So what was it that stopped me? A reluctance to admit to yet one more breach of trust; a reluctance to shed yet one more of those qualities which had originally formed part of my attraction? It seemed there was so little of me left, so painfully little of me left, as it was. Where had he gone to — that fellow, Samson Groves? (Ha! *Samson!*)

I looked up from the tablecloth. Nervously. "I don't know," I said.

"You don't know? You don't know what?"

I almost said, *Anything.* "I don't know whether or not... I do believe."

"But why did you encourage me to think you were so *sure?*"

I shrugged.

"After all, you already knew that — me — I had no faith whatsoever."

"Like everything else, it grew." (Or happened; had there been any time for growth?) "I suppose I felt... You'd got such expectations; I couldn't bear to disappoint them. I thought if that was what you were looking for... certainties... encouragement for a belief... then that's what I would try to give you. Certainties. Encouragement for a belief. Somehow. Perhaps in that way if not in any other I was even being a little selfless... " I shook my head, however. "No. Not selfless in any way at all. It was purely a means to an end. I wanted you so much."

"Wanted?" she said.

But it transpired it was merely my tense which she was querying and suddenly I realised that it *was* going to work out. Oh, it was, it was! The inquisition was over. Against all the odds: I had come through.

"Wanted. Want. Shall want. For ever and ever and always — amen. All the gerunds and gerundives and participles thrown in. Oh, darling, I shall change — I shall change — I shall change! I'm not basically a liar — never have been — but I am a lot of things I know I shouldn't be. Vain, selfish,

212

sexist, stupid, greedy — arrogant at times, intolerant — lacking in compassion and imagination — mean, calculating, unstable..."

She put her hand up, swiftly, with a laugh. "Whoa! Stop! This is *not* the way to sell yourself."

I wondered for a moment if indeed I'd overstepped the mark. "But I do have some fairly nice points, too. And all I need, deep down, is the love of a good woman."

She dispelled these latest doubts. Not by kissing me nor by the use of any reassuring phrase or endearment but simply by going to a cupboard and getting out the large iced cake with its haze of cottage garden colours. "I think we ought to have a slice of Granny's cake for afters."

"Junie's cake." And then, again not sure I'd said the right thing, I told her that Susie had been put down.

"Why?"

"Because Junie..." Then I paused and made a fresh start. "Because I suppose I should never have tried hanging on to her after the accident."

Loyalty had been another of my father's gods.

"Oh, Sammy, I am sorry. That must have been so... How did your children take it?"

I realised I hadn't thought very much about how my children had taken it.

"They were both of them pretty upset. Naturally."

Then I said: "But in a way Susie was more my dog than theirs."

"I can believe it."

I wondered for how long she would have to go through life assuring me she could believe it. I wondered for how long I would have to go through life asking myself whether or not she could believe it.

"How do they feel about your leaving home?"

"Badly." For the moment, though, I didn't want to think about that. Just those two syllables had been difficult enough.

"But, tell me, isn't there any slightest chance of a reconciliation? I mean, if it weren't for me, if I hadn't happened to walk into the shop looking for a present last weekend... ?"

"No. None," I said. "None whatsoever."

"Not even for the sake of the children?"

"No."

"Tell me about her. Just a little." She smiled. "She's obviously a good cook."

This was dangerous territory. I knew that someday I should need to loosen up but for the time being it seemed far better avoided. "Oh... We met and we married and were too young. We had no yardsticks and — and we didn't know that people changed; or that one of us could change and not the other. There ought to be a law: no one should marry under twenty-five."

I hoped that for the present this disposed of Junie. Yet when I thought of her on the telephone being made to look foolish in front of a former schoolfriend — and, worse, in front of a former schoolfriend's unknown wife — I had to add immediately: "But, yes, you're right. She's a good cook. And a good mother. A *very* good mother. And there've in fact been times when we've had fun. I'm not saying... that she didn't try to make things work. I'm not saying that at all."

I made myself think back ten hours. The steely set of her face. I must hold on to this. Anyway, I must hold on to it for tonight and tomorrow and probably the next few weeks. *So has she discovered yet you're not that good in bed?*

She had been hurt, of course. She had been very badly hurt.

Can't she bring herself to tell you how magnificent and strong you are, even when you feed her all the proper lines?

I wished just then we hadn't been sitting there eating her cake.

"The very final lie," I said; "or at least the very last omission. I've had a vasectomy. One gets no guarantees that they can be reversed."

She simply made a moue. I wasn't sure if this chiefly expressed sympathy for me or concern for herself; and I didn't like to ask.

It was after half-past-eight when we cleared away the

supper things. "Momentous question," I said. "Grave repercussions for the future. D'you prefer to wash or dry?"

"No, I'll see to that. To tell you the truth I'm getting worried about your being able to find yourself a room."

My face wouldn't have done too well for the diplomatic corps.

"Sammy," she said, "I've got to have a little time to think. I'm not going to let you spend the night here."

I nodded, rather slowly. Yes, I supposed. Not unreasonable.

"And anyway," she said, "Zach's coming back at nine."

"Will *he* be spending the night here?" Oh, how to win friends and change the path of history. Without even thinking about it.

"No, of course not! All we do is talk. He phones me when he's feeling down. When he came I couldn't say I wouldn't see him *at all* tonight. Especially since at the time of his phone call this afternoon... "

"What?"

"I was feeling rather down as well. He went to a lot of trouble to try to cheer me up."

No doubt by saying that she would soon get over me. That I really wasn't worth becoming depressed about. How much *detail* would she have given him?

"Then he obviously hasn't remarried?"

"No."

"But do you still fancy him?"

"Sam, I would advise you to leave it right there."

"After all, you said he looked a lot like me."

I wasn't being aggressive. I was being rational. Pulling at the skin through my open collar with a thoughtful, almost academic air. I just wanted to know the answer.

She wouldn't give me any answer.

"Well, I've a good mind to stay and... "

"And *what*?"

"Tell Mr Zach Whatever-His-Bloody-Name-Is just precisely where he gets off!" I agree that didn't sound, perhaps, so entirely academic.

"Oh God," she said.

"Because when he says he's feeling down how can you be sure that's really what it is? How can you be sure he's not just feeling bored? And sexy?"

"Oh, how can I be sure of anything?" she cried.

Her exasperation, or despair, was the corrective I much needed. I gave myself some hard knocks on the temple with the heel of one palm.

"I'm not normally like this; I swear I'm not. Can't think what's got into me! It's been a tough couple of days."

She smiled, a little wanly. "Yes; I'm sure it has."

"Forgive me?"

She nodded.

"No. I want to hear you say it."

"Sammy. I forgive you."

I still looked deep into her eyes, searching for that absolution, that state of grace, I'd so much need to help me sleep. Despite her gentle words — her tired but gentle words — I wasn't totally convinced that it had been conferred on me. Not wholly conferred.

What was conferred on me — without question — was painstaking advice on how to get to Kilburn.

"May I leave one of my suitcases?"

She had to consider this. "Yes, of course... but when will you be wanting it?"

"Why? Does it matter?"

"Not really. It's just that... "

"What?"

"I'd rather we didn't see anything of each other for a short time. Let's say — about a week."

"A week!"

"You see, I want to be as sure as possible of how I feel about things."

"So not until next Monday?"

"Don't look disconsolate! It really isn't that long! And you'll have so much to be getting on with."

"Oh, yes? Like what?"

"Like finding your bearings. Making arrangements. Looking for work." She paused. "Like getting things sorted out inside your own head."

"Thank you; but I don't think I have to get things sorted out inside my own head. *I* know what's good for me. *I* know what I want. Unlike *some*," I added — but only in a mutter as I went downstairs to bring up the suitcase which I wasn't going to need.

"Obviously, you've got all your wash things et cetera in the one you're taking? Socks? Shirts? Underwear?"

"It sounds like the end of the school holidays used to be. When I was five."

"Well, don't forget to wash behind the ears." She smiled. "Soap? Towel?"

I hadn't thought of bringing either. She supplied me with both.

"Pocket money?"

"Piss off."

She laughed.

"But I *will* take that cake." I decided. Guard against night starvation; give me succour through the long dark hours. Make bloody sure that bloody Zach — Zachary? — Zachariah? — what sort of poncy moniker was that: him in his yellow jacket and green trousers! — that bloody Zach wasn't going to be comfortably tucking into it five minutes after I had finished (less comfortably) doing the same. Junie hadn't made that cake for any cheap philandering fantasist.

"Sensible," she said.

I wondered also about asking for the pie and soup; partly for purposes of economy.

But for some reason couldn't bring myself to do so.

Moira left the cake in her own tin; added a couple of plates, a mug and some cutlery. A tea towel. Jiffy Cloth. Screws of coffee, Coffee-Mate and sugar; a few tea bags. She tied the tin with the same hairy string Junie had put around the box; but neither the knot nor the loop were nearly as secure as

Junie's. Inevitably this raised a point; how well was she going to make out, then, stationed at the entrance to a maze?

"You should've used that golden thread," I told her, "so long as you meant to keep a firm hold on it, while it unravelled. Me journeying this night into the darkest reaches of the heart of Kilburn."

"I supposed you had in mind something more interesting round which to tie that," she commented, drily.

I smiled. She'd given the right answer. "Are you teasing me, Pandora?"

"Pandora again? I thought my name was Ariadne."

"Tonight I'm all at sea. Ariadne is the land girl; Pandora's the self-sacrificing angel of release who will swim out to my boat. Two sides of the same coin. You're both beautiful. Both bringers of salvation."

"Oh, good," she observed. "Almost the perfect setup. Almost... dare one say it... the Captain's paradise?"

But before I'd had much opportunity to react to this either clumsily or with grace (and I'd always wanted life to imitate the movies) she added, "Now be away with you! Enough of this! I don't want the two of you to meet upon the stairs."

"Why not?" I wondered if she'd told him I was there. "Afraid he'll think he's seen his Doppelgänger and imagine only death can now await him?"

"Idiot." As she said it she reached up and briefly kissed my lips. But twisted away the moment I tried to hold her with my free hand. "Sammy?"

I'd already started down the staircase.

Up one minute; down the next.

"If you should find yourself slipping into the doldrums at all," she said, "and feel you must either talk to somebody or bust... Well, I'm usually here from six; and our embargo needn't comprehend the telephone."

"Right, then."

"And Sammy?"

"What?"

"No... nothing."

"Go on. Say it."

"Oh, it isn't unpleasant. Could maybe sound a tad sentimental."

"I'm all for sentiment."

"I was only going to mention... however this turns out... whatever we decide... "

"Yes?"

"Well, we're always going to stay friends, aren't we? We're always going to have a bit of a soft spot for one another? That's all. I wanted to make sure you understood this." Then she blew me a last kiss and withdrew into her flat and closed the door.

Abruptly.

29

Despite the continuing drizzle I stood on a corner out of sight of Moira's window and kept cave. Finally I saw him. His umbrella partly screened his face but there wasn't any doubt. He all but cannoned into me. "Sorry," he said. "Sorry," I said. Ships that pass in the night, exchanging a brief toot. Golden boys that pass in the rain, smiling an apology. Little trace of tarnishing. After a moment I saw him glance back. Something of sympathy flashed between us. Something containing a charge that was almost — !

Christ, no! Not true!

But the closer I got to Kilburn the greyer everything became. In one sense, of course, this was scarcely to be wondered at: it was now approaching ten. As I stood outside the underground looking at the notices on a newsagent's board to which some passersby had drawn my attention it occurred to me she hadn't said, Come back if you can't find anywhere; or Give me a ring to let me know you're settled.

It occurred to me she hadn't asked what was likely to happen to Treasure Island. Nor had she refloated, or remembered, that bolstering notion of my maybe writing off to university.

There was a private hotel advertised in Admiral Road. There was also a scrappy piece of paper offering in red crayon a single room, not large but clean, in a quiet house in the same street. Any nationality. Thirty-five pounds per week. Three spelling mistakes in just four lines.

The woman who came to the door was small and wizened and lumpy. Lumpy, because she had on several layers of clothing including a jumper, cardigan and overcoat. The overcoat was only partly buttoned. There was a grey woollen scarf — long, like a college student's — wrapped around the head and tied beneath the chin and she wore fingerless grey mittens.

But I didn't see those mittens, nor the fingernails which accompanied them, until I'd told her why I was there, twice apologised for having come so late (this had been my day for apologising to everyone for everything) and until she'd at last decided to remove the chain. A welcome contrast: the hall appeared well-heated. Well-carpeted and furnished, too, although the light seemed pretty dim. The landlady was Polish. She'd lived in this country for seventeen years and said she had the toothache and had been just about to go to bed. Also that her husband lived in the basement; her own bedroom was the coldest room in the house; and the summer wasn't going to get here till July. Her English was as weird as her apparel but she was amiable enough. While I waited in the doorway of her fuggy, cluttered, cat-infested room she collected a key and a rent book and an After Eight mint chocolate which she pulled out of its envelope and held hospitably towards my mouth. I couldn't really fancy it but didn't have the heart to shake my head.

She led me slowly up three flights of stairs, breathing heavily and pausing on every landing. During our initial stop she asked about my home. Home? She hadn't heard of Deal but when I told her it was on the sea and was the spot where Julius Caesar had first landed in Britain she puzzlingly supposed it was also the place from which Sir Walter Raleigh had set sail for El Dorado. I felt vaguely surprised she should have known of either the man or the destination but she then informed me — and with an air of clearing up any mystification on this or any other topic — that she had a daughter married to a drunken docker in Limehouse.

On the next landing she pointed out the bathroom — with its enormous, maybe prehistoric geyser — and the separate lavatory, which, even from a distance, smelled as though the drunken docker might recently have used it to be a drunken docker in.

It brought back certain memories.

The vacant room was one of two on the top floor. My

prospective neighbour was playing glee songs at a volume that belied the advertised kwiet (*glee* songs, I ask you, surely the ultimate irony?) and on this landing the yet dimmer light bulb had no shade and the paintwork and carpet looked neglected. But certainly the room itself, after the old woman had fumbled with its heavy key, appeared relatively ungrubby. Nor was it as small as I'd imagined, although the crude wallpaper, repeatedly emblazoned with the three plucky galleons proudly conveying their master towards his glorious discovery of the New World, did nothing to open things up. It seemed instead to make a mockery of the gimcrack wardrobe, table, bed, chair — cooker, tiny fridge and sink: a mockery of everything. But in fact the room was about the right size. A refuge. Sanctuary. The proper place to lick one's wounds.

I gave the woman forty pounds. Told her I'd collect the change tomorrow — also the rent book, which she'd been going to fill in then and there. But all I wanted was to close my door. Close my door upon the world.

She showed me where the meters were and showed me the little trick required to light the gas fire. My bed was made up but she explained about the laundering of the sheets and pillowcases. Hoover and dustpan kept downstairs. I didn't mention I might just be there one week: *The Passing of the Third Floor Back*: at last, you see, I get to play the title role.

But I didn't mention that.

The moment she'd gone I took off my raincoat... and discovered there weren't any hangers; nor coat hook on the door. I was about to call after her — simply couldn't face it. I removed my spattered shoes. Remembered I hadn't brought any shoetrees, or even brushes and polish, and felt hot tears come rushing to my eyes.

Crybaby! Crybaby!

I set my suitcase on the bed but as soon as I'd done so decided I couldn't face that either — the unpacking.

What was I going to do? No polish; no shoetrees, probably

a score of other things that I'd forgotten. All equally essential.

And could I afford to replace them?

I was missing my wife and family; that's what it all came down to.

Missing them like hell.

But I knew I couldn't go back. I knew this with a certainty that underlaid the ache and emptiness and sense of loss: my feeling of impending doom; my conviction that nothing could ever work for me again. Underlaid and overlaid and wrapped it all about.

I was going to be on my own. Forever. Unloved; uncherished. Ill-equipped to deal with just the ordinary details of everyday existence. Afraid of them, even. Crybabily afraid.

And it stuck like a sickness in my throat and a pressure on my stomach: the ever-present yet recurring knowledge: that I had truly burned my boats.

Just bits of debris scattered on the water. With nothing remotely hopeful I could salvage.

Nothing.

No use pretending. I wasn't like Zach. I was *not* like Zach. Poor devil! I could empathise; even feel drawn to him; but I would never be like Zach.

I'd left the cake tin on the table. Listlessly I started to untie the string. Caught sight of my reflection in the window. Was distracted; even startled — for one split second imagined I had seen a stranger.

Obviously no stranger. My own double. Yet as I moved towards him I had the laughable illusion he looked much nicer than me. (*Nicer*: what a feeble word!) But anyone not knowing might have thought — wow! There's someone I should like to meet. Make a friend of. Model myself on, even. There's someone I could really trust… Cleaner; shinier; more golden.

I stood for a moment by the window. It was now so dark I wouldn't normally have seen a lot but someone on the ground floor had their light on: probably my landlady: her room was at the back and I retained an impression of its having tall French doors and of the curtains being undrawn. Even so I couldn't see a great deal: merely a patch of scrubby grass, with, at its centre, a birdbath that instantly made me think of my grandmother's garden — made me think, too, of the night I'd climbed out on the windowsill which overlooked it.

There, as well, it had been the original sash window.

Just as before, the bottom half now proved immovable. The top had also jammed. But, just as before, I finally managed — a bit like an automaton, an automaton *possessed* — to jerk the top half all the way down.

Just as before, I straddled the peeling frame.

At my grandmother's house there had been concrete where I would have fallen. It was the same thing here.

I was soon fully on the outside. For support I hooked my elbows over the double thickness of window. The sill creaked beneath my weight but in spite of its deteriorating paintwork remained firm.

Presently the light went off downstairs; the grass and birdbath disappeared. My own room's forty watts gave only scant illumination. No moon; no stars. Now left with all but nothing.

Nothing.

I braced myself. Sought to reinfuse my dissipating courage.

In just three seconds — five? — it could all be over. Splat! Like being caught by the full force of an explosion. Nothing.

I really didn't mind.

Nothing?

And if I myself didn't mind — then who on earth should?

I thought about the landlady, my funny little Polish landlady, who had presumably just settled down to sleep.

I thought about the effect of a body falling right outside her bedroom. The ground-shaking thud, or squelch; the shock it must produce; the mess and horror left behind.

I remembered she was suffering from a toothache.

And wasn't it just possible she might already — doped —

be drifting out towards oblivion?

Then how could I do this to her?

Could I do this to her?

Yes!

I felt deeply sorry for her but I could. I had to. I knew I'd reached the point of no return.

Besides. It's an ill wind. And every cloud. Once she'd recovered from that initial trauma, that first horrendous impact, mightn't the self-destruction of a golden boy make the rest of her own life seem marginally more bearable?

The passing of the third floor back.

Eponymous hero.

Which reminded me: I'd never got around to finishing that paperback. Damn. Though I knew, of course, how things were going to turn out: justice would surely be done, reparation made, personal growth achieved. On earth as it is in heaven. For ever and ever. Amen.

Exterminating Jack Bradley. The title was a good one but misleading. Even without his hugely missed family I knew only too well a happy ending lay in store for that particular eponymous hero. Lucky guy.

But, no, I'd got it wrong. The book wasn't called *Exterminating Jack Bradley*; it was called *Exterminating Jack Mangam.* Mr Bradley had been the old man on that other train journey, the old man I'd meant someday to take Junie and the kids to visit, the one who was chiefly waiting, so he'd said, to be reunited with his wife. Jack, I only hope you make it, I assured him now; and soon — if that's really what you're after. Though not, of course, as the result of being exterminated. As the result of something a whole lot gentler and more merciful. Please.

Actually I wasn't aware of even being sardonic.

Then, believe it or not, I laughed. Poised on a ledge in rainy darkness, some forty or fifty feet above my own apparently ungentle fate, I honestly did laugh.

Ascribe it to hysteria or insanity. Or to what you will.

"Exterminate! Exterminate!"

And for an instant I was back with my children and we were all watching reruns of *Doctor Who*; Junie was there as well — in the TV room, I mean — but it was principally me who was being chased all through the house and having to clutch my chest or belly and die as histrionically as ever I knew how. This — to promote the triumphant malevolence of a pair of ecstatically rule-breaking Daleks, amidst the lickings and excitement of a white-haired, tail-wagging, black-eyed pup.

"Exterminate the brute!"

It seemed like yesterday.

Yesterday… I was a big man yesterday but Lord you ought to see me now.

Now I was a little boy lost.

A lost boy.

A lost boy without the prospect of an awfully big adventure?

You know what? I wished I could have measured up to that reflection in the window.

(I've always said it: it's absurd the things that'll flash across your mind at moments of maximum tension.)

A Broadway musical, yes, but since the writers — or producers or angels or whatever — had chosen to name it as they had you'd have thought there'd be at least some glancing reference. Wouldn't you?

And you'd have thought my neighbour wouldn't suddenly turn up the volume of his gleeful choristers at something getting on for midnight. Wouldn't you? After all, tomorrow was another day. And people had to rise and shine.

Now *there* was a coincidence.

For what had he decided in his wisdom ought perhaps to be my swan song?

> "… Gentlemen songsters off on a spree,
> Doomed from here to eternity!
> Lord have mercy on such as we…
> Baa, baa, baa!"

But surely there was too much relish in it — reaffirmation — vigour. Even freshness. It sounded more like a dawn chorus.